Grand Floridians

Grand Floridians

Richard Haight

iUniverse, Inc.
New York Bloomington

Grand Floridians

This is a work of fiction. All of the characters, names, incidents, organizations, and dialogue
in this novel are either the products of the author's imagination or are used fictitiously.

iUniverse books may be ordered through booksellers or by contacting:

iUniverse
1663 Liberty Drive
Bloomington, IN 47403
www.iuniverse.com
1-800-Authors (1-800-288-4677)

Because of the dynamic nature of the Internet, any Web addresses or links contained in this book
may have changed since publication and may no longer be valid. The views expressed in this work
are solely those of the author and do not necessarily reflect the views of the publisher, and the
publisher hereby disclaims any responsibility for them.

ISBN: 978-1-4401-3362-6 (pbk)
ISBN: 978-1-4401-3364-0 (dj)
ISBN: 978-1-4401-3363-3 (ebk)

Printed in the United States of America

iUniverse rev. date: 4/30/2009

For Michael, Cory, Erin, and Josh

From the Author

I wish to thank all my friends and colleagues who supported me in my first effort, *Winter Beach Dog Trot*, and encouraged me to get *Grand Floridians* to press. I'm also grateful for the inspiration of the residents of the Treasure Coast, especially those who struggle to stay one step ahead of the game.

Once again, I owe a great debt of gratitude to my wife Denise for her careful editing and support. Thanks also to Cory Haight, my daughter-in-law, for lending her word processing skills to the project. Finally, I would like to thank the professional staff at iUniverse. These folks make it possible for those who would likely go unheard to reach their audience with a truly professional product.

ONE

Ten miles south of the Florida border Eldridge Dewitt eased the blue Buick Electra onto the off-ramp. He and his wife Verbena had been driving for four hours straight and now he had to pee so badly his teeth were floating. A quarter mile west of the ramp, just past the Bob Evans, the golden arches of McDonald's filled the skyline like a urine stream. On the south side of the road stood a thirty-foot grinning plastic gator named Gabriel. In one gator hand he held a long golden trumpet to his lips. In the crook of his left arm rested a black-and-gold Bible. He was mired in a swamp of billboards: *This is it! Exit Now! T-Shirts, Discount Disney Tickets, Free Orange Juice, Souvenirs, Bibles!*

Beyond the commercial extravaganza lay vast pastures of stubble grass dotted with scrub pine where white cattle egrets and cows grazed under a cloudless blue sky. Verbena let out an audible sigh. "We're home, Eldridge!"

"Jesus. It makes me want to piss my pants," he grumbled as he approached the line of traffic at the intersection. He hoped he could make it to McDonald's before he did.

"Eldridge, you never talked like that when Father was alive." Verbena thrust her lower lip forward in a pout, her intonation that of a petulant child at a candy counter. For Eldridge, a root canal held more appeal than her whining.

"If our goddamn luck doesn't change, this won't be home for long, and I wouldn't talk like this if your father hadn't croaked and left us holding the Save-A-Buck bag."

"My father spent his entire life managing the first Save-A-Buck discount store in Wisconsin. He bought their stock every chance he got, and Daddy even invented their slogan *A buck saved is a Badger buck earned!* Save-A-Buck made him a millionaire and he bought us the cottage in Deerfield Beach. He worked harder in a year than you have in your whole life. He was smarter, too."

"If getting his Badger butt hole kicked by Wal-Mart was smart I guess he was a fuckin' genius."

"Stop it, Eldridge. Just stop it about Daddy." Verbena braced her fleshy forearms against the dash and began to hyperventilate. Her heavy breasts heaved rhythmically as she strained against the seat belt.

Eldridge just shook his head; he knew he was right. In the years since Verbena's mother's death, Save-A-Buck had been crushed by the discount chains while her despondent father sulked in his study and watched his stock plummet. Finally, in a panic, he sold his stock at rock bottom just before Wal-Mart bought out the chain at a premium. Her Daddy died of a coronary two months later, leaving only the house, his Buick, and the cottage to never-employed Verbena and unemployed Eldridge.

Forty-five minutes further south, Leon Eckerman fumbled with the radio dial of his seafoam-colored '98 Taurus as he cruised along at eighty miles an hour. He was trying to find one channel that wasn't either appealing to his everlasting soul or playing the Dixie Debutantes' *I Bought a Gun; He Bought the Farm*. He finally settled on a combat psychologist's show and listened to a woman whine about her live-in boyfriend.

"Dr. Spikeman," (woman sobbing) "I … aaah … Help me!"

"Ma'am, get ahold of yourself. We are on the air. Please state your name."

Woman's voice again, sniffling and honking, nose blowing. "Lydia, sir."

"All right, Lydiasir. Calm down and tell us what happened."

"It's my boyfriend."

Dr. Spikeman sighs. "And you live with him. Am I correct?"

"Well, it's more like he lives with me in my trailer."

"Because he doesn't have a job, does he Lydiasir?"

"How'd you know? But he can't work on account of his back."

An audible yawn. "So you've rescued him and support him now. Is Lydiasir one of those Eastern European names?"

"It's Lydia, sir. Anyways, I work nights at Waffle World."

"It sounds idyllic, Lydiasir. What could be wrong?"

"It's the other women." —sob— *"He's in our bed with them when I get home. I can't get comfortable on the couch"* — more sobbing. *"I need some rest!"*

"With that bad back, you can't expect him to perform on the couch and let you have the bed."

"He says he loves me, and if I really loved him I would trust him."

"Has he considered manipulation?"

"The girls at work say he's manipulating me."

"No, Lydiasir. I mean chiropractic manipulation for his back."

"No, sir, but…"

"Lydiasir, your home is the man's castle. I suggest you either buy a sofa sleeper for yourself or get a king-size chiropractic mattress and join them. No pictures pleeeze!" Big laugh in the background. *"And that brings us to today's sponsor, the Chiropractic Club Mattress. Throw your back into a really hard one tonight."*

"But, Dr. Spikeman."

"Good-bye, Lydiasir."

Last night Leon had slept in a North Georgia rest stop parked between two semis, and he'd tried all morning to work out the crick in his neck. His ears were still ringing from the constant hum of the trucks' generators and it would take another five hours to reach Melbourne.

Leon had been forced into early retirement. After thirty-five years, ten in middle management, they downsized him and showed him the door. As a result, he received sixty percent of his entitled pension and had to pick up his own health insurance. At sixty, he was still two years away from collecting Social Security and five years from Medicare.

Corporate assigned a snot-nosed acne-scarred kid from personnel to his case to help him relocate. After a few meetings in which he was encouraged to let go of his anger and write a creative resume, he told the condescending little prick to shove it up his ass and walked out.

No one wanted a washed-up office equipment salesman who couldn't program his own Tivo much less keep up with the new developments in office technology. When he started this business, high tech was an electric typewriter. Now he couldn't even find a ribbon to fit his. Shit, he might as well take himself and the Selectric down to the resale shop.

Leon had never been to Florida but had always assumed he would move there because that is where retired people go. God's waiting room. Through a friend, he had rented a condo in Melbourne near the ocean. Dahlia Dunes, an adult community, had it all: bingo, mahjongg, horseshoes, tennis, water exercises, and line dancing. The only thing missing were dahlias and sand dunes.

TWO

Nero Venditto could feel the sweat trickling slowly down the middle of his spine. It was over ninety degrees, and without an ocean breeze the barrier island wasn't any cooler than the mainland. He wanted to turn the car around and return to Melbourne. The opulence and conspicuous consumption of Premier Island, a fortified gated community, made him edgy. It didn't matter that he had aspired to it his entire life.

"Y'all could have stayed home and let me handle this," Helen said. "It's not like I haven't worked for Colonel Collins before, honey."

"This could be dangerous. I'm not letting you do this alone. You said you wanted a man to be there for you; here I am."

"Just because he's rich and powerful doesn't mean he's a treacherous man."

"It doesn't make him fuckin' stable either."

"He's a refined gentleman who always treats me like a lady."

"I wish you had turned him down."

"Nero, that wouldn't be polite and we need this ten thousand dollars to set up your little ol' project. That French Connection thing you're so passionate about."

They slowed to a stop at the gatehouse and picked up their pass from an earnest-looking silver-haired guard, whom Helen ventured was retired military police. It comforted Nero to be driving his previously owned Cadillac De Ville which he had received in trade for his '97 Saturn four door. At least he looked like he belonged.

Nero proceeded along a curved palm-lined drive leading to a sprawling white Caribbean-style clubhouse with a sloping green metal roof. He noted that the parking lot was almost full: Lincolns,

Mercedes, BMWs, Cadillacs, and cars foreign even to himself. Bronze faced men in lime, plum, sky blue, and cream-colored blazers escorted brightly dressed women in matching wide-brimmed hats, their wide, botoxed eyes scanning the scene with nervous anticipation. It was as if, in their otherwise empty lives, they expected something no less than the second coming of Elvis or that Obama was the IRS's answer to the anti-Christ.

"Must be some kind of shindig going on here," Nero said.

"Probably their Sunday polo match. The colonel will surely be playing. Mercy, I hope we're not late," Helen effused.

"The guard said it would be just past the clubhouse."

Helen seemed to know a lot about the Colonel, Nero thought, as he turned into a sweeping circular drive of soft-toned gray pavers and rolled to a stop in front of a Spanish stucco mansion with an orange barrel-tile roof. Tall white turrets finished off each corner giving it the appearance of a Mediterranean fortress. Bougainvillea crept up the walls while royal palms and peach-colored hibiscus filled the landscape around the drive.

"Damn!" exclaimed Nero. "The Colonel has built himself quite a place here."

"Don't kid yourself, honey; it's just a little ol' spec home. The Colonel doesn't have time to design and decorate mansions in the proper fashion. He bought it furnished from the Atlanta developer."

"Fuckin' A. A four million dollar spec home. I don't believe it."

"Hush your mouth and pull your Yankee self together. We're not in Jersey any more, Toto."

Just then the dark planked front door opened and a muscular young man appeared. His attitude, physique, and short cropped hair gave him a military presence not unlike the guard at the gate. As he walked around to Helen's side of the car and opened her door, Helen quickly checked her make-up and lipstick in the visor mirror then turned to Nero. "Remember, this is my show."

THREE

Eldridge danced on his bowed legs toward the men's room at McDonald's while Verbena wedged herself into a booth. Verbena was fat. She'd weighed ten pounds five ounces at birth and, during childbirth, had nearly killed her mother. Subsequently the only child of Bill and Roberta Billingsly, she was a fat kindergartner and at Ambrose Pierce High School in Waterford, Wisconsin, the big-boned girl with the pretty face.

But Verbena wasn't a wall flower who sat in the back row, smelled bad, and wouldn't shower after phys. ed. An outgoing girl Verbena collected lots of friends. The pretty girls took her into their confidence because she could keep a secret and didn't present a threat.

If high school were a beauty contest, she could claim Miss Congeniality and Forever Secretary: Class secretary, French Club secretary, Pep Club secretary, and secretary for Future Homemakers. Not-so-glamorous Verbena got the not-so-glamorous jobs.

Eldridge eventually reappeared shaking his still wet hands over the heads of small children and toddlers who swarmed just below him. "You want your usual, Babe?" he called as he positioned himself in line.

Verbena smiled and nodded while she focused on the throng of children. Eldridge didn't like children and made it clear from the start that they wouldn't be having any. Shortly after they married, he sealed their fate with a vasectomy.

Verbena had cried briefly, even though she was herself ambivalent. On every single birthday her mother Roberta would recount her long and exhausting labor. At three in the morning during a violent thunderstorm, Roberta dreamed she was being soaked by the rain and awakened in a pool of amniotic fluid.

Verbena's father panicked, and as he navigated the flooded streets of Waterford they prayed they'd get to the hospital in time. Neither of them had taken time to notice that she wasn't having contractions. It took six hours for the first wave of pain to commence, and twelve more hours before a completely exhausted Roberta felt the urge to push. Roberta's oral history of the event never varied.

"The nurse who had admitted me the night before returned to her shift fresh and rested. She was a coarse tiny woman with an eagle-beak nose. I can still see those long black hairs curling out of her nostrils." Roberta shuddered. "That witch frightened me more than the delivery itself. It was only later I learned she belonged to those Voracheks who farmed west of town, and that behind her back the other nurses called her the labor Nazi. She forced my legs apart, jabbed them against my stomach like I was a Vorachek heifer, and hissed at me to push. I strained to do as she commanded but, to my own horror, instead of pushing you out, Verbena, I defecated right on the labor bed. The whole room smelled like Grandma Gifford's outhouse."

At this point in the story Verbena lost interest in her birthday cake and had a good notion why she was an only child.

"I pushed for three hours until all the veins in my face burst. I was black and blue for a week and wouldn't let anyone see me except your father."

Roberta would pause and Verbena would say she was sorry she had been so much trouble, even though she had no control over the circumstances of her birth. Verbena would never have a sister to play with but she had only herself to blame.

Late at night after Bill and Roberta were in bed, Verbena would slip back to the kitchen with her doll and teddy bear for her own private birthday party where she finished the entire cake. She talked it out with Bear and Doll saying, "I was bad in the beginning and prevented my little sister from ever being born, but I'll work hard to be good from now on." It was a covenant not inconsistent with her Methodist upbringing.

When Verbena grew up and it became apparent that she would always be fat, Roberta frequently expressed her concern that Verbena herself would have a great deal of trouble in labor. Verbena had no reason to doubt her mother's prophecy.

Eldridge returned to the table balancing a tray containing his super-sized triple cheeseburger combo and Verbena's Big Mac and fries with a Diet Coke. Between mouthfuls of cheeseburger he began to speak of the cottage. "I don't know how we can afford to keep the place after this year. The beach front it's sitting on is worth more than the structure and we could get along for quite awhile on that money."

"No, Eldridge. We are not selling." Verbena stopped chewing her Big Mac and stared past Eldridge at the line of women and children ordering Happy Meals. Some of the kids were starting to cry because the manager announced that they had run out of the little toys. Some Happy Meal.

The beach cottage defined her life just like the toys defined the Happy Meal. She loved her winters in Florida more than life itself and certainly more than she did Eldridge. She couldn't bear the thought of trudging through the slush of Waterford in her wool coat and earmuffs trading frozen smiles with her former classmates.

"They don't know about your escapades down here, Eldridge, so maybe you can get a job teaching at the junior college."

"You fool, they don't teach phys. ed. at junior colleges. And my knees are ruined for any other job." He was silent for a minute except for the crunching of his fries as he stuffed them into his mouth. Finally he added, "Didn't I ask you not to bring up my *escapades*?"

"If you hadn't gotten into trouble you'd still have a job."

"And how in the hell would I be able to leave Waterford for the winter? The town doesn't shut down just because you, the princess, take your leave."

Eldridge always had an answer when it came to working but Verbena would not give up her cottage. She was Scarlet and Deerfield Beach her Tara. Deerfield Beach did define her and set her apart from the rest of Waterford. Eldridge would never understand why she needed to go on living in Waterford and have the rest of them watch her leave for Florida at the first frost.

"Maybe you should find a job down here during the tourist season, Verbena."

"Well what can I do? All I've ever done is take from my parents." A tear began to trickle down Verbena's cheek and she dropped her Big Mac into her fries.

"Just forget it." Eldridge picked up the local sports page from the next table and finished his cheeseburger in silence. And then, since Verbena had returned to the car, he finished her fries and ordered a chocolate shake to go.

FOUR

Nero and Helen stood alone under a sparkling crystal chandelier in the marble foyer of the Colonel's mansion. Helen seemed quite composed, while Nero found it difficult to act nonchalant. He began to fidget as his eyes darted from the chandelier above to the marble tile below. French doors led to the pool area beyond.

"Hold still, dammit," Helen snapped, her words echoing off the tile enclosure. "I can't think."

"Hold still yourself, dammit." In the distance they could hear the faint click of heels. The sound grew louder and suddenly Colonel "Suicide" Collins towered over them. He extended his hand to Helen and smiled perfunctorily then adopted a military at-ease stance, feet apart and hands crossed in the small of his back. He wore riding pants, black boots, and a navy-blue silk polo jersey that bore his name and the number six. A military cut shaped the gray hair around his deeply tanned face. Steel blue eyes took in Nero briefly, as if he were a new recruit, but other than that the Colonel didn't acknowledge his presence.

"It's been a long time, Helen. Have you been well?" He looked past Helen toward the door as if something else were on his mind.

"Tolerable, Sir, despite this frightful heat and dampness that's afflicted us. How about yourself? You certainly don't plan to brave this humid weather and ride today, do you?"

The Colonel turned and smiled at his assistant, then scanned Nero again before proceeding. "Helen, I need someone of your demeanor and discretion to make a delivery for me in the near future. I believe Michael quoted you the terms and you find them agreeable?"

"Yes, and they are generous, Colonel." Helen smiled warmly.

Nero coughed and reached under his silk Hawaiian shirt to scratch his ribs.

The Colonel turned to his assistant and spoke. "Michael, show Helen's guest to his car while Helen and I discuss the details."

"Yes, Sir." In one fluid motion Michael escorted Nero out the door like a dog who was about to puke on the carpet.

As the door slammed the Colonel continued. "I'm sorry if I've offended your friend."

"Really?" Helen mocked.

"Where did you hook up with him?"

"He's a good man. Nero can spot a mark faster than a hound can scent a coon."

"You could have fooled me."

"Successful men like yourself tend to intimidate him. He knows you can't be fooled."

"As do you, Helen."

Helen blushed and smiled.

"I swear you've traded your hillbilly Missouri accent for that of a Georgia peach, though I think that coonhound thing gives you away."

Helen stiffened. "Missouri was so long ago; I almost can't remember."

"From sharecropper's daughter to Northeast Missouri Pork Queen and you never looked back."

"It's marvelous how you can recall such detail, Sir." Helen's voice had lost its honeydew tone and now had the edge of a woman wary of men like the Colonel. "When will you need me?" Helen continued.

"That I can't answer yet." He tapped his riding crop against his forehead. "Arrangements still need to be made; then I will be in touch." He turned to Michael, who had just returned from depositing Nero, and nodded. Michael produced a set of keys and a credit card from his pocket and handed them to Helen. "You remember my condo at Dahlia Dunes?"

Helen nodded. "It's a lovely spot."

"A bit too communal for me I'm afraid. Everyone's involved in everyone else's business. In any case, I want you to move in and wait for my call. Move in alone … as a divorcee or whatever but alone. Am I clear?"

"Yes, Sir; that won't be a problem. Is there anything else?"

"No, that will be all, Helen." The Colonel opened the front door and darted a glance at Nero, who stood fuming next to the De Ville. "It was nice seeing you again, but I'm running late and must join my fellow equestrians. Otherwise I would ask you and your friend to stay and join me for some fresh iced tea by the pool." The Colonel smiled a noncommittal smile. "Michael will show you out." Then he turned and disappeared down the hallway, heels clicking against the marble floor tiles.

Nero managed to contain himself until they were in the car. "What the fuck was that all about?" He slammed his fist into the dash then winced in pain. "We drive all the way out here in weather like a fuckin' sauna for two minutes of his time."

"He needs to show he's in control by giving the orders in person."

"He treated me like I was your fuckin' chauffeur. No, worse, like I was your goddamn servant." Nero's hands flew about in desperation as if he had been enveloped by a swarm of yellow jackets. "The guy thinks he's still a fucking general."

"I told you to stay home. I didn't need any help. And I don't need your Jersey home-boy language either. Let's go."

"Jesus H. Christ! He acted as if I didn't exist. And what's with the General Patton boots and pants?" Nero briefly fingered the gold shark's tooth that hung from a gold chain around his neck before he swiped the sides of his Poncho Villa mustache and stared straight ahead.

"You need to dye your mustache again. The gray doesn't match your toupee."

"Where the hell is that coming from?"

"Start the car, Nero, and let's get out of here."

Nero gripped the wheel hard, but did as he was told leaving his foot on the brake as he accelerated. The tires squealed leaving black skid marks on the brick drive. As they passed the clubhouse, he slammed on the brakes and made a hard right into the parking lot just missing a man in a plum jacket and cream-colored slacks. "These must be some of the Colonel's *equestrian fellows*."

To Helen's dismay he turned off the ignition and jumped out of the car. "Excuse me, sir. Do you have any Grey Poupon?"

The wife of the man in the plum jacket took his arm as they huddled together like two lost puppies in the rain. Nero speculated that they had purchased here to avoid uncomfortable encounters such as this. "I beg your pardon?" the man finally ventured.

"Just kidding, Old Bean." Nero smiled broadly as if he were on his best behavior. "Actually my wife and I were hoping to join our fellow equestrian aficionados, but we seem to have lost our way."

Just then the car door opened and Helen shrieked, "Nero, get in the fucking car now!"

Both Nero and the old couple jumped. Then Nero dashed back to the car. "Sorry, chaps, the little lady can't stay: low estrogen, hot flashes, and all that rubbish. Tah tah for now."

As they headed for the gate they passed the guard driving his golf cart at full throttle toward the parking lot. "It's lucky we've got a head start on him," Nero remarked.

Helen's response was ice cold. Her hands shook as she lit a cigarette. "You don't fuck with the Colonel."

FIVE

Nero Venditto grew up in Newark as the son of Mario *The Torch* Venditto. Mario was an arsonist for the Protano family before their hostile takeover by the Guilones. One night after too much Chianti, Mario announced that his son should be named after the most famous of all Italian arsonists and thus christened the infant Nero.

When Nero turned fourteen, Mario was waylaid by the Bellotti family while torching one of their Laundromats and never seen again. Nero learned that while crime did pay, the days of the independent hood were over. Like corporate America, a few families would soon control everything.

He was sixty-two, but he'd been working cons on the east coast of Florida since age eighteen. Lately, while Helen waited in her condo for a call from the Colonel, he spent his mornings at the Pelican's Pantry scouting new pilgrims from the North.

Today he noticed a man his own age reading *USA Today*. The stranger sipped his coffee slowly and seemed in no particular hurry. Nero picked up his cup and worked his way over to the table. "Excuse me. Do you mind if I look at a section of your paper?"

"No, go right ahead." The man smiled and handed over the sports section as Nero sat down to join him.

A Midwesterner, thought Nero. They're such easy marks. Nero feigned interest in the paper for a moment, then spoke to his quarry. "You must be new to the area; from the Midwest? How ya doin'?"

"Cedar Rapids, Iowa, but how did you know I was new?" His smile was Midwest friendly and his eyes curious. Experience taught Nero that

Midwesterners were inquisitive herd creatures incapable of thriving in a vacuum like the Eastern city dweller.

"It's your skin," Nero said

Leon looked down at his arms and laughed. "I guess I do stand out like a Yorkshire hog in a field of Durocs."

"Charming analogy. Are you down for the winter?"

"I'm renting a place from a fellow over at Dahlia Dunes. It's just this side of the river on the mainland, less expensive than being on the barrier island. It's my first winter down here. How about yourself?"

"I never could afford to live near the beach. I'm west of here near I 95. I work three doors down at Mattress World; been there two years. Sales is my thing but never too long in one place. Management's always screwing you over. More sales for less pay. Then as soon as they make a little headway, they want to stay open twenty-four hours a day without increasing the staff." Improv lying came naturally to Nero after so many years.

"Tell me about it," agreed Leon. "I give one company the best years of my life and they downsize me. I sold office equipment."

"*Early retirement* they call it, like it's a fucking favor. Pardon my French. Are you going to get another job?"

"Who wants a guy my age, unless I want to bag groceries at Publix?"

"No kidding. Look, I gotta be going or I'll be bagging groceries for a living. I usually take a coffee break here this time every morning, so maybe I'll see you again. My name's Nero Venditto." Nero grinned and extended his hand.

"Leon Eckerman, Nero. It's a pleasure to talk to a working man." Leon took Nero's hand.

Ten minutes later Nero was on the phone to Helen. "Listen, I found just the guy to keep you occupied while you wait for GI Joe to call."

"I don't think this is a good idea, Nero. The Colonel could call any time."

"You said yourself that it could be weeks or months."

"Yes, that's how he operates. He's terribly careful; everything must be in place before he moves."

"Then we have plenty of time. Besides, once the Colonel does get off his ass, his job is only going to take a couple of hours. We've got our own future to worry about."

"Our future? Have you been reading *Modern Maturity* again?"

"We need to think about our future, Helen. That magazine said that most people don't put enough away for retirement, and Social Security won't cover a fraction of their needs.

"And you've put away how much?"

"Zip, nada. That's why we need a score, but even with that we'll probably have to ship off to old Mexico or Costa Rica to make it last."

"So you have nothing in the bank?"

"My God haven't you been listening to CNN at all? The banks are a scam and those corporate pricks the biggest cons of them all. They're worse than me and they're legal. They squeeze the lifeblood out of their employees and reward themselves with millions in bonuses. And the brokerage houses are in their pockets. Accepting big bribes on the front end to take the stock public, they soak the little guy with commissions on the back end. If the stock falls, they collect another commission to get the putz out. Meanwhile, corporations shell out peanuts in dividends and grant executives and board members huge stock options so they can manipulate their stock's price.

"Insider trading. That's where the money is made, Helen. I know 'cause my cousin Vito was a broker. He told me all this shit right after they threw him out for breaking a guy's arm. The guy deserved it; he gave Vito a bogus insider tip. CEO's make the Godfathers look like fuckin' amateurs.

"All that's left for the people like us is Social Security and that's an even bigger joke. You never saw me put a goddamn dime into Social Security. Like we should trust those bozo politicians. Why should I put up money just so they can hand it to some fat bald guumba on the beach? They expect me to believe that some yokel from Elkfuck, Wyoming, will be willing to put money in for me when it's my turn on the beach? When I need a Social Security number I make one up.

"Gold, Helen! That's the answer; put your savings in gold. There's no politics or hidden agenda in gold."

Helen sighed. "All right. 'Tis what ah' do best, honey. I could play the Colonel's lonely widow. His picture's all over the place."

Helen hadn't worried her pretty little head about the world of economics like Nero had, but she had never put away anything for a rainy day either. Her whole adult life had been spent with men who had assured her they would take care of her. Of course, none had followed through on their promises.

Now her last hope lay with Nero, whose only apparent asset was the gold shark's tooth hanging from his neck. She had her doubts. It wasn't because she thought Nero wouldn't come through, but rather her anxiety concerning the finality of spending her remaining years in some sterile retirement complex with this good fella wannabe from Jersey.

Her career had started long ago when she captured fourth runner-up as Missouri's Pork Queen and jumped at the chance to follow a contest judge back to Atlanta to begin a modeling career. He lied, of course, as did most of the other men in the years that followed. But Helen shrugged off the disappointment and successively learned from her mistakes. Nothing they could do to her compared to her previous life of poverty on a pig farm swilling hogs, a life lived in a cultural vacuum.

Once she thought of *retiring* and marrying the Colonel. Despite his ability to offer her everything, he wasn't like the men who had led Eisenhower's armies. He was driven in a way that frightened her. Money satisfied her but he craved power. Wealth was merely the means to obtain it. She suspected that he and the CEOs Nero preached about answered a common calling. No, despite all his failings, she felt safer with Nero.

SIX

The Colonel had finished his morning workout of sixty laps in his pool and now sat in his white cotton robe savoring a cup of freshly brewed Kona coffee. Michael had delivered his raisin bran, whole wheat toast, and an imperial red grapefruit half on a silver tray upon which also rested a copy of the *New York Times*. Michael drove five miles to the nearest Snatch 'n Go every morning and returned with the paper before the Colonel finished his swim. The Colonel expected it and never commented.

Out of the corner of his eye the Colonel caught sight of a small chameleon darting across the deck and into the green-and-red-splashed bromeliads. Their long slender blades pointed skyward and reminded the Colonel of bloody bayonets. He scanned the headlines but his thoughts were on Helen. He could trust her. She was uncomplicated; she liked money and had an aversion to poverty. For this kind of money she had no reason to disobey orders. The world needed more women like that. He needed a woman like that. Damn her for leaving!

But Venditto was a different story. A low budget con artist who made his money off confused little old ladies wasn't part of the plan. In fact, his quick temper could ruin the whole deal. "Michael, get your ass out here," Colonel Collins shouted to a shadow waiting just the other side of the French doors.

"Yes, Sir." Then the sound of heels striking the tile floor. Michael drew up just short of the Colonel.

The Colonel smiled at his power to bring men running and relaxed in his chair. "Sit down, Michael. Do you want some toast?"

"No thank you, Sir. I just ate in the kitchen." Michael sat down opposite the Colonel.

"Have we heard from Estefan yet?"

"No, he's still working the Boca area raising money for the guns."

"What the hell is taking so long?"

"It seems one of the universities down there is campaigning hard to raise money for a Division One football team and a new stadium. They've hired TJ Estrada as their front man and eventual coach."

"That spic analyst from ESPN? You're kidding."

"Yes, he is Latino but he was an all-pro running back with the Dolphins before he blew out his knee."

"The television offer was easier than the rehab. He's not tough enough to be a coach."

"Just the same, Sir, he's got a big following in the Latin community and he's sucking in a lot of money."

"I can't goddamn believe it. We let those Cuban patriots into our country and now they're all going soft on us. They talk about a free, democratic Cuba but you won't see a one of the rich bastards lined up to get back on the boat after the revolution."

"I'm afraid Helen may have to wait awhile," Michael said.

"She'll wait. Are you sure that credit card you gave her was encrypted?"

"Yes, Sir. I tested it myself. Every transaction will be immediately recorded at the Agency. Within minutes of her using it, we can pinpoint the amount and location. It's as if we had planted a transmitter in her purse."

"Excellent, but I'm also worried about that sneaking dago boyfriend of hers. I want to know where he lives and how he spends his time. Put somebody on it today."

"Yes, Sir." Michael rose to leave and then waited for permission to speak.

"What is it, Michael?"

"It's just that I'm Italian too, Sir. You called that man a sneaking dago. So how can you trust me?"

"Because you're *my* goddamn dago. That's why. Now get the hell out of here."

"Yes, Sir." Michael forced a smile and turned to leave.

"Michael, wait."

"Sir?"

"You don't have any spic blood do you?"

"No, Sir."

"Good, because I just realized we should eliminate Estrada for strategic purposes."

"Excuse me?"

"You heard what I said, Michael. If Coach Estrada is standing in the way of a free Cuba he must be sacrificed. I want to send a message to the Cuban community. Arrange it with demolitions; they'll know what to do." The Colonel inspected his grapefruit to be sure it had been sectioned properly. Without looking up he said, "The high command has spoken, Michael. Get moving."

SEVEN

After their marriage, Eldridge Dewitt began to travel to Florida with Verbena and her father. Like a manatee near a power plant in January, Eldridge adapted well to the warm weather, the lifestyle, and the restaurant food. He could be found most days under a striped umbrella on the boardwalk playing Hearts for a penny a point with the prune-faced old-timers who lived from one Social Security check to the next. Hunkered down in his aluminum arm chair beside his cooler of Miller beer, he was wearing his red-and-yellow bamboo print trunks and his Cleveland Indians cap. Eldridge's sunburned face and peeling gut perfectly matched the hue of the Chief Wahoo logo. This winter proved to be no different.

Verbena stood at the open window facing the ocean breeze and watched as Eldridge slapped down what she surmised was the queen of spades. "You're going to bed with the slut queen!" he shouted.

Winning at Hearts wasn't going to pay the rent. Her stomach spasmed whenever she thought about it and she involuntarily clasped her hand over it to make the rumble stop. She contemplated a Moon Pie to settle her stomach and take her mind off her troubles.

As she walked barefoot to the kitchen she could feel the gritty sand under her feet and stopped to write herself a note to call the repair shop and find out if the vacuum had been fixed. The disinterested young man who'd picked it up had assured her it would be ready by now.

Returning to the window with its faded yellow chintz curtains she noticed their neighbor descending his back steps. He was wrestling with a red-striped umbrella and a pink beach chair. She stripped the cellophane off the Moon Pie and sunk her teeth into its soft marshmallow center.

Verbena rapped on the window and waved. Tom looked up, startled, and subsequently missed the last step. As he struggled to maintain his balance Verbena squealed in dismay and waddled out her back door to Tom's side. Eldridge looked up briefly then resumed arranging his cards.

"I'm so sorry, Tom. Are you all right?"

"I'm fine, Verbena. No harm done." He grinned sheepishly. Verbena shifted her pudgy feet in the hot sand and felt herself blush for no apparent reason. She guessed Tom's age as late thirties or early forties. His brown hair had a natural wave enhanced to a cascade of curls by the Florida humidity. Tiny white tan lines emanated from the corners of his eyes due to a constant squint because he was forever misplacing his sunglasses. The rest of his features were undistinguished although a bit effeminate: average height and build with an even caramel tan.

"Will you sit with me, Verbena?"

"Okay, I'll go get a lawn chair." It usually took her two months in Florida to change from *lawn* to *beach chair*. The reverse occurred when she returned to Waterford causing the locals to comment on how uppity she had become. If Tom noticed her error he didn't comment.

"Don't bother; I've got to get the cooler. I'll bring you one. You want an Orange Crush with your Moon Pie?"

"That would be nice, Tom." Eldridge used to be thoughtful like that before her father died. Now he just ignored her. They rarely even had sex but Verbena didn't care. Eldridge's idea of sex involved jumping into bed naked and shouting, "Here I come with Big Boy!" He'd climb on top of her and last about thirty seconds, groan, and roll off. He seemed quite sure of his prowess, and felt compelled to let Verbena know from his vast experience as a phys. ed. teacher that all men were pretty much equally endowed in the Big Boy department. Like she cared.

Tom disappeared into his cottage and returned moments later with a blue and white Playmate cooler and a webbed chair. "Sit here, Verbena, while I set the umbrella." He unfolded the chair and proceeded with intense effort to corkscrew the umbrella deep into the sand. "There, how's that?"

"Wonderful, Tom," Verbena responded as she popped the top on the Orange Crush.

Tom pulled a chair beside her and cracked open a Dr. Pepper. He leaned back and sighed. "What a day! I couldn't work inside a minute longer."

He reached for his suntan oil and began to squeeze copious amounts into his hands, filling the air with the aroma of coconut. Verbena closed her eyes and inhaled the fragrance as she sipped her orange soda. Then she wiggled her chubby toes in the hot sand and giggled.

"What's that about?" Tom looked over and asked.

It was Verbena's turn to sigh. "It doesn't get any better than this." She began to hum and sway to the tune *Tuxedo Junction*, which she'd heard on her father's cherished Glenn Miller album. Her parents would never let her buy those trashy albums the other kids listened to.

"I rented this place to write my novel but I'm afraid I should have picked somewhere more dismal. I can't concentrate."

"How far along are you?"

"I'm still on the first chapter. I can't decide if I should start in the present and then flash back, or start in the past and work up to the present. I originally thought of starting where the mother of my hero moves back in with him after his divorce and tries to console him by denouncing his wife for the slut she is. Then I would flash back to the courtship, marriage, and eventual breakup which would bring me back to the present when my hero would confront his mother with his newly discovered homosexual orientation. What do you think?"

"Are you asking me, Tom? I'm flattered but I'm afraid I'm not very creative." Verbena burped softly and took another bite of Moon Pie. "The only writing I did in high school was as a club secretary."

"Didn't you take creative writing?"

"No, but sometimes my mind wandered during the meetings and I would have to make up some filler. Nobody read the minutes anyway."

"Did you really meet Eldridge in high school?"

"Not really. I was always fat." The aluminum frame of her chair groaned as she shifted self-consciously in her chair. "Most boys didn't know I was alive. Eldridge was the star quarterback and they went to state his senior year. He even got a football scholarship to Wisconsin but he ruined his knee freshman year."

"And he never talked to you in high school?"

"Well, one time." Her voice trailed off and she began to make designs with her toes in the sand.

"And?"

"It's sort of embarrassing."

"Listen, Verbena, I'm a writer. We handle *embarrassing* with discretion." Tom squinted at Verbena as if he was trying to look deeply into her eyes, and Verbena realized she had no idea what color Tom's eyes were.

"Well, one time I confided in Andrea Thorson, who I thought was my best friend. I admitted I had never been lucky in love. Andrea, who's now married to Henry Streator, our pharmacist, was a Homesteader cheerleader and homecoming queen."

The intuitive writer smiled and shook his head as if he knew what was coming.

"She defined *lucky in love* as getting your period every month." Verbena blushed again but when Tom laughed she suddenly felt comfortable with her confession.

A now-animated Verbena began to reenact the incident playing the roles of both Andrea and herself.

"But there must be somebody," Andrea said.

"I've never even gotten a valentine, except from Mom and Dad."

"But there must be somebody," she kept insisting.

"Well, Eldridge is pretty cute but he doesn't know I'm alive, even though he sits next to me in fifth hour history."

"Eldridge? Eldridge Dewitt our quarterback?" She had that annoying habit of covering her mouth with her hand to stifle a giggle.

"It's a cheerleader thing," Tom interrupted. "So what did you answer?"

"I said, 'Yes, but swear to God you won't tell.' Of course she said, 'Swear to God.'"

"God, cheerleaders can be so bitchy."

Verbena laughed and looked at Tom. "Whose story is this?"

"Sorry." Tom drew an imaginary zipper across his lips.

"I can still picture Andrea with her head cocked as she began to twirl a strand of her long black hair and smiled a smile that suggested her mind was already somewhere else. My stomach did a flip flop just like before you get diarrhea.

"Andrea, true to form, spread the news all over school by fifth hour. As I stepped into the classroom everyone looked at me and I knew. My face burned as deep within me a rumble began that sent me straight for the bathroom where I threw up. The diarrhea came later. I felt so betrayed and embarrassed that I ran all the way home from school. No small feat for a fat girl."

Verbena noticed a tear trickling down Tom's cheek. "That must have been so awful for you."

"It was, but the next day I returned to class and in a few days the teasing and smirks disappeared. To my immense relief, Eldridge acted as if nothing had happened and even offered to lend me his notes from my missed history class."

"Did you confront that bitch, Andrea?"

"I was pretty swamped by my secretary duties and soon forgot about it. Andrea Thorson did notice later that the poignant remarks she had made regarding the French Club's visit to the art exhibit at the university in Madison never made the minutes."

"Ha! So you got even, girl."

"I guess I did but I always wished I had confronted her. I've rewritten that dialogue in my head a thousand times. But that's a long time ago. A small scar on a big body … but with a pretty face," Verbena mocked.

Verbena had never developed her own circle of friends in Florida but chose instead the friends of her parents, who had begun their pilgrimages in the late 70's. The older generation appreciated her attentiveness and sincerity, and they doted on her as if she was their own child. The women remarked again and again on her pretty face and her long blond hair.

Shiny headed bald men in madras jackets and who smelled of Aqua Velva asked her to dance to the music of Guy Lombardo. Their Lincoln Continentals, Cadillacs, and Buick Electras sported eight-track tape decks blaring Sinatra's *Strangers in the Night* or Dean Martin's *Volare* as if the whole world were hearing impaired. Verbena acquiesced to this lifestyle, becoming an anachronism in her own generation.

But now her parents' friends were slipping away. While some returned to their homes in the North to live near their own children, others entered nursing homes marketed as *progressive care facilities* to those with the hefty down payment and enough residual cash to pay the monthly fees.

The less financially endowed secluded themselves in their condos, wearing a path between their hot plates and their recliners. They watched Jerry Springer and prayed God would take them before his guests, or people like them, broke down their doors and murdered them in their beds. Eventually God answered their prayers, and their remains were quietly air-freighted North while their obituaries, meaningless to most of Deerfield Beach, went unnoticed.

Tom Poole was the only friend near her own age that Verbena had. The fact that he was gay and a writer made him much more exotic than the Andrea Thorson Streator types of Waterford. Verbena didn't see him as gay but rather as a man with a strong feminine side. She could share things with him that she never could with Eldridge, like why she could never give up the beach house.

Verbena could hear the sound of Eldridge's tangerine flip-flops as he approached the cottage from the beach. She looked up from her reading and smiled as he dumped a pocketful of change on the counter. "Looks like you did well at Hearts today, dear."

"No challenge today, Babe. Fred keeps having senior moments and forgets what's already been played. And his vision isn't too hot either. I played the jack of spades and he mistook it for the jack of clubs and threw on the queen and had to take the trick. Man, I wish we were playing for a buck a point."

Verbena watched as he and his flip-flops trailed sand to the refrigerator door. He let out a loud belch then bent over to drag out more beer for his cooler. His sunburned butt crack peeked out of the waistband of his suit but Verbena didn't comment.

"I see you and that fag writer were having a nice chat on the beach." Eldridge's voice echoed from deep within the refrigerator.

"Don't call Tom a fag, Eldridge. He's a nice man who's just trying to find himself."

"I hope you didn't mention that *little problem* I had up North."

"Heavens no, Eldridge. Like Father said that first winter we all came down here together, that stays in the family. Besides, it's all in the past."

"You're right it's in the goddamn past. Like it was some big fuckin' deal anyway."

"You were the football coach and phys. ed. teacher, Eldridge. You could have gone to jail."

"Bullshit!" Eldridge belched again as his face reddened. "It was just a little peep show."

"You were making video tapes through a peep hole in the girls' locker room."

"What did it matter to those girls? Always flaunting their tight little asses and big tits in the hallways. 'I can't come to phys. ed. today, Mr. Dewitt. I have cramps,' or 'Please don't give us a test today, Mr. Dewitt.' 'I have a pass to go to the dentist, Mr. Dewitt.' All the time batting their eyelashes and wiggling their butts or bending over to let me have a little peek down their blouses."

"It was wrong, Eldridge. They didn't deserve that."

"Hell, you didn't even know me then." He banged his beer can on the counter.

"You're right. You never came around until you were fired."

"It was all because of the fuss put up by those lesbo feminists." Eldridge snorted and hitched up his trunks.

"Eldridge!" Talking about Eldridge's past made her uncomfortable. Verbena plucked the dish towel off the counter and patted her sweat-dampened face and arms. She had run out of baby powder.

"It's true. You yourself even said that Andrea Streator, your old friend and born again Christian, said that they were lesbos for a fact and should have been fired themselves."

At the mention of Andrea, Verbena began to laugh softly. "It was kind of funny. Her church volleyball league played at the high school on Wednesday night and she told everyone in town that she'd be mortified if she showed up on one of your tapes. She always finished with that nervous little laugh that ended with an annoying snort."

"I think she would have been more disappointed if she hadn't appeared on those tapes." Eldridge tipped his head back and chugged the rest of his Miller beer.

"Eldridge, you didn't?"

"Hell, no. Besides she wasn't exactly a vision worth preserving." Eldridge scratched his big belly and stared off into the distance, his alcohol-induced gaze almost whimsical. He sighed. "You know, Verbena, I hadn't had a winning season in four years. That's the real reason they fired me."

Verbena knew there was no point in arguing further with a sports legend. Verbena had been so happy when Eldridge first paid attention to her. He helped her plant the pansies, laughing as they reminded him of his former football teams. When it came time for her errands, he insisted on driving Verbena chauffeur style.

Verbena also knew the Streators were not a kind couple in tiny Waterford, where gossip and a harsh word travel at Internet speed. Andrea sniped, "At least the poor thing has somebody." And Henry commented that Eldridge hopped around like a damn monkey on a string while he waited on Verbena. These comments all reached and wounded her. But if that wasn't enough, Verbena, who had taken a childlike pride in her shapeless hibiscus print shifts gleaned from the beach shops of Florida, heard that Andrea had referred to her as the Muumuu Queen.

She knew it was wrong but deep down inside she wanted to kill that snotty bitch. And if there was anything between Eldridge and her she'd kill them both and sell the story rights to her new friend Tom.

EIGHT

Vinnie D.'s experience in both the U.S. Army's Special Forces and the School of the Americas qualified him for the top spot in Colonel Collins' Clandestine Activities Group, CAG as the Colonel insisted it be called. In fact, as far as Vinnie knew, he was the only member of the Colonel's elite group.

When the orders came down to eliminate Coach Estrada, he skillfully masterminded a plan, which included designing the perfect bomb and hiring a local Cuban anarchist to carry out the mission. The Colonel felt strongly that Cubans should be employed in their own liberation. Besides, if they were exposed, the incident could be blamed on the militant faction of the Cuban community.

That's why Vinnie was sitting on this particular park bench in South Miami in smoldering ninety-degree heat waiting for a man he had never met. On the sidewalk nearby, hordes of fire ants swarmed the liquid remains of a cherry Popsicle.

It was eleven a.m. The joggers and walkers had cleared out before nine to avoid the suffocating humidity, and the park stood empty except for four sweat-drenched retirees on the distant tennis courts.

A young Latino approached from the west entrance. Vinnie groaned. His contact was wearing an orange silk shirt and pleated gray slacks. His shoes were black patent leather and Vinnie could hear the rhythmic click of steel heel clips as they struck the concrete. The guy was a cross between a jockey and a pimp. "Jesus Christ!" he muttered.

As the man approached, Vinnie folded his newspaper and stood. "Carlos Delgado?"

His contact stopped abruptly as if someone had slapped him in the face. "Shhh! Don't call me that. I am wanted." He looked nervously over his shoulder as if he expected to be apprehended momentarily. "I am Carlos *El Gato,* the cat," he whispered.

"Whatever you say, Mr. Gato. Sit."

El Gato looked around again then took a seat. "I congratulate you, sir. You have selected a most talented assassin when you asked for *El Gato.*"

"Who do you work for?"

"I work for no one. They call me *El Gato Solo, el hombre de muerto!*"

"It's a pretty long goddamn name. Must be hard to order return address labels."

Carlos jumped to his feet. "You would make fun of me. I kill for less!"

"Sit down, Poncho. I just need to know your credentials if you are going to work for us."

El Gato twitched nervously and returned to his seat. The men on the tennis court finished their game and departed.

"Who have you worked for, Gato?"

"El Gato has contracted with *Siempre Libre, Los Tigres, Los Desperados,* and many others. If there is danger, El Gato is there."

"Impressive. Maybe we can use you," Vinnie lied. The groups Carlos had mentioned were nothing more than frustrated street gangs, but enough of a connection to distance El Gato from the Colonel if necessary.

"There is no job too difficult or dangerous for El Gato."

Great, thought Vinnie. *A guy who thinks he's fuckin' Zorro.* "We just need an assassin."

"Excellent, Jefe. Will El Gato be smuggled into Cuba?"

"No, more like Coral Gables." *And probably not as easy,* thought Vinnie. "I will make a bomb for you to place under the car of a man who is spying for Castro."

"*Hijo de puta*! El Gato will slash the bastard's throat."

"Sorry, Gato. We just want to blow him the fuck up. *Comprende?*"

NINE

"I tell ya I woke up and the damn dog's head is lying in my crotch right on my balls. He's just lying there looking up at me with those big brown eyes of his. Helen says they're sooo expressive. They're expressive all right. I so much as make one move and he bares his fangs and growls." Leon Eckerman nervously adjusted the waistline of his turquoise Sansabelt slacks. It had been two months since he had met Helen and moved in with her.

Leon studied his reflection in the window of Melbourne's Mattress World, took out his comb, and combed back what remained of his thinning pompadour. Someone once said he looked like Elvis but that was years ago. At sixty his hair was thinning and it took more than Sansabelt slacks to restrain his paunch. Sometimes Leon thought it was better to be like John F. Kennedy or Princess Di. Exit young — leave a handsome corpse.

Leon liked Nero. They had been meeting for coffee almost daily for the past two months. Nero's banter made Leon laugh. His friendship and Helen's companionship made his mundane life as a business machine salesman seem a long time ago and his firing just a bad dream.

"I'll loan you my thirty-eight special and you can blow his fuckin' head off."

"Jesus, Nero. What are you thinking? This is my balls we're talking about here. Christ!"

"Like you need them, Eckerman. Unless you're taking that Vee-agra." Nero smoothed the crease in his cream-colored pleated slacks and patted his cigarettes in the pocket of his Tommy Bahama floral print shirt. Leon wondered if the gold chain around Nero's neck sported a genuine gold-dipped shark's tooth.

"I don't see you moving in with anybody."

"I got a job. Remember? I don't need to walk no dog with a gonad fetish." Nero took one last drag on his cigarette and crushed it under his black tasseled loafer into the sidewalk. "Look, I gotta' get back inside. I'm expecting a buyer from Sea Grape, that new golf resort. We're talking five hundred mattresses. Plus, I think she wants me." Nero turned and checked his reflection in the window adjusting his coal black toupee. "I'll see ya tomorrow, man. Y'all sleep tight now ya hear!"

"Bullshit!" Leon replied.

Leon slid behind the wheel of Helen's midnight blue Lincoln Mark IV. He had parked his seafoam Taurus when he moved in with Helen and her damn dog. Helen was the kind of woman who couldn't function without a man around. Some women were like that.

They met at the condo association's weekly bingo night. Leon only attended because he wanted to win a fifth of cheap bourbon. At the time he was barely able to pay the rent on his place.

Helen approached him during the break. "Leon, I do believe you haven't taken your eyes off of me all night," she drawled. "It is Leon isn't it? Bertie said you were the new fellow in the J building."

She was a striking blond probably a six petite, the kind of woman that turned men's heads and earned women's scowls. Gold chains adorned her neck and complemented her four finger rings. From her deep tan and skin tone Leon could only surmise her age to be anywhere between fifty and sixty five.

Leon habitually studied women, but he wasn't used to being called on it and felt the sudden rush of heat in his face. "That's me, ma'am. Bertie must have told everyone about me. I hope it was good." He couldn't remember for the life of him who Bertie was.

Her necklaces rattled softly as she laughed. "Yes, Leon. I know all about you." She reached out and touched his forearm and Leon instantly relaxed as if he had been touched by a magic wand. "A single man doesn't have any secrets for long around here. Leon, these streets are so poorly lit. Would you mind escorting me to my condo after bingo? I could possibly offer you a bourbon." Before he could answer, she winked then spun around and quickly returned to her friends.

Surprised at his luck, Leon could barely concentrate on the game. The caller, a tall skinny guy in horn-rimmed glasses, looked eighty and had a visible tremor whenever he reached for a ball. His dentures fit so badly that when he called out the numbers it sounded as if he had marbles in his mouth. Leon missed one bingo, then blurted out *Bingo* later in error. He felt the glare as everyone's eyes fixed on him, then noticed Helen who smiled and winked again.

Amazingly their conversation flowed effortlessly as they walked home in the dark. When Helen suggested he needed to work on his bingo skills, his laugh came easy, and he was only mildly surprised when she really did invite him in for a nightcap.

Helen gave him a quick tour of the two-bedroom place stating that her deceased husband had been career army; they had lived all over the world. Pale peach grasscloth wall coverings were adorned with art from the Far East interspersed between photos Leon presumed were of her late husband. There were pictures of him with politicians that looked familiar but Leon couldn't recall their names. Then there was a picture of him standing with George Bush, and another on the edge of a desert in full battle gear with General Schwarzkopf. Her husband was always the same, grim faced and serious, a man with a mission.

In the living room Helen pointed to a black lacquered oriental liquor cabinet. "Won't you fix us something, hon?"

"Sure. What would you like?" Leon perused the stock which included Maker's Mark and Wild Turkey as well as brandy, scotch, and gin. The general certainly knew his bourbon.

"Anything as long as it's with bourbon. I simply cannot tolerate scotch. I've concluded it's a Yankee drink." Suddenly she flushed. "Y'all aren't a Yankee are you? At least you don't talk like one."

"I guess it depends on what you call a Yankee. I'm a Midwesterner from Iowa. We did fight for the Union."

"How awful. You lived practically next door to that terrible Mr. Lincoln from Illinois."

Leon started to pour the Maker's Mark as he cursed his lineage. He figured he'd be thrown out any minute.

Helen appeared to pout for a moment then pronounced, "A

Midwesterner is not a Yankee. A Yankee has to be from a place with the word *new* in front of it, like New York, or New England, or New Jersey."

"I'll drink to that." A relieved Leon passed a tumbler of bourbon to Helen and lifted his own.

Helen smiled and raised her glass. "Here's to new friends and the end of Yankee tyranny and tourism."

Eventually when they were both a little drunk Helen suddenly began to cry. "I was raised in Atlanta and used to being cared for. Father was an executive at Coca Cola and we lived in a fine home with colored servants. Jack came along and looked so handsome and strong in his fine uniform, but he couldn't fathom why I wasn't more self-sufficient. Always the military man, he took charge whenever I got befuddled by a situation."

"I'll bet you were a very beautiful and supportive officer's wife."

"I gave such wonderful parties and teas. Everyone loved them but I don't think Jack ever fully appreciated their importance to his career. By the time Jack retired, he was a colonel and knew nothing but uniforms, salutes, and being addressed as 'Sir.' Civilian life was a terrible adjustment for him, even though we settled here in Melbourne near the air base."

"I'm sure giving up all that power created a sense of impotence."

"Oh, you're more right than you know!" Helen smiled and held her cold glass against her flushing cheek. "When he gave up the uniform, he no longer had any idea who he was and became cranky and distant. Then he died of a coronary leaving me helpless without enough sense to even get the little ol' oil changed in the car. You can't imagine what a struggle it has been for me to become the self-sufficient woman I am today," Helen concluded.

Leon nodded with drunken sympathy. He had served in Vietnam as an enlisted man and thought officers were morons. Internally he thought Jack got just what he deserved when he retired. He almost smiled as he pictured him with cropped hair and knobby knees standing ramrod straight trying to appear the man of leisure in walking shorts and a Hawaiian luau shirt. But he didn't let on to Helen.

In fact, he found himself more attracted to Helen because she had been an officer's wife. He envisioned himself, an enlisted man, having an affair with an officer's wife and it all seemed just a bit more forbidden. Leon realized he was aroused and was about to move over to the couch next to Helen when he heard the growl. A white toy poodle stood in the doorway to the sun porch, fangs bared.

"Oh, there's my Pookie. Come here to Mama." Helen made kissing sounds as Pookie wiggled across the threshold and leapt into her lap. Leon felt his amorous feelings drain away. "Pookie, this is Leon," she cooed. Leon was amazed at the sudden change in Helen's behavior. From a sexually attractive lady she had instantly morphed into a blubbering doting old grandmother. It unnerved Leon.

Pookie licked at Helen's ear and Helen pretended he whispered sweet nothings. "Pookie says you were in sales, Leon."

"Pookie's pretty smart. I sold office supplies for a small company until I was downsized and kicked out. It cost me half my pension."

"I hope your pension is protected. Jack said there's no safer pension than the U.S. government. What would happen if your little company went bankrupt?" At this point she cooed again to Pookie and kissed him on his little doggie lips. Leon squirmed and took another swallow of bourbon.

"I could have taken a lump sum distribution and I still could. I suppose that might be safe but if I live a long time it wouldn't nearly cover what the monthly payout would."

"Well, as Jack always said, *A bird in the hand* ... well, you know what I mean."

"Sure." Leon wanted to change the subject. He was uneasy about his finances as it was and didn't need any advice from a dead prick colonel.

But that was two months ago. Helen's advances and encouragement drew Iowa Leon like a hog to clover. Within three days they behaved like two hormonally-charged teenagers in heat. A long-deprived Leon saw no incongruity between the soft Southern belle he'd met at bingo and the tigress he bedded. He almost wept as he ran his hands in amazement over her soft pillowy breasts and down across her well preserved thighs with only a hint of early spider veins. Clearly he beheld the temple of a body that had born no children.

When he moved in with Helen, she persisted with her suggestion that he take that safe lump sum pension and sublet his place. With her husband's pension, they could pool their resources and maybe even move into more upscale accommodations. Leon guessed the only thing that held him back was her damn dog Pookie. He wondered how much more life the little dust muffin had in him.

TEN

Vinnie parked his car in the lot of a shiny new fast food place that served seasoned Cuban chicken with black beans and rice. It reminded him of a Latino Kenny Rogers. It was pouring rain, so he turned on the radio and watched the windows fog up as he waited for Gato.

Soon he heard a rap at the window and looked out to see Gato in a white shirt, red bow tie, and the franchise's paper hat. He unlocked the doors and let him in.

"Man it's pouring. I'm soaked."

"Yeah, it's raining *gatos* and dogs, buddy. You didn't tell me you worked at this place."

"It's a cover, man. Who would suspect El Gato, the assassin, to work here?" His paper hat was melting. Red and yellow dye ran down his face.

"You're right, Gato. Who would suspect?"

El Gato beamed at the apparent compliment. "Did you bring the package?"

"It's here in the back seat." Vinnie reached back and retrieved a small black bundle. "This is a complex bomb but all you need to know is how to arm it."

"How does it work?"

"It's based on velocity. I've set it so it will go off when the vehicle reaches a speed of 55 which usually means an interstate on-ramp. It avoids the risk of blowing away some school kids or a nun. Much cleaner."

"I see, Mr. Vinnie. So El Gato doesn't give the revolutionaries a bad name."

"That's right, Cisco."

"Hey, didn't I see this in a movie? Yes, that funny actress driving a bus."

"It was called *Speed*. I think it starred Bruce Willis and Madonna."

"No, I don't think it was Madonna."

"Who the fuck cares? The point is that in the movie the bomb goes off if the bus slows down. That's why they called it *Speed*. This bomb goes off when the car accelerates."

"Yes, El Gato understands clearly. But I know it wasn't Madonna."

"Just take the fuckin' bomb and wait for my call. You activate it by turning on this switch after you tape it to the chassis near the gas tank."

"Piece of cake, *Jefe*."

"Just get the hell out. You're dripping all over my car."

ELEVEN

Bennett Durant stood over the entangled pile of used vacuum cleaners, hoses, and electric cords that he had just dumped out of his boss's rusted Country Squire wagon. *What's he going to do with all this stuff?* he thought. *There can't be a dozen functional parts in all this garbage.* Besides it stunk of dog hair, mildew, and even fish.

Who the hell would vacuum fish guts? He imagined some of the old farts he delivered to and envisioned them sucking up spilled fish guts from the fish they weren't supposed to be gutting in the house anyway – getting their butts chewed out by their wives because they'd ruined a perfectly good vacuum cleaner.

He pulled a cigarette out of his pocket, lit it, and inhaled deeply taking pleasure in the tobacco's aroma. Sometimes it seemed like the entire male population of Florida consisted of retired old men with skinny white legs dangling below baggy plaid shorts, not to mention their cheap Taiwan tennis shoes accessorized with brown dress socks. And baseball caps with stupid slogans like *Wish I were Fishin,' Spending My Children's Inheritance,* or simply *Old Fart.* Fish and Wildlife ought to declare open season once a year just to cull the population. Open season. Like shooting ducks in a barrel.

It wasn't like this when he was a kid, before or after his father disappeared and left his mother and him to fend for themselves. Before the booze sunk its hooks too deep, young and middle-aged males flocked around their house. His mother was beautiful then and it was always open season on those men.

When they were short of money, which was most of the time, she'd shower and powder herself and slip into her pale blue dress with the scooped neckline, fitted bodice, and flared skirt. Once outfitted, she'd put up her hair in front of the mirror while Bennett fastened her pearls around her neck. He could still recall her perfume and the twinkle in her eye as she transformed into June Cleaver, the Beaver's mom.

The men and their money were drawn from miles around like drone ants to their queen. Bennett would dress up in his creased Sunday pants and his plaid cotton shirt just like the Beaver. Then his mother would reach over and make a spit curl in the middle of his forehead, and Bennett made her laugh when he furrowed his brow and asked, "Gee, Lumpy, do you think Wally and Mary Ellen Rogers use a rubber?"

When the guest arrived, Bennett would take his hat and serve the drinks while his mother perched on the couch, her skirt splayed out to each side. They played their roles well, the only difference being that rather than Theodore, she called him Beaver. She'd casually cross her legs at the mention of his name and wink at her caller invariably causing him to lick his lips and twitch uncontrollably.

She could tease and lead men on this way for hours before she took them back to her bedroom. Often the callers would just lie naked on the bed while she talked dirty but sometimes when she had drunk too much she undressed and joined them. Her johns always treated her with respect and tipped well because she was the queen of the television moms.

Bennett played the game because he didn't know any better. Everyone laughed and had fun. His mother said, "We need the money to live and these men have it to spare. It's not a crime as long as no one gets hurt."

But his mother lived in a world of booze and make-believe. In the real world, Bennett ended up at Glades doing three to five for fraud. Duping blue-haired ladies out of their credit card numbers had been so simple. "We think some juvenile delinquent used your card at the mall, ma'am. If you could just give us your number to confirm our suspicions." God, it was as easy as playing the Beaver. Nothing disarmed an old lady quicker than the sound of an official's voice casting aspersions on today's misguided youth.

"Yo, Bennett." It was Roy, Bennett's boss, breaking the reverie. "You gonna' stand and look at that shit all day or put it away before sundown?" Roy was both Bennett's boss and his parole officer's brother-in-law.

"Sure, Roy. I'll get right to it. No problem, Roy." He flashed his best con artist smile revealing straight white teeth through a deep Florida tan.

Roy was a skinny-necked, nervous pain in the ass who dressed in light gray shirts and coordinated charcoal gray chinos. His shirt even had a red-and-white patch over the pocket embroidered with his name.

Bennett suspected he dressed that way because he was a frustrated auto mechanic. Roy always bragged about his Country Squire and how it didn't burn oil because he took such good care of the engine. But he wasn't a mechanic. Instead he ran a run down vacuum cleaner sales and repair shop. It sat two miles from the beach on an unpaved side street next to a discount tropical fish and reptile shop run by a born-again biker and his common-law wife.

Bennett wasn't very big himself – five ten, 160 pounds – but no fat. He pumped a lot of iron at Glades and ran laps, at first to kill time and then because it made him feel good about himself. Penned up at Glades with the *Who's Who* of dealers, pimps, molesters, and shooters of South Florida made Bennett feel about as secure as a butt hole at a proctologist convention, but the exercise helped Bennett work off that stress.

"Listen, Durant, I want you to get this stuff put away then run this vacuum cleaner out to the beach. It's the Billingsly place, where they want to put that Ramada Inn. You know it?"

"Yeah. The nice fat lady in the tent dress."

"That's the one but get cash. I'll bet they don't have two nickels to rub together. The Ramada people are just waiting for the city to foreclose on the place for back taxes."

"No problem, Roy. I'll get the money." Roy and the beach developers were no different than he was, thought Bennett. They just robbed them legally. Get the old folks' money while you can, and when they die clear the land for a hotel and, who knows, maybe a casino if you can find a real live Indian to claim the site.

Bennett decided he would take the wagon and go home. Why fight all the traffic to the beach now? Instead he'd stop over early in the morning to collect before coming in to work. Roy wouldn't know the difference.

Verbena did her best to forget Eldridge's dire financial predictions. She would not give up her cottage – her Tara.

Eldridge still chauffeured her to the dances every week but he claimed his bum knee prevented him from participating. Eldridge wasn't himself, however. He'd lost interest in his card game on the boardwalk preferring to sit alone and watch T.V.

"Eldridge, it's time for me to go."

"Huh, where?"

"You know. It's my mahjongg night with the girls." Every Wednesday night those remaining friends of her mother's gathered for mahjongg. They donned cocktail dresses and sipped sherry while they compared the best early bird specials and their grown children's successes. Verbena felt a safety and warmth similar to the reaction she experienced watching reruns of *Father Knows Best*, and she never missed a gathering.

"Well, I'm not takin' you. You can just drive yourself tonight. I got more important things to do."

"Why… what do you mean?"

"Somebody's got to consider our financial situation. Go ahead and live in your fantasy world if you want, but I've got an appointment with a realtor tonight to find out what we can get for this place."

"You can't. It's mine!" Her face paled and she began to tremble.

"It won't be yours for long. It's fourth down and fifteen and we can't afford the damn taxes here or in Waterford."

"But my daddy always took care of us."

"We won't have any place to live. But you just go along and play your silly games with the nice ladies."

"You never cared about me. You only wanted Daddy's money."

"If that's all I gave a damn about I'd have been gone long ago, sweetie. In case you haven't noticed, he pissed it away before he died."

"Well, I'd rather die than sell. I won't sign any papers."

Eldridge put his head in his hands. "Verbena, we simply can't survive like this. I'm trying to save a little for us both."

"You don't care about me. You never did. Give me the keys and I'll take care of myself."

"Fine. Just fine and dandy." He tossed her the keys and turned back to Whoopi Goldberg's oversized grin on *Hollywood Squares* as Verbena wedged through the door and slammed it.

Verbena sensed an impending diarrhea attack but for the first time she drove herself to her party. Tears rolled off her swollen cheeks onto her muumuu. She had lived her entire life as a marionette manipulated by her mother Roberta, Andrea Streator, and even Eldridge. As Forever Secretary, she had sat on the periphery and recorded the actions of those with real power, the ones who pulled her strings. She played the Beaver to the Eddie Haskels and the Lumpies of the world. The realization made her flabby arms and chubby legs feel very heavy, and suddenly she didn't have the strength to continue as the big boned girl with the pretty face.

When interviewed later, Verbena's friends said she appeared unsettled when she arrived for mahjongg. She ran straight for the bathroom. Her play was erratic and someone remembered that she did have more sherry than usual. Yes, she seemed a bit forgetful and preoccupied. In fact, she couldn't remember where she parked the car and thought she'd lost her keys, only to discover them in the ignition.

TWELVE

By 8:00 the next morning, the thermometer already read eighty-five degrees. Despite the fact that Bennett had left the windows down, the wagon felt like a sauna, a sauna used to store dead fish. He lit another cigarette and headed for the beach. Fortunately the breeze off the ocean began to cool the car as the smell of tobacco and salt air supplanted the fish odor. With one hand on the wheel, his other arm resting on the window and the wind rustling through his hair, Bennett felt at peace again.

At the stop light, he smiled and nodded to a young girl in white tennis shorts and a pink visor as she sat in her yellow convertible. She frowned and looked away but it didn't matter. He was free; his time in Glades had taught him to value freedom. If she had any appreciation of her own freedom she would have smiled back.

When he turned into the Billingslys' driveway, the place looked vacated. Since Roy wanted cash, he left the vacuum cleaner in the wagon. As he walked up and knocked on the front door, he noticed a dark towering cloud bank looming in the East over the ocean. The storm would slam the beach within the hour. No one answered, so Bennett knocked again. Then he noticed the smell, one he couldn't quite identify. Instinctively he turned the door handle and it opened into a small living room.

The fat woman in the recliner next to a clamoring window air conditioner appeared to be asleep, but something wasn't right. Her bright pink cheeks looked different than a simple sunburn. The color went deeper. Secondly, Bennett couldn't detect any respiration.

Perplexed, Bennett looked to his left and noticed the open door to an attached garage and all at once it came together in his mind. Carbon monoxide poisoning. He'd learned all about it in drivers ed.

Bennett slammed the door as he lunged back outside and fought back the bile rising in his throat. His first thought was that his discovery would somehow result in his return to Glades. He took a few deep breaths and calmed himself. After all, he was just an errand boy. He hadn't stolen anything and the door was unlocked. He could drive away and no one would be the wiser but that wouldn't be right. Besides, he wasn't sure anyone was dead.

Finally, after a brief internal debate, Bennett made what should have been a relatively simple decision and ran next door to notify a neighbor. If the octogenarian who answered the door seemed timid at first, she was absolutely terrified by what Bennett imparted.

"I'm calling the police," she rasped and slammed the door in his face. The deadbolt snapped shut as he ran back to the Billingslys to do the only thing he could, which was to open every window he could find. The car's engine was still warm and Bennett surmised that it had run out of gas.

Bennett returned to Roy's car and nervously lit a cigarette as a patrol car rounded the corner and stopped behind his wagon blocking his escape. The older of the two officers spoke briefly into his radio, then slowly got out of his car and walked over to Bennett's window. Bennett's palms began to sweat so he slapped them onto the steering wheel and hoped it would go unnoticed.

"You the one that found the body?" the officer asked Bennett.

"Yeah. She's in the living room but might not be dead. And the door was unlocked," he quickly added.

"An ambulance is right behind us. What's your business here?"

"I came to deliver their vacuum cleaner." He jerked his thumb toward the rear of the station wagon.

"You work for Bill's brother Roy?"

"Yeah." Evidently everyone knew about Bill and Roy's rehabilitation business. Bennett gripped the wheel harder to keep his hands from trembling. His cigarette smoldered in the ash tray.

"You on parole?"

"Been off two months. I'm about to find a new job."

"No one stays with Roy long after their time's done." He looked over his shoulder at his partner. "Let's get this over with, Martin." Turning back to Bennett he muttered, "College boy – first month on the force. Jumpy as hell."

The rookie got out of the car and nervously adjusted his belt as he approached his partner. He nodded solemnly at Bennett, then waited as if expecting a written invitation to enter the house. "What are you waiting for, Martin?" Together they turned and approached the house.

Bennett peeled his hands off the steering wheel and quickly lit another cigarette. His hands still shook. He inhaled deeply and sighed with relief. He'd find another line of work as soon as he got his next paycheck. Roy's constant babble was bad enough but he couldn't hack this. Dead bodies and cops were just too hard on his nerves.

Just then the rookie stumbled through the front door and threw up on the front lawn. Bennett smiled. Eventually his partner appeared and spoke into the radio strapped to his shoulder. He stopped when he reached Bennett. "Her husband is in the bedroom – dead. She's got a weak pulse."

"Will she be all right?"

"I don't think she'll make it. She's as pink as a South Beach hotel. Must be loaded with carbon monoxide. No signs of B and E or trauma. I get your name and number and you can go."

"No problem, officer. You think the rookie could move the squad car?"

The cop looked over at the retching youngster. "Shit, I'll do it myself. You'd better pull out so the ambulance can get in." Bennett glanced over his shoulder toward the sound of an approaching siren.

THIRTEEN

Helen reached the phone on the second ring. "No, the Colonel hasn't called yet. Yes, it's safe to talk; Leon's lap swimming at the pool."

"What do you suppose he's up to?" Nero asked

"Who knows, but it probably has to do with guns."

"Yeah?"

"Yes, but you can't call here if you want this Leon con to work."

"And how is that going?"

"Since the Colonel decorated the condo in his own image, it's been simple to convince Leon that the living Colonel *Suicide* Jack Collins is my dear deceased husband. He'd be surprised to find old Jack still alive and living in the little ol' Cold War fighting the spread of communism: El Salvador, Cuba, Colombia, or wherever. He's the only man I know who thinks John Wayne's death was the work of communist assassins."

"Didn't he fuckin' die of the big C?"

"The Colonel says that's what the liberal press wants us to think." Helen inhaled deeply on her cigarette.

"Any progress with Leon?"

"Nothing yet." Pookie whined at Helen's feet so she put down her cigarette and picked him up. "Kisses," she whispered and he promptly licked her cheek. "Pookie and I can't tolerate this much longer, Nero. He's driving me crazier than a one-armed peach picker and I hate playing the role of the poor vulnerable Southern girl. What if the Colonel finds out I've got a live-in boyfriend?"

"I didn't think it would take this long for the Colonel to make his move."

"Please, God, make it soon. I can't watch *Field of Dreams* with Iowa Boy again. He gets all teary eyed every time."

"How much is in his pension plan?"

"He says about three hundred and fifty thousand."

Nero let out a low whistle. "Amazing what honest work and tax-free accumulation gets you. Now if we can just liberate that account and get him to deposit it into yours."

"I hope you've been working yourself while I'm doing all this."

"I talked with Carver, my cousin's brother-in-law in Orlando, and he's writing the letter that we'll send to John Q Veteran from the French government. He guaran-fucking-tees he can create the loopholes to keep us in the clear if anyone tries to slap us with fraud charges."

"What's he charging us?"

"Ten G's up front and ten more later."

"That's a hell of a lot for a little ol' letter. Stop it, Pookie!"

"Is Pookie there? Put him up to the phone."

"I think he knows it's you. He's been trying to get at the receiver. Here, Pookie, listen to Daddy." Helen brought the receiver to Pookie's ear so he could hear Nero's voice. Pookie cocked his head right then left. Finally in recognition he let out a squeal of joy and began to bark.

"Kisses," Nero pleaded. Pookie promptly began to lick the receiver.

"Nero, I better get off the line. I think I hear Leon coming."

"Okay, but don't forget we need Leon's money. I still have to locate someone to set us up on the Internet and make our web page for Carver's letter. Once we have that we can score this thing from the islands or whatever."

"Sure, hon. Gotta go." Helen had put Pookie down and he began to circle her feet yipping wildly. Helen hung up just as Leon walked in the door.

"Are you all right, Helen? You look like you're about to cry."

"It's nothing, Leon. I'll be all right."

"It *is* something. What?"

"Oh, just that nasty bank. They say I'm overdrawn but that can't be."

"Did you check your book?"

"Yes, first thing. That's why I can't be overdrawn, because I still have checks in it!"

"Helen, Helen." Leon smiled and took her in his arms, oblivious to Pookie's low growl. "I told you that you have to record those checks and calculate your balance each time. It doesn't matter how many blank checks you have."

"Leon, I'm such a fool." Helen choked back a well-rehearsed sob. "What shall I do? I can't manage all this. Jack always did it before and he said not to worry my pretty little head about these details."

"It will be all right. Ouch!"

Helen jerked back. "What is it?"

"Pookie just sank his teeth into my ankle. Dammit to hell!"

"Pookie, baaad dog." Pookie quickly feigned remorse by hanging his head and Helen swept him up into her arms again. "Pookie mustn't bite Leon. Be good. Kisses." Helen made smacking sounds as Leon hopped on one foot and rubbed his ankle. Pookie perked up immediately at the sound of kisses and licked Helen's face.

"I'm sorry, Leon, but Pookie isn't used to competing for my attention. He must sense how much I care for you and he's threatened by it. I love you both so much but he'll have to learn to share. Give Pookie a pat and say you love him."

Leon looked dumbfounded. He hesitated then patted Pookie.

"Come on. Say you love him." Pookie whined and cocked his head.

"I ... I ... I can't talk to a dog."

"Come on, Leon. Ease his pain. Kevin Costner would do it."

"His pain? What about my pain?"

"Love is unconditional, Leon."

Leon grudgingly bent toward Pookie. "Kevin Costner my sweet butt," he mumbled. "Okay, I love you, dog."

Pookie squirmed and licked Leon's face. "That's enough," Leon said as he pulled away.

"You're so wonderful to us both, Leon. I couldn't make it without your help. Please examine my check book. I have to figure this out before my next condo payment is due."

"All right, set Pookie down and let's have a look."

As she feigned awe at Leon's skill, he patiently explained each step.

Helen felt her heart melt just slightly for this man. He cried at movies and really did care for her. Finally, a tear came to her eye as Leon finished his explanation of automatic withdrawal. "Helen, I believe you're going to cry again. There's no need now."

"Silly man," was all she said. Then she got up, locked Pookie in his plastic kennel, and led Leon, still in his wet suit, into the bedroom.

FOURTEEN

This was the big break Carlos El Gato, a.k.a. El Gato and El Gato el Hombre de Muerte, had waited for. He had desperately sought his niche in the Cuban revolutionary community ever since he'd lost his job as stock boy at Best Buy. It hadn't been easy, since he was actually Puerto Rican.

The only contracts he could claim with the Cuban gangs were his former employer's overpriced extended service agreements. They would slit his throat before letting him join *La Causa*. But now he had been given his chance to become a real hero in the Latin community. The man who called himself Vinnie wouldn't be sorry he dealt with El Gato.

Just like Vinnie said, he found the silver BMW with the Miami Dolphins plates parked in the university staff parking lot. He parked his rusted-out Yugo a few rows away and got out the Sony Walkman he had liberated from Best Buy. He slipped on the headset and listened to Ricky Martin while he waited for the Cuban spy bastard to return.

He snapped his fingers and rocked to the beat of *Livin' La Vida Loca* for several minutes before he noticed the bomb on the seat next to him. "*Madre de Dios*!" he exclaimed as he frantically peeled off the headsets. "I forgot to plant the bomb."

No one lingered in the parking lot since the temperature was one hundred and two, but clever Carlos had thought to disguise himself as an auto mechanic and had borrowed his cousin's Midas coveralls. If anyone questioned him, he would claim in broken English that he was just making a routine service call. "Yes, I be just making a, how you say, adjustment to blow the *cajones* of the filthy spy through his fucking sun roof." El Gato smiled at his own wit.

Carlos lay on the ground and eased himself under the BMW. He pulled a roll of one-inch masking tape from his coveralls and proceeded to strap the bomb to the muffler. The bomb weighed more than he thought, and he wished he had stolen duct tape instead of this cheap masking tape, but it was too late to worry about that now. He hurriedly finished and rushed back to his own car.

"*Ay yi yi*, it is hot," he muttered as he slipped out of his disguise and returned to Ricky Martin. He wanted to leave and find a bar that served cold Corona but he knew a good terrorist stayed until the job was finished. So he waited in the sweltering heat.

An hour later a near delirious sweat-drenched El Gato saw a familiar looking Latino approach the BMW. Through sweat-stung eyes he witnessed the spy climb into his car and proceed toward the exit. "Now you die, pig!" the assassin quipped. It was all he could come up with, but he felt obligated to make a pronouncement at this historic moment.

Suddenly the entire scene changed. As the BMW pulled away Carlos noticed the bomb lying ineffectively on the pavement. "Shit!" he shouted as he leapt from his Yugo and retrieved the bomb. Visions of the fiery explosion on the freeway evaporated as he looked around frantically for his prey. The BMW eased itself into traffic and headed north.

Carlos ran to his car and threw the bomb onto the passenger seat. He couldn't fail now. He must follow his victim and pray to God he stopped for a drink or his laundry, so Carlos could replace the bomb.

The handsome Latino in the dark designer glasses eased the BMW effortlessly from one lane to the other as he sped north toward the interstate. Carlos cursed as he wiped the sweat from his eyes and pleaded with his stuttering Yugo to keep up the pace. The spy steadily distanced himself from his stalker, making it apparent he didn't plan to stop. Carlos reconciled himself to the fact that he would have to be patient and follow his prey *a su casa* to replant the bomb. "Damn, I should have stolen the fucking duct tape!"

As he approached the on-ramp, Carlos El Gato punched the accelerator of the struggling Yugo one more time pleading, "*Para la*

Causa." As if it understood the revolutionary verve of its driver, the Yugo gave one last cough and charged up the ramp at nearly fifty-five miles an hour.

"*Arriba!*" shouted an ecstatic Carlos who for the first time during the chase looked over at the ticking bomb on the seat next to him.

If Carlos realized the imminent danger, it was too late to matter. The Yugo, sensing the importance of the chase and possibly the humiliation of the more powerful BMW, surged to sixty miles an hour.

Witnesses later described the body of a man in a pair of coveralls, as well as a small box that looked like a Walkman, explode through the roof of a small foreign car as it burst into a ball of flame. Neither the make of the car nor the body of Carlos were ever identified, although the police suspected a Latino since they found a charred Ricky Martin CD near the scene.

FIFTEEN

Leon awakened from his post-coital slumber to Helen's smiling face. He could hear Pookie scratching at the door. "I dreamt we had our own place, Helen."

Helen smiled and clasped her hands together. "Did it have three bedrooms?"

"I don't remember but I was in the lap pool and you were working in your flower garden. We were having friends over for bridge."

"It sounds so wonderful, Leon."

"But I don't know how to play bridge."

"You can learn."

"I've made up my mind, Helen. I'm going to cash out my pension and invest it in our future together. How's that sound?"

Helen threw her arms around Leon. "Oh, honey. Y'all are the most romantic man I ever knew."

They took a seat in the waiting area of the bank and couldn't help but overhear the customer service rep painstakingly review the merits of the various CD's to a shriveled old man in a Marlins T-shirt and baggy plaid Bermudas.

"You'll have to speak up, miss!" he shouted. "My hearing aid is on the fritz. It's a Wonder Ear but they won't honor the damn warranty."

"I'm sorry to hear that, Mr. Wulterkins," the rep shouted back.

"The Citrus Farmers Bank will pay a quarter percent more than you folks."

"Yes, but they require a minimum deposit of twenty thousand and you only have ten, sir."

The deflated financial wizard placed a wrinkled brown bag on the service rep's desk.

Leon rose from his chair impatiently and poured coffee into Styrofoam cups for Helen and himself as the rep began to explain compound interest for the third time. As he sat down he leaned over to Helen and muttered, "When I get that bad just shoot me."

"Oh, Leon, be patient." A small part of her felt guilty but a larger part kept reinforcing the notion that men are all alike. Her motto: *Screw them before they screw you.* She had taken too many chances with men over the years and time was running out. She was tired of the hustles and wanted a normal retirement for Pookie and herself. And Nero if it worked out.

Eventually the old man surprised everyone and decided on a five-year CD. Helen felt certain that the wizened old guy would cash in before the CD did. The service rep forced one last smile and looked beyond her customer who struggled to extricate himself from his chair and leave. "May I help you?" She directed a Prozac-deficient smile at Helen and Leon.

"We'd like to open a joint account," Helen said as she and Leon quickly settled into the chairs in front of the young woman's desk.

She was dressed appropriately for the job but Helen thought her suit looked cheap, and the coordinating oversized necklace and bracelet detracted from her deeply tanned skin and sun-bleached hair. Clearly the bank job was just a place she went for a break from the beach. Compared to this girl, Helen's life had been one great adventure.

Helen forced herself into character before she spoke again. "I'm sure you can help us, honey. My, what a beautiful necklace. Where on earth did you find it?"

The rep, probably a recent University of Florida grad, smiled enthusiastically as if Helen had just slipped her the secret Delta Gamma handshake. "Oh, it's nothing. I actually found it at the Bealls Outlet store. You can find some great bargains there."

"Aren't they just marvelous? And no one would even suspect." Helen surmised the girl wouldn't have been caught dead in the outlet store if Mommy and Daddy still covered her plastic.

"Miss," Helen continued. "I already have your Chronologically

Gifted Account, since I'm just over fifty and I would like to add my friend and companion Leon."

The rep smiled and winked at her new-found sister. "That won't be a problem. This is such a wonderful cost-free account we offer to our senior citizens."

"Oh my, yes. I don't think any other bank offers the annual bus tour to Cypress Gardens. It's a real Southern treasure."

"And this year we plan a side trip to Bok Tower to hear the chimes."

Helen sighed. "I hear they are just magnificent."

"Excuse me, ladies." It was Leon. "I believe there are some details we need to attend to."

"Yes, but it's quite simple. I have the forms right here." She brushed back her hair and reached into her drawer for the paperwork.

"I will be transferring a large sum from my pension to this account. I assume you're only insured for one hundred thousand?"

"That's correct but we have an in-house financial advisor and our own list of mutual funds. Those accounts are insured for over three million. You can order the transfer and I'll set up an appointment with Chuck – excuse me, I mean Mr. Fairchild. He'll arrange to put your money to work for you the minute it arrives."

Helen suspected from her wistful smile that Chuck was the man in her life. "Well, I'll leave all those financial decisions up to the men." She signed the form and passed it over to Leon. "What I want to look at is some new checks. Do you have any with beach scenes or cute little seashells? I just love those."

"They're so classy. It costs more but you'll really make a statement." The rep wiggled away with the enthusiasm of a kitten chasing a ball of string and returned moments later lugging a large book of selections.

Leon excused himself and poured some more coffee. As the two women bonded over what looked more like wallpaper than blank checks, he realized this would be about as much fun as watching paint dry.

Leon considered shopping for a ring with Helen but then changed his mind. When he was twenty he married Irene, his high school sweetheart, but it hadn't worked out. As expected in Catholic marriages, they did not practice birth control but were not blessed with children.

Irene, who believed she existed solely to conceive children, suffered more than Leon. In their small town, she knew people were talking and she was afraid they thought she was committing the birth control sin. She became more and more despondent and soon began avoiding the wedding dances and Knights of Columbus parties.

Then one day a revival tent appeared on the south side of the railroad tracks. The minister was a brown haired sleepy-eyed boy who looked more like James Dean than an evangelist. Irene met him at the Red Owl where she worked as a checker. The moment he smiled at her she knew that he felt her pain.

That night she snuck out of the house and sat in the back of his tent, terrified of being recognized and reported to Father O'Malley. The summer air was hot and sticky when the young evangelist took the podium. He spoke so softly that Irene and the others had to lean forward straining to hear, but as he began to build momentum his voice raised to a fevered pitch. "Jesus is coming and only he that is born again will be saved!" It was a simple message.

Leon always suspected it was that born-again part that got to Irene, since she obsessed about birth in the first place. That night changed her forever. First, there were nightly prayer meetings and Bible study groups. Then she left her job at Red Owl to hand out pamphlets on the street corner.

This all occurred before Leon entered the office supply business, before he had to leave town. In those days he drove a milk route for the local creamery. Rising early every morning of the week, he picked up milk cans from the surrounding farms and delivered, emptied, washed and restacked them onto his truck in time to get home for a mid-afternoon nap.

One afternoon he caught Irene in bed with the sixteen-year-old neighbor boy, whom she had been trying to save for Jesus. That ended their marriage and though he could have, Leon never bothered to have it annulled by the church. In fact he'd had enough of churches and saving.

Ironically Irene did get pregnant and that's when Leon felt compelled to leave town. He could face the fact that he had been cheated on and even enjoyed the sympathy. But to have it known that his sterility had played a role in Irene's downfall was more than he could bear. Realizing he would suffocate if he remained, he moved to the relative anonymity of Cedar Rapids.

A few years later he received a letter from one of Irene's sisters informing him that Irene had been diagnosed as manic depressive. The family had committed her to the state mental hospital at Strawberry Point and were raising her five children. Her illness saddened Leon and further heightened his guilt for not standing by her. He decided he didn't deserve to ever be anyone's husband again.

SIXTEEN

Leon looked over the top of his *USA Today* as Nero entered the Pelican's Pantry. He anticipated sharing Helen's and his news about combining their resources but sensed something was wrong with Nero.

Nero's rug sat slightly askew on his head. He sported a wrinkled Hawaiian silk shirt that he hadn't bothered to tuck in and his feet were sockless in his tasseled loafers. "We can start meeting anywhere we want for coffee now, Leon. They fired my ass."

"You're kidding. You're their top salesman."

"*Was*, Leon, fuckin' *was*." Nero slumped into the chair next to Leon and waved off the waitress as she approached with coffee.

"You going to tell me about it?"

"Keep it down, will ya? Everybody's looking over here and turning up their hearing aids."

Leon put down the paper and leaned toward Nero. "So what happened?"

Nero fingered his gold-plated sharks tooth. "It was that bitch from the new resort. I told you she was hot for me. She always wore a beige business suit with a really tight skirt that rode up her thighs every time she sat on one of our beds. Underneath the jacket she wore one of those sheer silk blouses that clung to the sweetest pair of knockers you can imagine, Leon." Nero held up cupped hands, as a fisherman might, to approximate their size. "Damn fine tan she had, and when she bent over to test the fabric I could look down that blouse and see that tan going on forever."

"Well, she begged me to meet at the store after hours to demonstrate our vibrating mattress. I should've known better." Nero winked knowingly and patted down his toupee.

"I didn't know they still made vibrating mattresses."

"You want to fuckin' hear this or not, Leon? Put the damn paper down!"

Leon dutifully put down his paper and picked up his coffee cup. "How old was she?"

"I don't know, forty-five maybe. She was just the right age; like my old man used to say, 'Won't swell, won't tell, and appreciates it like hell.'"

Leon smiled and sipped his coffee. "So, go on."

"Anyway, we get there see, and she tells me to leave the lights off, then lies on the bed while I'm crawling around in the dark like a teenager, trying to plug the fuckin' thing in. So I get it set and look up to see her purring like a kitten with her jacket off and skirt vibrating up around black lace panties. I got stiffer than a Stuckey's pecan log.

"Next thing you know she's tearing her clothes off and I've got my face between her tits with her rock hard nipples vibrating in my ears." Nero paused and sighed.

Leon shifted in his chair slightly embarrassed by his own arousal but impatient to hear more. "And …?"

"How was I supposed to fuckin' know the boss was coming back?"

"Oh, Jesus," Leon responded, more deflated than sympathetic.

"He caught us in the altogether right there in the main fuckin' showroom." Nero let out a low chuckle. "You should have seen that woman scramble to get her clothes. As the lights flooded the showroom, she tried to crouch behind the *Clearance* sign. I can still see her ass quivering like a bowl of Jello at the Ramada's early bird buffet. You can bet she won't be back … so I lost the sale and my job."

"Nero, I can't believe it." In fact Leon was pretty sure he didn't. Sometimes Nero's stories took the spin of a locker room teenager.

"I can't help it, Leon. I'm virile. Women are attracted to me and I get those urges. I have needs you know. At least I'm honest."

"Doesn't sound like you had a chance, being caught like you were. What are you going to do?"

Nero banged his cigarette pack against his first finger then drew out a Marlboro with his lips. He started to light up and stared off the waitress who approached to chastise him for smoking. "Damn Snow White over there ought to go back to fuckin' Fantasyland."

Nero's cigarette bobbed between his lips as he spoke. "Actually, Leon, I've been working on something with some friends in Orlando. There might be a spot for you, too. We're thinking of opening a branch office right here in Melbourne with the air base being so much closer."

"Well, I don't know. I'd have to talk to Helen."

Nero stood up, hitched his pants and threw two dollars down on the table. "Fuckin' A, Leon, how did you make it in sales as long as you did? Let's take a ride." He waved his cigarette toward the waitress. "See ya, Snow!"

"Can you believe this car, Leon?" They were heading east on New Haven toward the beach. The car was a cream-colored Cadillac De Ville. Leon had heard the story fifty times but knew he was going to hear it again. "This car is sitting on the lot with only twenty-four thousand miles on the odometer. And the kid salesman doesn't know a fuckin' thing about cars. He wants twenty five and I get him down to twenty thousand. What a steal. These Florida punks wouldn't last a month in Jersey."

"Amazing," Leon answered without enthusiasm. The only thing Florida had more of than strip malls was used low-mileage Cadillacs. Their former owners put more miles on their golf carts.

"You remember the article in the paper recently about the French giving medals to surviving soldiers of World War I? Of course, there's like one alive. So now these cheap bastard French decide to hand out medals for a war no one remembers. Well, what about the vets from the big one, WWII? How long they gonna have to wait to be honored for saving France's butt?"

"When did you get so concerned about the veterans?" He wondered if Helen's husband, good old sound-advice Jack, had served in France.

"Since that big Tom Hanks movie about saving some private and since I been talkin' to the boys in Orlando. Here's the deal, see? We want to honor those fellas, too. Half of them must live right here in Florida. We're going to send them all letters, very official with those French Flowery de Lays on them, telling them they are entitled to this special award suitable for framing. For a small fee, say $79.95, we will make all the arrangements and mail it to them in honor of their meritorious service in France."

"What's the French government got to say about this?" Leon sensed a scam but at the same time thought of Jack proudly displaying his certificate right next to Bush.

"They don't know anything about it. But they ought to be damn grateful that someone is rectifying a slight they should have corrected ages ago. They might even give us a goddamn medal when they find out."

"You sure this isn't mail fraud, Nero?"

"Forget about it. I took it to a shylock in Orlando and he worded the letter very carefully. No fraud my friend. If just one vet in ten, or even their widow – can't leave them out – sends for his certificate we'll be wiping our asses with ten dollar bills. I'm letting you in on the ground floor. You can move in with me and no more dog walking for your supper."

Nero swung into the parking lot at the public beach and parked. He waved one hand toward the scene: clear blue sky, hot sand, young girls in thong bikinis. Rolling down the window he inhaled deeply. "I've always wanted to live on the beach. How about you, Leon?"

Leon looked out across the sand at the Atlantic Ocean. Making a profit on the boys who went over there and risked their lives didn't seem right. Having a lawyer okay the deal made it certifiably wrong. Still, he'd think about it. He decided not to mention anything to Nero about his plans with Helen.

"By the way, Leon, you ever figure out how to get that dog off your nuts?"

"Yeah." Leon felt the heat of a blush coming on.

"And?"

"It's just … well, I fart."

SEVENTEEN

Leon slowly climbed the stairs to Helen's condo. Near the top he felt his chest tighten just slightly but as he stopped to catch his breath it disappeared. This little event had been occurring on a regular basis the past two weeks and Leon vowed he'd get in better shape soon. Maybe he'd start getting up early and walk a couple laps around the compound before it got so goddamn hot.

Helen stood in the kitchen bent over the sink. She'd put her hair up in rollers the size of concentrated orange juice cans but now seemed preoccupied. Leon startled her. "Mercy, I didn't hear y'all comin' in, hon. Where've you been?"

"I was just over to the Citrus Mall having coffee with Nero. You okay?"

"Sure, I'm fine." She fumbled at her curlers and started for the bathroom. "I hate it when anyone catches me in these little ol' things. Go sit in the living room, Leon, while I make myself respectable."

Leon slumped into a chair and rubbed his aching arm. "God, I'm out of shape," he muttered.

"What'd you say, dear? I can't hear you."

"I said Nero got fired from Mattress World."

Helen returned to the living room and sat opposite Leon. The right side of her head was still in rollers while her hair hung down limply on the left. The color had drained from her face. "I'm so sorry, Leon. What's he going to do? How will he make out?"

"Oh, Nero will be fine. He's got some scheme going already." Leon proceeded to sketch out Nero's plan, anxious to see if Helen had the same reaction he did.

"It doesn't sound honest to me, Leon." Helen appeared to be deep in thought as she absently tugged at the remaining rollers dropping them one at a time on the floor. Pookie sat at her feet, looked at her, then at the rollers, then back at Helen. "I hate to think what my late husband Jack would do to Nero if he knew he was behind this scam."

"You think I should stay out of it then?"

"Oh, Leon!" She was suddenly crying as she sprang from her chair and ran over to hug him. "Don't even think about it." She released him and stood up. Turning away to face the water fountain on the retention pond behind their condo she continued. "What's happening to our society? Men like you and Nero are loyal to their employers and then used up and thrown away. Retired folks driving Cadillacs are starving on Social Security because their entire check goes for their medications. It's like that man said on *Sixty Minutes* the other night. 'We're all just one step away from living on the streets.' I'm so frightened, Leon. We've got to be careful and be there for each other. It's just … Pookie!"

Leon turned toward a crunching noise where Helen's rollers had lain. Pookie was happily gnawing on the remains.

"Leon, you've got to watch him! The poor baby could have choked." Helen swept up Pookie and her rollers and retreated to the bathroom leaving Leon alone again.

She's right, Leon thought, even though sometimes he suspected she cared more about that dog than she did him.

"You can't trust the government and you certainly can't trust your employer," Nero had said. "You've got to look out for yourself." Nero had found his ticket, and while pedaling French commendations still didn't feel completely right for Leon, he could've done a lot worse than throwing in his lot with Helen and Pookie.

EIGHTEEN

Gerald O'Brien was worth millions but his fortune had more to do with his being fortunate than brilliant. Twenty-five years ago he had gone to Iowa State on a wrestling scholarship and soon gained the nickname Underdog after the cartoon character. It seemed everyone on the team had more talent than he, but through hard work and injuries to two wrestlers ahead of him on the roster, he made the team his senior year and went on to upset the reigning national champion from Oklahoma State.

After college he drove his VW Microbus back and forth across Iowa selling wrestling mats and giving motivational speeches at high school athletic banquets. Underdogs, regardless of their politics, became not only his mission but his obsession. He campaigned for Dukakis and bled purple for the Minnesota Vikings. He championed his ignored Iowa home, the state folks drove through on their way somewhere else more exciting and exotic like Wyoming or California.

He could sell mats, give speeches, and promote losing causes forever, but the high cost of liability insurance was killing the business. The company he worked for decided to discontinue wrestling mats altogether.

Gerald never kept a neat desk and one night while sitting at his computer he absentmindedly set his mouse down on a sample square of wresting mat and noticed how easily it rolled about. Gerald's life changed forever that night; he had invented the mouse pad.

His first pads were simple colors, but soon companies wanted logos and students wanted their college mascots printed on the surface. Gerald realized how big mouse pads were really going to be when he was approached by a Wall Street firm to go public. He subsequently realized that simply adding *.com* to the end of *Mouse Pad* would make the shares of his IPO soar. And they did. In fact, another high priced *.com* company, that had yet to make a profit, quickly stepped in and bought Gerald out.

Gerald's acquired net worth was so high that he drove monthly from his newly acquired estate in Boca Raton to Palm Beach for meetings with his accountant to recalculate his estimated taxes and figure out how to give away more money to his favorite charities. As a champion of the underdog, he was prone to disappointment because he'd lost sight of the fact that underdogs are labeled as such for a reason – they usually lose. He was instead overcome by the limited philosophical viewpoint that losing was a symptom of the moral decay in American society. The stark cultural contrast between Boca Raton and his humble Iowa upbringing certainly reinforced this concept.

He sent James Dobson and Pat Robertson large sums of money along with Notre Dame, which he considered the ultimate Christian sports institution. Since the Fighting Irish were without an athletic conference and everyone was out to beat them, Gerald legitimized them as an underdog; besides, they usually won. Then there was the dummy charity in New York which converted his donations into guns for the IRA's freedom fight in Northern Ireland.

This month's visit had particularly disturbed Gerald. While his net worth and subsequently his tax liabilities were on the rise, due in no small part to his excellent timing in unloading large blocks of Microsoft and Yahoo, his accountant had urged removing the charity in New York from his favorites list. Gerald frowned. It would leave a big hole in his charitable giving.

Gerald's accountant was a tall lean Scandinavian with pale white untannable skin. Any sun exposure at all merely burned him cherry pink, so he constantly smelled of sun block and his handshake left an oily impression. "Gerald, the New York charity is getting passé. Since Clinton and Blair negotiated a peace agreement, all the guns are off the table so to speak. No one is interested in seeing that war start up again. The Bureau of Alcohol, Tobacco, and Firearms will make every effort to dry up the separatists' supply and brand them as terrorists. If that happens and you get audited, you could owe back taxes and substantial penalties."

"I thought this outfit would pass IRS muster."

"Before 9/11, maybe. But now peace is the politically correct issue. Everyone is tired of the fighting in Ireland, and besides we are achieving the peace by turning the little Irish terrorists into computer programmers with mouse pads. The outsourcing and investment opportunities are significant. I wouldn't risk sending any more money to New York."

"Dammit, I'm sick of all this politically correct shit. Now, it's politically correct to be an anti-Christian bigot and to support the faggot lifestyle. They've even gotten to Budweiser, John, the rock of American sporting events."

"Budweiser?"

"Their marketing department approached my old company to make a mouse pad with two guys holding hands and saying something like 'Be yourself.' God, I almost puked. Can you imagine what my former teammates would think if I manufactured that crap?"

"That would be inconsistent with wrestling?"

"My God, John. Don't even go there! Budweiser of all people. I don't think I'll ever watch another Bud sponsored stock car race again. And it was such good family entertainment."

"Well, all correctness aside, we can't send any more money to Ireland."

"Piss." Gerald knew his accountant's advice was on target and that he would follow it. He always did. He had picked John Petersen for two reasons. In the first place, he didn't have to worry about him always being on his boat or on the golf course with that fair skin of his. Also, despite being raised Lutheran, John Petersen had graduated from Notre Dame. Since Gerald was Catholic he could practically claim alumni status. In fact they had met at an alumni meeting. "Well, John, I guess we'll have to find something else."

"You can always keep the money and pay the taxes."

Gerald ran his fingers through his thinning red hair and sighed. "I like supporting underdogs in noble causes, John. It makes me feel good when I go to mass."

"The university is raising funds for their new football program. They seem to think it's a noble cause."

"I considered it until that son-of-a-bitch coach started claiming they would become the Notre Dame of the South. I don't care if he and the rest of the Cuban donors are Catholic; it just isn't right, them saying that."

"Well there's always Cuba itself," John said with a smile.

"You mean freeing Cuba of Castro?" Gerald furrowed his brow and looked down at his financial statement. "That's a great idea, John."

"I was just kidding, Gerald."

"No, it's a great idea and something made you say it. Work on that angle, John, and find me a charity that wants to free Cuba. It shouldn't be too tough to accomplish down here. Look what happened when they tried to send that Elian kid back to his father. These Cubans care about freedom and family values." Gerald collected his statements and rose to leave. He was smiling now. "This is a winner, John. I love a winner."

NINETEEN

The Colonel was bored and that made him edgy. He had taken his bass boat out at dawn because he couldn't sleep, but the weather had been hot and the fish weren't biting. His favorite pony had come up lame on Sunday and was still hobbling. His warehouse sat full of munitions while he waited for word from Estefan, who was having trouble raising the money. Then there was the matter of his demolitions unit, which had botched the assassination of the third-rate football coach.

Helen waited at Dahlia Dunes but according to Michael she'd found a live-in guest. It appeared she and Nero were running another scam. She'd disobeyed his orders and that could complicate things.

From his office the Colonel could look out over the twelfth fairway. The black storm clouds that had formed at sunrise were now almost overhead. Brightly dressed golfers scrambled for their carts and sped in the direction of the clubhouse as torrents of rain spilled from above and rolled directly toward the Colonel. He stood at the window unafraid, waiting for the storm to hit the house, and took it as an omen that something big was about to happen. He welcomed the change.

Later when the storm had passed and the air hung over the estate like a wet cotton blanket ready to smother anyone who ventured out, Michael returned from Boca with the news. The Colonel had returned to the window and watched as the black groundskeepers removed branches and other debris from the fairway. They moved slowly and deliberately in the suffocating heat. Unlike most days, they worked in silence. As they bent over their task, the Colonel half expected the arrival of the plantation master, wearing a broad-brimmed straw hat and black riding boots, astride a chestnut-colored stallion. Shortly the greens keeper appeared instead, riding on a golf cart rather than a stallion. He was tall and white, and when he stepped from the cart the Colonel noticed he was wearing calf-high black rubber boots. As he began gesturing impatiently, the Colonel surmised that he might be the grandson of the plantation owner. In any case, not much had changed in one hundred fifty years.

"Sir, I've just heard from Estefan. He has found a benefactor and we can proceed with the delivery."

The Colonel turned from his reverie and seemed almost surprised to see Michael standing there. "It's about time. I was beginning to think he wouldn't find one. Do we know the man? Not that it matters."

"An Irishman by the name of Gerald O'Brien."

The Colonel smiled. "I know the name. We've dealt with his favorite charity in New York in the past. He keeps his distance from the actual transaction so as to draw little attention from the Feds. That's good."

"Shall I make the arrangements, Sir?"

"You arrange for Estefan to receive the goods and I'll arrange for Helen to collect."

"Two hundred and fifty thousand doesn't buy him much of a war these days."

"That's his problem, Michael. I've fought my wars, and I learned that all the money in the world won't win one if you don't have men of purpose."

"Yes, Sir. Do you think Helen can be trusted? I'll contact her myself if you like."

"Helen will be fine. We need someone anonymous, Michael. Besides we can still track her with the credit card if necessary."

"Yes, I've had it tested several times. We're receiving notice less than a half hour after she makes a transaction."

"God bless technology! If only my demolition unit were as effective."

The phone rang three times before Helen answered. The Colonel was relieved to hear her voice. "Hello, Helen."

"Colonel, is it time?"

"The pickup should take place in the next twenty-four hours. I understand that despite my specific orders you have complications. I assume you'll handle them and get away?"

"It won't be a problem. My poor little 'ol widow routine attracted some male attention but it actually solidified my cover. Once I walk away from here and deliver y'all the money I'm gone."

"That's probably bullshit, Helen. If you get caught in your scam my name better not surface."

"Of course not." Helen's voice took on a hard edge and the Colonel could sense she was not afraid. "If I implicated you, it would only add to my troubles."

"You should have stayed with me, Helen. Life would have been easier for you."

A pause at the other end. "It's just that I can't afford to be dependent on anybody, no matter how generous they are. I think it's a control issue."

"And you're in control with Nero?"

"I'm not as sure about things as I used to be. I'm too old to do this anymore but I'm not sure I can retire. I've never done anything else. Nero and I are alike; we're equal partners I think."

"Be careful, Helen. Nero isn't powerful enough to be trusted."

"Thanks for the advice but no one could possess enough power to impress you." Silence on the line. "You'll call me back about the time?"

"Yes," answered the Colonel.

"Will we use that Denny's near the airport again? It's simply dreary."

"That's fine. Keep it safe and out in the open. These people are not desperate. It's not like the Nicaraguans this time."

"My, they were intense! I'll expect your call."

TWENTY

Helen wasted no time in contacting Nero. Leon's money had been deposited in the bank and the arms delivery was imminent. He suggested that they meet at a Tiki bar on the beach two miles north of the New Haven causeway. Leon played in the golf league at Dahlia Dunes and would be gone until early evening. All she needed to do was lock Pookie in his kennel.

Pookie followed her into the bedroom and whined as she readied herself. He sensed her preparations meant confinement for him. As Helen checked her lipstick and reached for her purse he took refuge under the bed.

"Oh, Pookie, baby. It's okay; Mommy will be right back." Helen was on her knees now coaxing. "Come on, baby." No luck.

Finally, Helen got up and walked to the kitchen. All she had to do was rattle the lid to the cookie jar and she could hear Pookie's toenails clicking on the floor. In an instant he was sitting at her feet with his right paw extended. "Pookie, you are so gullible; you fall for this every time." She shook Pookie's paw and handed him a bit of cookie, then swept him up and shoved him into his kennel. "You're too trusting for your own good," she said as she slammed the door to his escape. "Mommy will be back soon, baby."

Ten minutes later Helen was crossing the causeway to the beach. The width of the Indian River Lagoon stretched for at least a mile at Melbourne. Under a cloudless azure sky, egrets, little blue herons, and pelicans worked the shoreline. Further out, small bass boats floated on the glassy surface while in the distance a smattering of high-rises configured the skyline of the barrier island.

Compared to the spectacular approach, Helen found the barrier island itself anticlimactic. As the causeway ended she was greeted by a Speedway gas station promoting free orange juice. Just beyond, a Kmart-anchored strip mall sprawled toward the nondescript brown stucco ranch homes that filled the gap between the causeway and the beach hotels. Helen turned north on A1A and two streets later turned into the deserted asphalt lot of the Tiki bar.

As she entered the darkened bar she stopped to allow her eyes to adjust. A dark silhouette, which she assumed to be Nero, beckoned her from the distant veranda. She walked past brightly decorated rattan chairs and the bamboo-trimmed bar and found herself facing Nero. They stood under a thatched roof on a raised veranda overlooking the white sand beach and the endless ocean. It was as if Helen had stepped into a time warp onto a private island in the South Pacific.

Nero reached for Helen and gave her a quick hug. Releasing her he turned away and leaned on the bamboo railing with both arms extended. As if sensing her approval of this setting, he looked out over the ocean and began to speak. "We'll have our own place just like this, Helen. Soon. But it won't be a frickin' bar. It'll be our own beach home. We'll make this delivery and then all I have to do is tie up a few loose ends on this French Connection plan. I've figured it out so we can run the whole job from the islands."

"And just how would we do that?" Helen asked smiling. She took a seat at a small table.

"It's so easy, Helen. Modern technology allows us to scam anyone from anywhere in the world. The Internet, Helen."

The bartender appeared at the door and Helen ordered a mojito while Nero pointed to his can of Bud Light and nodded. As he disappeared, Helen's gaze returned to Nero. "What do you know about computers or the Internet for that matter?"

"Nothing yet. I admit it, but we have to change with the fuckin' times."

"I don't like change and neither do you, remember?"

"Well, I'm a new man and I embrace change," Nero said.

"You've been reading *Business Weekly* again haven't you?"

"It's better than gambling."

"I'm not so sure," Helen quipped.

"What the hell else am I supposed to do while you seduce our Hawkeye friend and wait for Colonel Sanders to make his move?"

"You do have a tough life, Nero."

"Look, here's the plan. I got us a place we can rent for a week or so while we wait for things to cool down. It's in a furnished high-rise just south of Lauderdale on the beach. We'll close out your account with Iowa Boy by wiring it to a Caribbean bank, then trash our credit cards so we can't be traced, and spend the cash you earn from the Colonel.

"When we get to the condo, I'll hire someone to help me buy the computer and set up our web page. When it's all set, we'll hire a plane for the islands and set up shop on the Internet. No one can touch us."

The waiter returned with their drinks and set them on the table. "You want to start a tab?"

"Why not," Nero responded. "Hey, we're kinda celebrating here. You got any of those Hawaiian poo-poo trays? You know, hors d'oeuvres and shit."

"It's off season. You want to celebrate I got Beer Nuts."

"Beer Nuts." Nero shook his head in disbelief. "Fine, bring me a fuckin' order of Beer Nuts."

"Sure." The bartender left and returned moments later to drop a bag of Beer Nuts in front of Nero.

"Just put it on the tab."

"No problem. Anything else?" the bartender continued in his monotone.

"Gosh, I can't think of a thing," Nero mocked.

The waiter shrugged his shoulders and left them alone again.

"God, I've got to get out of this home-boy town, Helen. In the islands we'll have our own houseboy just dying to please us."

"I hope he can cook, Nero, because I won't."

"If he can't we'll hire a cook, and send the boy into the village to fetch a live chicken and our mail with the checks from MasterCard and Visa."

"You're sure this island of yours will be Internet ready?"

"Of course, Helen. It's the modern fucking age and even the most backward countries have Internet access. Haven't you seen those IBM commercials?"

"Okay, you win. I'll make the transfer before I run the Colonel's little errand. We'll drop his money off at his place and keep heading south."

"I'll go with you to the drop site," Nero interjected.

"No, I'll do it alone."

"I'm not sending you out on some dark back road alone."

"For Christ's sake, Nero, it's at the Denny's near the airport. This is the modern age!"

Nero looked a bit crestfallen. "I should go anyway."

"No. Whoever it is will be expecting a woman alone."

"Fine, I'll stay in the car and leave it running just in case."

"Oh Jesus, Nero. Fine, but don't get out of the car. We'll go straight to the Colonel's from there."

"Perfect," Nero replied as he struggled to open the Beer Nuts with his teeth. Suddenly the bag ripped and the nuts scattered in all directions. "Hell, let's get out of here before he makes us sweep this shit up."

Helen sucked on the last of her mojito, making a conspicuous slurping sound with her straw. Then she took one last look at the ocean. *God, I hope we can settle in a place like this,* she thought. *But then what am I doing trusting my future to a man who can't even open a bag of Beer Nuts.*

TWENTY ONE

Rick Brindle tipped back in his government-issue desk chair and gazed out his office window across the Ft. Lauderdale landscape. He had been with the ATF (Bureau of Alcohol, Tobacco, and Firearms) for twenty years. It was too early to get out and he felt too old to learn a new game. He ran both hands through his thinning brown hair.

He had survived three administrations and the aftermath of the Waco, Texas, debacle. In the shake-up that followed Waco, he was transferred to Florida to spend his time inspecting legal gun dealers and assisting them in deciphering the 1994 Crime Bill which, among other things, defined which assault rifles were legal and which weren't.

To Rick the solution had been simple; civilians had absolutely no reason to own any kind of assault rifle, so they should all be banned.

The second part of Brindle's job proved more interesting, although no less political. A lot of weapons and munitions moved into and out of Florida illegally and it was his job to keep track of the importers and exporters and report their activities upwards through channels. Superiors decided when and if any action should be taken. Guns for Central America or Mexico were out. Guns against Castro were always good, but guns for Ireland which had been politically correct in the past were to be stopped now.

That's why Rick kept a file on the local philanthropist Gerald O'Brien. The file lay on his desk at this moment and included a copy of the old Sports Illustrated article that covered his dramatic national title bout. As a former high school wrestler himself, Rick enjoyed the article. He reread it every time he pulled the file, admiring the picture of

O'Brien slapping on a bear hug and throwing to the mat the surprised defending champion, Tedaki Nakayama, from Oklahoma State.

A former athletic overachiever, O'Brien now had a soft spot for lost causes, but unbeknownst to him the Treasury Department via ATF was fully aware of his donations to the assorted factions of the IRA. Rick Brindle had been given orders to sever his supply line to the rebels.

Recently two pieces of seemingly related information had reached Brindle. First, O'Brien had sold a large block of stock and subsequently transferred a significant amount of cash from his account. Second, a Cuban known only as Estefan had been soliciting funds from wealthy locals but had suddenly closed up shop and gone underground. Brindle suspected he had obtained his funds and an arms deal was about to materialize.

The New York office confirmed that O'Brien's favorite charity had not received any recent infusions. Had O'Brien switched causes? Or was he shrewd enough to play the Hispanic angle in Florida and hire Estefan as his front man? Brindle had unwritten orders not to interfere with the Cuban traffic but he saw no choice but to follow Estefan to the guns. It wouldn't be hard; his sources had already given him all the probables.

Rick picked up the phone and dialed Merritt Nixon. Three rings later, "Nixon."

"Merritt, this is Brindle."

"Hey, buddy. What's up? Some little old ladies making bootleg wine again?"

"I need you to go with me to monitor a gun deal in Melbourne."

"No kidding? Our man Estefan?"

"Looks like it. Word has it that the transfer of funds is to take place at a Denny's at the airport but we don't have any idea where the guns are being warehoused. I thought we might drive up together and rent a second car."

Nixon suddenly began a coughing fit that lasted for nearly a minute, then responded. "Sorry. I've got to quit these damn cigarettes. So we tail them both to their respective sources?"

Brindle had a mental picture of Nixon's red face and teary eyes. "That's it ... And next time cover the mouth piece."

"Sorry, Rick."

"Look, this isn't a big bust or anything. Just a little reconnaissance. Lord knows the bureau isn't looking for more publicity. I just need to know where the guns are going. There'll be plenty of time to stop the transfer later."

"You packing this trip?" asked Nixon.

"Hell, no. You know I hate guns. They should be outlawed."

"Well, you know what the Constitution says, chief. 'If we outlaw guns, only the outlaws will have guns.'"

"Yeah, them and the postal employees."

"Oh well, I suppose we've got to save the world. What's the Denny's dress code? I forget."

"White shirt and tie. I'll explain later. Pack an overnight bag just in case. And, Merritt, buy some of that nicotine gum."

"Hey, why do you think I joined the bureau? Alcohol, tobacco, and firearms – a man's best friends."

"See you in the morning." Rick hung up the phone.

Ironically Brindle had joined the bureau for the opposite reason. Born and raised in Utah as a Mormon, his ATF career choice was merely an extension of his conservative religious beliefs. The son of a policeman and a stay-at-home mom, he was the poster boy for the family values that the politicians of both parties now embraced. Except for Uncle Carl, who kept three wives, scandal had never touched the family.

When he turned nineteen just after his freshman year at BYU, he decided to complete his obligatory missionary work and found himself in Atlanta, Georgia. The city's sharp contrast to Salt Lake City awed him. It was awash with liquor, tobacco, and firearms while the extremes of wealth and poverty were as oppressive as the heat and humidity itself. The very fiber of its culture ran contrary to his upbringing.

As he immersed himself in his mission of converting the unenlightened Southern masses, he began to feel like an anachronism. His sense of being an outsider was only enhanced by the requirement that he work with a partner. Pairs created a necessary sense of security but also a sense of superiority. In most cases, two of them proselytized to one nonbeliever. Together they spouted the doctrine of founder Joseph Smith.

But merely offering answers to the uninitiated left a void in Rick. He couldn't understand why these people lived the way they did and consequently was full of questions himself. At night he began to read history books about the South and soon found excuses to avoid his partner so he could work alone. Cautiously he walked the streets of Atlanta to frequent its coffee shops. He made acquaintances, asked questions, and forgot he was supposedly the one supplying the answers.

That's how he met Helen, the woman he would never forget. Helen was fifteen years older than Rick and outwardly manifested all the gentility and mystery of Southern womanhood. Helen approached him one morning as he sat at his table in the corner poring over *The Atlanta Journal-Constitution*. "Excuse me, but do y'all mind if I join you? This place is so crowded."

Rick looked up into sparkling blue eyes and a face framed by thick blond hair. Her perfume permeated the stale air around him and evoked the creamy-white exotic flowers he had seen on magnolia trees in the suburbs. He had fantasized about women like this as they passed him on the street never giving him a second glance. As a Mormon, Rick had never known intoxication until this very moment.

"Are you that preacher fella they're all talking about?" she asked demurely as she swept her skirt under her and sat across from him. Her blue eyes suggested both mischief and genuine interest.

"No, ma'am. Actually I'm a missionary for the Church of Jesus Christ of the Latter-Day Saints." Rick looked uncomfortably at his worn *Book of Mormon* on the table.

"Mormon, right?"

"Sure, it's easier. Or LDS – except some people started confusing it with LSD and thought we all did drugs." Rick blushed.

"Short hair, white shirt, and tie. You don't look like you do drugs, Mr. … ?"

"Brindle, Richard Brindle." He said *Richard* because he suddenly wanted to be older – her age.

"I'm Helen, Richard. Pleased to make your acquaintance. Is that your book of verse?"

"Yes, do you want to hear about it?"

Helen smiled as she reached out and touched Rick's hand. "Mormons are honest people, right?"

"Well, yes, you could say that," Rick stammered as he struggled to put the image of Uncle Carl and his three aunts out of his mind.

"Then that's all I need to know. You can keep the book." She pushed it slowly towards Rick. "I'm so tired of dishonest men. Tell me about yourself, Richard."

That's how their affair began and how Rick Brindle discovered sex. Her sexual moods varied from instructive and patient to wild passion and abandonment. She laughed or cried, talked about herself or was reticent. Regardless of her disposition, Rick became her devoted student. He loved Helen and promised to be there for her even though he knew his superiors planned to move him to another city soon. It didn't matter, because he would find a way to return for her. He was, after all, an honest Mormon.

Rick was still young and couldn't foresee that his betrayal would take a different, unavoidable form. One warm night as he hurried to Helen through a torrential Atlanta downpour, he was struck by a van delivering *The Christian Science Monitor* and suffered a compound fracture to his left leg. He was rushed to surgery at Grady Memorial Hospital and awoke to the weary face of his mother, who never left his side until they flew home to the safety of Salt Lake City.

His family never asked about his mission, leading Rick to believe they knew more than they let on. As his leg healed and he walked his homogenized Mormon neighborhood, his mind was racked with confusion and guilt. That fall he returned to BYU, determined that Atlanta become a finished chapter of his life: unsettling, haunting, painful, but always near the surface. He never tried to contact Helen again.

TWENTY TWO

Bennett Durant, former vacuum repairman, sat searching the want ads. The coverage of the Eldridge Dewitt death was old news. His wife, the former Verbena Billingsly, had originally been reported in critical condition, but as the days dragged on Bennett had lost interest and didn't know whether she'd survived or not.

He had been right: it was carbon monoxide poisoning. It seems Verbena, after returning home from mahjongg, had forgotten to turn off the car after closing the garage door. The fact that they were in debt and about to lose the cottage had raised the question of suicide. Bennett didn't believe it. Nobody who wasn't doing time and had a cottage on the beach would go and kill themselves.

Probably just stupidity or senility; it didn't matter which. It reminded him of a T-shirt he had seen the other day that said, "I don't have Alzheimer's, I have CRS (Can't remember shit!)" He wondered who the hell would wear that.

The ad for a computer operator caught his eye. He had completed his rehabilitation work on the computer at Glades. He couldn't program but he could run basic Microsoft and had learned to set up web pages with site links. It came easy to him and would be like stealing to get paid for it, so he answered the ad.

TWENTY THREE

Helen spent two days pacing the condo, desperately craving a cigarette. She arranged the transfer of Leon's pension to her account in the islands and it would only be a short time before he discovered it was gone. In fact, he had an appointment with the bank's investment advisor tomorrow.

If the call didn't come today, she would have to feign illness and pray he'd cancel it. Leon sat across the room reading the paper but had already sensed her apprehension. She told him she was anxious about some blood work the vet had drawn on Pookie.

Suddenly the phone rang. Helen fought to retain her composure as she picked up the receiver and spoke softly into the phone. "Yes? Certainly I can come over. Right away? Certainly if it's urgent. I'll be right there." When she hung up there were tears in her eyes.

"What's the matter, dear? What's wrong?"

"That was the vet clinic. It seems something's horribly wrong with Pookie's blood work and I have to rush him back right away."

"I'll go with you. I'm sure it's nothing." Leon started to push himself out of the recliner.

"No, you stay here and don't fret. I'll take Pookie alone." She ran over and hugged Leon hard. Leon retracted, surprised by the sudden display of affection. "I'm sorry to put you through this, Leon honey."

"That's all right. Don't worry; Pookie will be fine."

"Yeah, sure. I best be going." She picked up her purse and called for Pookie.

Once settled behind the wheel of her Lincoln, she felt a wave of relief. Even though her commitment to Leon had been a lie, she felt smothered and trapped when they talked about spending the rest of their lives together. Having listened to his life story and having fabricated a story of her own, she now found it hard to find things to talk about.

What more could he say about his golf game or about the number of laps he swam in the pool? The weekly discussion about whether or not they should join the bingo crowd at the clubhouse had also become tedious.

Dahlia Dunes suffocated Helen. Her neighbors were blue-haired widows who timed their trips to the mailbox to match Helen's so they could discuss the comings and goings of their neighbors. They wondered how the couple in G-2 could afford to eat out almost every night, even if they did go to the early bird specials. Or how Henry from G-6 could stay out after eight o'clock when he had cataracts and shouldn't drive after dark. And did she know that Betty Rubin's grandchildren peed on the hibiscus behind the carport? Just who would pay for that if it died?

She felt sorry for Leon and a bit guilty about her deception. She assuaged her guilt by telling herself that she was saving him from a slow monotonous death in Dahlia Dunes. Yes, she certainly was doing him a favor. Her life with Nero would be different; they wouldn't fall into this trap.

Helen drove straight to Nero's dingy efficiency on the west side near the interstate. Nero unhooked the chain on the door and walked back into the room to switch off the Marlins game. Blue smoke hung in the air and Helen inhaled deeply to satisfy her own craving.

"It's about goddamn time that bastard called." Nero stood unshaven in his wrinkled luau shirt. Of course every hair on his head lay in place but it wasn't his own. He snuffed out a half-smoked cigarette, then reached under his shirt to scratch his gut.

"Are you ready? We haven't got much time."

"Bag's fuckin' packed." Nero pointed to the small suitcase by the door next to his tasseled loafers. Helen wished she had slipped a few of her own things into the car but it wasn't worth the risk.

"We'll have to take the back roads; New Haven Avenue is too busy," Helen said.

"Then let's hit it." Nero smiled as he pulled a screwdriver out of his pocket. "I can feel the adrenaline pumping, babe."

"What's that for?"

"Just a little dance routine – a precaution. It's called the Jersey Shuffle. We'll leave my car here and trade your plate with the kid's next door. He works nights and sleeps days. It won't be long before Leon figures out you're not coming back and the first thing police will ask him is your license plate number. He might actually remember it."

"Sometimes you actually amaze me, Nero." Helen bent forward and gave him a kiss on the cheek. "Let's do it." She felt a rush not unlike the ladies entering the bingo hall at the Dunes.

Rick Brindle's plan was simple. He and Merritt Nixon drove up I 95 from Lauderdale and rented a second car at the airport so they could each follow a suspect from the drop site. "But why do I have to wear this white shirt and tie?" Nixon asked. "We stand out like Jesse Jackson at a Klan rally."

"Here, take this," Brindle responded and handed him a book.

"What is it?"

"The *Book of Mormon*. You're going to be a missionary." Brindle smiled at the baffled Nixon.

"You've got to be kidding. Nineteen year olds do this, not guys like us."

"You haven't been keeping up, friend. It's the rage for retired Mormons who shirked their duty as teenagers. Retired rich men with time on their hands start to wonder if they'll make it into heaven."

Nixon took the book and shook his head. "Me, a Mormon. I'll get an academy award if I pull this one off."

"A half hour of clean living won't kill you. Let's go."

They found a vacant booth that afforded a view of the premises. Nixon instinctively reached for a menu but Brindle stopped him. "Open your book and pretend you can read."

"Asshole. Hey, what's a Jack Mormon?"

"You might say they've fallen from grace. They're Mormons in name only because almost everyone else in Utah is. It's good business to be part of the religious community. But they drink alcohol and even smoke. I believe you Southern Baptists call them backsliders."

"I think I'll be one of those Jack Mormons. I never took to being called a backslider."

"Not today. We'll have to discuss your conversion later."

"Do I have to go to confession or burn up all my old clothes?"

"No, but I get 25,000 frequent flyer miles if I bring you in alive." Rick looked up and saw a young waitress approaching. About sixteen, her red hair was piled on top of her head. She had the bouncy walk and toothy smile of a high school cheerleader on her class trip to Sea World. Her Denny's tag bore the name *Tiffany.* "Hi, fellas. Can I get you something to drink?"

Nixon beamed back at their pretty visitor. "Sure thing, hon. I'll have regular coffee…" He felt Rick's foot kick him under the table. "I mean iced tea." Another kick. "Lemonade?" He looked quizzically at Brindle.

"We'll both have lemonade, thanks," Rick interjected.

"Two lemonades. I'll be right back." Tiffany turned and bounced off toward the counter.

"Nice ass," mused Nixon.

"Stay in character."

"Sorry." Nixon bowed his head and opened his book.

Tiffany returned shortly with the lemonades. "Hey, neat. You two are reading the same book. Is it like for a class or something?"

"Sort of," replied Rick.

"The *Book of Mormon*," she mused. "It sounds like a series, like V.C. Andrews writes."

"Well, it's not quite V.C. Andrews, but something like that."

"Cool!"

"Riii…ght. Listen, Tiffany, we're going to sit here and read to each other for awhile and maybe order later. Okay?"

"No problem. I just came on, so I'll be here if you need anything." Tiffany turned and bounded for another booth with the enthusiasm of a golden retriever puppy.

Nixon leaned forward and whispered. "Looks like this could be fertile ground for spreading the word, Rick. In fact, I'd say you're in virgin territory, no pun intended."

"Shut up and watch for the bad guys."

Nero eased the Lincoln into the parking lot and maneuvered into a slot facing forward. "Are you sure you want to handle these guys alone?" he asked turning to Helen.

Helen remained patient. "Thanks, honey, but I know what I'm doing. Whoever makes the drop expects just little ol' me."

"I'll keep the car running."

"If you don't, Pookie will suffocate." Pookie whined at the mention of his name and Helen leaned into the back seat, peering through the grate on the pink plastic kennel. "Mommy won't be long," she cooed. She turned around and took one last look at her makeup in the mirror, smoothed her dress with both hands, and got out of the car. She smiled at Nero before she turned and casually walked into the restaurant without looking back.

Once inside she proceeded toward an empty booth. Her muscles tensed when she noticed two clean-cut men in white shirts and ties across the room. She initially thought that they were federal agents but then she noticed their reading material and smiled. *They must have run out of pretty young boys*, she thought to herself.

She ordered an iced tea from a disinterested middle-aged waitress. Mormons. That seemed like such a long time ago. She lived in Atlanta then and thought she could do anything. On a dare she had seduced a young Mormon missionary in a coffee shop. He was so naïve, just like she had once been, and so easy.

At first she reveled in her power but soon sensed the boy had a power of his own. He was a fool but no one had ever given her unconditional love before. When his devotion finally won her over, she became the fool and actually believed it would work. But one day he, like all the rest, left without a word. Helen won her bet but learned her bitter lesson. Men weren't to be trusted.

A tall Hispanic man wearing dark sunglasses entered the restaurant. He stood, briefcase in hand, and surveyed the scene. Expectant. Helen looked up and caught his eye. He analyzed her coldly for a moment, then walked over and sat down opposite her. "Helen?"

"Yes."

"Estefan." He extended his hand.

"Have you brought me something for the Colonel?"

"Possibly, but I must check first." Estefan reached into his pocket and removed his cell phone. He proceeded to dial a number and waited. "*Hola. El cargo, esta allí?*" A pause while someone spoke at the other end. "*Verdad? Si, adios.*" Estefan closed the phone and returned it to his pocket. "Everything is in order, *Señora*. I have the briefcase for you and you may count it if you like, but not here."

"It's not necessary. The Colonel will find you if it doesn't add up." Something suddenly caught Helen's attention. She smiled broadly at Estefan and reached out to shake his hand. "Don't panic but we've been made."

"What!" Estefan's steel façade immediately melted.

"That Mormon over there just lit up a cigarette. You don't know what that means but we have to get out of here. Slide the briefcase over and escort me to the door."

Estefan began to visibly tremble. "Eemigration, they'll send me back. I can't go back."

"They can't send you back if they don't catch you. Listen to me. We'll leave here and head in separate directions. Whatever you do don't lead them back to the warehouse. And don't use your cell phone again. They have no proof that you've done anything wrong. I'll lead them away from the Colonel. Let's go." Helen slid from the booth, briefcase in hand, and laid five dollars down on the table to cover the iced tea. Estefan remained frozen in his seat. Beads of sweat formed on his brow.

Helen sensed this was going to get ugly. She took one last look at Estefan, shook her head, and slapped him as hard as she could with her free hand. "Bastard!" she screamed.

The slap and Helen's shriek resounded throughout the dining room and was followed by absolute silence as everyone turned to look. They witnessed the back of a neatly dressed woman exiting quickly with a large purse or briefcase and a well-dressed Hispanic man huddled on the floor pleading to her. "*No te vayá!*"

Rick Brindle sat momentarily paralyzed as the scene unfolded before him. The minute she had entered the restaurant he knew something was wrong. Her walk and aura of self-confidence created a sense of *déjà vu*. Her face was familiar but older. Suddenly it hit him like a lightning bolt out of his Bible. It was Helen.

His first reaction was to call out to her but once again fate would keep them apart. He looked over at Merritt, now engrossed in the Book of Mormon, and reminded himself they were on a stake-out. His focus returned to Helen. She spoke to the waitress and would undoubtedly order iced tea – lemon, no sugar. Her fingers briefly touched her cheek as she feigned indecision.

When the waitress left she looked his way but without recognition. She focused on the book and he thought she smiled. *God, was she thinking about Atlanta and them?* She was twenty years older now but still attractive. In fact she had kept herself up much better than he had. His thinning brown hair was cut regulation short. He had developed a bit of a paunch and at his last departmental physical he didn't even measure five eleven anymore. He was five foot ten in his threadbare stocking feet. No wonder she didn't recognize him.

The waitress returned with Helen's iced tea just as a tall, dark man in sunglasses entered the restaurant and stood near the entrance. Rick recognized Estefan from his photo.

Estefan's gaze rested on Helen and he walked confidently to her booth and sat down, resting a large briefcase near her foot. So Helen had been reduced to this, a courier for gun smugglers. A sense of sadness and loss crept over Rick. He didn't even notice as Merritt lit up a cigarette until he smelled the smoke. "Jesus, Merritt. Put that out."

"Sorry, Rick. Old habits die hard." Merritt quickly snuffed out his cigarette but Rick could see that it was too late. They had been spotted. Helen stood with the briefcase in hand and spoke sharply to Estefan.

"You follow Estefan, Merritt, and I'll stay with the woman." Suddenly Estefan lay on the floor crying, the result of a blow from Helen. Rick jumped up, ran to the window, and watched as Helen got into a waiting dark blue Lincoln driven by a man wearing a bad rug, dark glasses, and what looked like a gold shark's tooth on a chain around his neck. He waited until they turned south on Babcock, then keys in hand he strolled calmly out of Denny's to begin his pursuit. He had already committed the license plate to memory.

TWENTY FOUR

Leon had spent the rest of the morning in the condo reading the paper, watching *The View*, and napping. He awakened initially feeling guilty that he hadn't vacuumed like he'd promised, but then he realized he should have heard from Helen by now. He picked up the phone and called the vet.

A young girl whose voice Leon recognized answered the phone. "Melbourne Vet Clinic. This is Missy. How may I direct your call?"

"I'm not sure. I'm calling about Helen and Pookie."

"Oh, Pookie. How is he?" she giggled.

"That's what I want to know. You called Helen this morning to bring Pookie in for more tests."

"I don't believe so but let me check." Leon was suddenly on hold listening to a recorded voice of the same terminally cheerful girl who reminded him to protect his pet from heartworm and fleas by purchasing products sold at their clinic.

He only had to listen to the same message four times along with *Your call is important to us. Please stay on the line*, before Miss Cheerful returned. "I'm sorry, sir, but we didn't call Helen. There must be some mistake."

If Leon was surprised by the first call, he was dumbfounded by the call he received a few minutes later.

"Hello, this is Colonel Collins. May I speak to Helen?"

"Colonel Collins? But Helen said you were dead."

"I don't give a good goddamn what Helen said. Where is she?"

"I don't know. She said she was taking her dog to the vet."

"Helen is renting my condo and she's a month behind on her payments. I want to talk to her now or she's out of there by sunrise."

"Just a minute," replied Leon. "Did you dial 407-831-5341?"

"That's the number, ace."

"Oh, shit." Leon hung up on the Colonel. A sick feeling, not unlike getting kicked in the nuts by a Holstein calf, gripped the pit of his stomach as he began to grasp the meaning of the call.

Leon called for a cab as he cursed the day he'd parked his Taurus. Turning the key in the ignition had elicited the clickety-clackety sound of a dead battery. He paced back and forth in front of what now appeared to be the very alive Colonel's condo but stopped and flinched as the crushing pain gripped his chest. "Damn, I wish I had brought some Tums."

When the cab arrived, he ordered the driver to take him to the Winn-Dixie. Once there he fumbled through his wallet for his debit card and headed straight for the cash machine. Signaling for the driver to wait he entered his personal code and asked for his bank balance. *Accounts Closed* flashed before him as he stared in horror. "My God, she and her friggin' dog took it all!"

Leon staggered. He felt an uncontrollable urge to vomit, then did, on what he now realized were his bare feet. The cab driver suddenly appeared beside him and helped him back into the cab. Leon's arm hurt like hell.

"You don't look too good, mister. I should maybe take you to a hospital."

"No, I need to find Nero. He'll know what to do. Take me to Mattress World." Leon rolled down the window and sucked in the fresh air as they drove and the pain in his chest began to subside. He noticed for the first time that he was sweating through his silk floral shirt and admitted to himself that when this was settled he needed to see a doctor.

But how could this have happened? How could sensible refined Helen do this? They even slept together for Christ's sake.

"Here we are, man. You sure you're okay?"

"I'm fine. Wait here; we'll be going to the beach from here."

Leon walked slowly and deliberately to the counter at the back of Mattress World so as not to exacerbate his chest pain. He approached a smallish brunette woman about his own age. "I'm sorry to bother you but I'm looking for a friend who used to work here. It's rather important I get in touch with him."

"I'll help if I can, honey." *Another sweet-talking Southerner,* thought Leon. He thought he might puke again. "What's his name?"

"Nero Venditto. He was let go a couple of months ago. Had dark hair and was a smart dresser. Always wore a gold shark's tooth."

"That name doesn't ring a bell but a man of that description used to hang out in here. I haven't seen him in awhile though."

"Maybe I could talk to the manager. He'd know."

"Honey, I am the manager and have been for five years. We've never had anybody by that name work here. I'm sorry. Are you okay? You don't look well."

Luckily Leon was standing in front of a Sealy Perfect Sleeper when his coronary artery occluded. He flew backwards onto the bed as if he'd been shot in the chest with a twelve-gauge shotgun. Cecile, the manager, dialed 911 and began CPR. She knew exactly what had happened since her first husband had done the same thing in the middle of the all-you-can-eat buffet at the Golden Corral three years ago.

TWENTY FIVE

Nero and Helen sped south on Babcock as ominous black clouds rolled in from the west. "Who do you think made you, locals or Feds?" asked Nero.

"Feds, the locals wouldn't have heard from Leon yet and they'd have no reason to stake out Denny's. Somebody tipped off the Feds about the Colonel's operation. We can't take this money to him yet."

"Did you see what they were driving?" Nero looked nervously in the rear view mirror.

"No, they were already there when I arrived. Jesus, I can't believe this is happening."

"I didn't see you followed out. Maybe we're okay."

"I doubt it; they could have had someone waiting outside. God, the Colonel is going to be so pissed."

"Don't panic. Here's what we'll do. We'll drive around and take evasive action. Once we're sure no one is following us we'll head south on 95 to this place I've rented in Deerfield Beach. We'll have to switch plates again, too, just in case one of those agents made these."

"What about the Colonel and his money?"

"Forget about it. Like you said, the money is hot now. Hell, that little spic might've marked it. You don't know who fuckin' set us up."

"Maybe we better just get out of the country now, Nero." Nero turned west and, from the distant flashes of lightning, Helen surmised the storm had already struck the interstate.

"Don't panic, dammit. I've already rented the place in another name and placed the blind ad for our programmer. We can be in and out of there in forty-eight hours. And then there's the money."

"Oh, yeah."

"How much do you think we're holding?"

"I have no clue. That's not a detail the Colonel shared with me. You see anybody behind us?" Helen looked nervously over her shoulder.

"Not yet." Nero turned north this time as big drops of water began to splash against the windshield. "No one will find us once this deluge starts. We're lucky."

Yes, real lucky, thought Helen. She'd never been near an agent before, yet one of those men looked familiar.

"My father brooded about rain. He was a torch you know." Nero changed the subject. Helen guessed this was his effort to calm her.

"A torch?"

"Yeah, he started little fires for the syndicate up in Jersey."

"That was steady work?" Helen asked as she stared absently out the window. The black sky whitened with a jarring thunder clap and rain pummeled down in torrents.

Nero laughed and shook his fist. "That's it. Pour! They'll never find us."

Helen wrapped her arms around herself and nestled into the thick upholstery. The sight of rain chilled her to the bone. "So what did your father care about the rain?"

"Rain puts out fires, Helen. It's bad for business."

"Oh, I see," Helen responded vaguely as she ruminated about the Colonel and his money.

"He was always listening to the weather reports and cursed the weather man when he was wrong. Once he even tried to get the Protanos to off the weatherman. It was a funny thing. His fires were so hot the rain never put them out. He'd always take me to watch them. So I asked him one night, 'What do you care about the rain? Your fires burn anyway.'

"He says to me, 'If it rains on my fires my bosses think I don't do the job right. They don't exactly drive down and watch you know, 'cause it ain't safe. I want you to listen to this, Nero.'

"'Okay, I'm listening, Papa.'

"'You gotta learn this. It's all about perception. You can do the best job in the world but if someone perceives you didn't do it right all your work doesn't matter.'

"'Yeah?' I says… I was a bit confused, Helen, being just a kid. So my father says, 'Michelangelo paints the beautiful Sistine Chapel and everyone says he's a great artist. But what if someone starts a rumor that the whole thing is paint by numbers? People start to perceive that as true and all his work is for nothing.'

"'I see, Papa.'"

"'You plan to be a great craftsman like your papa, you better see, Nero.'"

"Your father was a genius, Nero." Helen held herself tighter and leaned her aching head against the cool window.

"So, Helen, we'll just pull into this mall and pick up a new plate and head south. In two days, after we have the web page, you're gonna perceive what a great craftsman I am."

"I'm sure, Nero," Helen responded without enthusiasm. Right now the Colonel's perceptions and what he planned to do about them concerned her more.

In the back seat Pookie slept soundly.

Rick lost track of Nero and Helen almost immediately and cursed himself for not placing a backup in the lot. He zig-zagged back and forth across Babcock hoping to pick them up again but it was futile, especially in a thunderstorm. Suddenly his cell phone rang. "Brindle here."

"You can ease up on those bad guys, Rick. I got all the info we need right here at the restaurant."

"What happened?"

"Estefan froze. He just laid on the floor and cried like a baby begging me not to turn him in to immigration. He seems to have a serious phobia about returning to Cuba."

"So, were the guns going to Cuba or Ireland?"

"He got the money from O'Brien alright but planned to ship them to some Cuba Libre group all along, so we can back off."

"What's the cargo?"

"Colt AR15's, probably Air Force military police surplus."

"He name the vendor?"

"No, not yet. It seems the only thing that scares him more than returning to Cuba is his vendor."

"Probably the Colonel."

"That's my guess. I heard he owns a place up here. You want to pack up and go home, Rick?"

"We might as well go back and file a report. I'll meet you back at the restaurant."

"Take your time, partner. I'm just going over this *Book of Mormon* with our waitress Tiffany. She's pretty fascinated, especially after all the excitement on her shift."

"Sorry to disappoint you both but I'll just be a few minutes." Rick hung up the phone and his thoughts returned to Helen. She was out there somewhere with a lot of the Colonel's money and thought she was being followed. He didn't know what she might do, but he had a good idea what the Colonel would do if he didn't get his delivery. He wished he knew Helen's plans. Hell, he wished he could just talk to her again.

TWENTY SIX

It isn't easy to steal a plain Florida Sunshine State license plate. The state, in an effort to generate more income, has created a plate for almost any cause imaginable. The list is endless: Gators, Seminoles, Hurricanes and every other state institution of higher learning, three pro football teams, two basketball teams, and the hockey team, not to mention a plate for each of the state's endangered species, which itself is an endless list since Florida leads the nation in creating endangered species. Then there are plates for children, teachers, and the arts - created when those groups protested being left off the Florida endangered species list. Of course, the space industry contributed the Challenger plate.

People who buy the standard Florida plate don't care to make a statement and consequently don't notice when their plates have been swapped. Nero inched along through the parking lot of the Treasure Coast Mall for ten minutes in the pouring rain to spot such a plate. He finally found one, but by the time he made the exchange and returned to the car he looked like he'd lost a close match with an alligator at the Reptile Farm.

Except for the intermittent monsoons, the trip to Deerfield Beach was uneventful. The traffic intensified as they reached the Jupiter area and slowed to a crawl near West Palm Beach. Appearing to be just another retirement-age couple in a Lincoln, Nero and Helen didn't draw the attention of the state police, who were too busy trying to keep the SUVs of the phone-toting yuppies from plowing into the rusted out heaps of the lesser privileged.

Heron Quay sat among the other indistinct high-rises on the beach, its only unique feature being its large green and pink sign. The cracked asphalt parking lot surrounded by dying hibiscus bushes had been carefully painted to delineate each owner's assigned parking space. Along the side of the sand-colored stucco building a bougainvillea struggled to establish itself in the shadow of two green trash dumpsters.

The shoddy landscape around Heron Quay suggested the condos had been sold to those without the means of ownership. Instead, they put the minimal amount down and financed the payments by renting out their unit on a continual basis. With the aid of an aggressive realtor, they convinced themselves that a Florida condo made a great investment. Once the developer finished the project and pulled out, the monthly maintenance fees began to skyrocket while the financially stretched condo owners consistently refused to vote for any improvements. Before long, the complex began to take on the seedy appearance of most of its neighboring properties.

Helen remained oblivious to the specifics of her surroundings. Stress, fatigue, and hunger enveloped her. Conversation with Nero had been sparse. Other than his toupee, which seemed to have been heavily coated with some sort of water repellent, he looked like a refugee from a Havana typhoon. His dry-clean-only luau shirt had already shrunk and rode above his fleshy love handles.

Stopping for food would certainly have drawn unwanted attention. While Helen agonized about the Colonel, Nero vented his frustrations at the incompetent drivers around him. He screamed *Nazi capitalist cocksuckers* at a BMW or *Pacific rim job whore* at a black Lexus. A young woman in a red Dodge Durango with *Save the Manatee* plates and a *Bush* bumper sticker cut him off near PGA Boulevard and benefited from *Soccer mom slut*! Helen tried to sleep, only to be jolted awake by Nero's epithets.

Upon their arrival, Helen struggled to extract Pookie from the back seat while Nero claimed his suitcase and the Colonel's cash from the trunk. Pookie stopped to pee on a withered hibiscus. Then the three of them wearily rode the elevator to their new hideout on the third floor. The place was furnished better than Helen expected but she was too exhausted to care.

She slipped out of her dress and crawled into bed with Pookie. Pookie carefully sniffed the sheets for signs of a female of his species but, finding none, circled several times in the area of Helen's breasts and settled down to sleep. Helen had already preceded him to dreamland as Nero sat at the dining room table and counted the cash from the briefcase.

The next morning Helen awakened to Pookie's soft snoring, the distant sound of waves lapping the beach, and the smell of freshly perked coffee. She found Nero at the dining room table again, this time poring over the morning paper. The coffee seemed to have energized him. "Where'd you get the paper?" Helen asked.

"Just down the street. I went out while you slept. You okay?"

"I guess; I slept hard. Where's the briefcase?"

"Over there." Nero motioned toward the coffee table. "Two hundred seventy five thousand dollars just waiting to accompany us to the islands."

Helen let out a small gasp. "Nero, you don't understand. We've got to deliver that money to the Colonel and try to explain what happened."

"Think a damn minute, Helen. We shook the Feds but they probably caught Juan Valdez in the Denny's. I'll bet he gave up the Colonel in a minute to save his own hide. The Colonel is either in custody or under heavy fucking surveillance. He's a made man. It would be suicide to make contact."

"And if he isn't being watched but is sitting there waiting for us?"

"Then I'll bet he's pretty pissed about his little aborted mission and figures someone has to go down for it. I don't want to be there when he points the finger."

"But it wasn't our fault."

"That's our perception, dear. His perception is the only one that fucking counts; he's the boss. My father taught me that."

"We can't just keep this money!" Helen's voice rose in desperation.

"It's the only safe thing to do. Trust me."

"Is there anything about the Colonel or Leon in the papers?"

"*Nada*. Nothing about a gun bust and nothing about Leon being scammed. That hick probably hasn't figured it out yet."

"Oh, he's figured it out, Nero. And he should have reported it by now. Why hasn't it made the news?"

"I've got no clue but all the better for us. Now I've got work to do." Nero stood up and drained the last of his coffee. "I've got to meet a man about the computer job. Why don't you get dressed and shop or something while I handle the details." Nero leaned over and kissed Helen on the cheek in dismissal.

TWENTY SEVEN

"Hello, this is Rick Brindle's office."

"Mr. Brindle?"

"Speaking. May I help you?"

"I don't know if you remember me. My name is Helen Wilson." A pause. "From Atlanta?"

"And Denny's of Melbourne. Of course I remember but how did you . . . ?"

"I'm sorry I caused trouble there. I didn't recognize you at first but you looked familiar. Later it came to me."

"Where are you?"

"I can't say. It wouldn't be fair. Then I found the ATF office in the book and …"

"The investigation is over. Our people aren't after you."

"But …"

"You were just the courier, so as long as you didn't keep the money you're safe."

"That's just it. We still have it."

"My God. He'll come for you. Where are you, Helen? I can help."

"No, it's too late."

"We need to talk. Let me meet you somewhere."

"I waited. You never came back."

"What do you mean?"

"Atlanta."

"I couldn't. I was hit by a car and woke up in a hospital. My parents took me home. I never had a chance."

"And never gave me a second thought."

"That's not true but there were so many things. And college."

"And your career?"

"I didn't know how to reach you."

"I was in Atlanta, remember. In the book."

"I never married."

"That's supposed to mean something?"

"Look, we have to talk somewhere else. Please, I can help."

"I don't think so."

"Then why'd you call, Helen?"

"I'm not sure. A lot of men have let me down but I always thought you were different. But you were just an infatuated kid and I still believed in you."

"I meant to ..."

"I'm real sorry about your accident. And sorry to have bothered you but I guess I just needed to know. Good-bye, Rick."

"Don't ..." The line went dead.

TWENTY EIGHT

"Mr. Eckerman? Leon Eckerman?"

Leon tore himself away from the heart monitor, where he had feared each blip would be his last, and faced a portly dark-skinned man in a long white coat. He guessed he was Pakistani or Indian. "Yes?"

"I am Dr. Singh." He smiled broadly with anxious relief. "And you are one lucky fellow, no?"

Leon looked down at the burn marks on his chest from the shock paddles. His throat felt like Herefords were grazing in it, and all he could remember was that Helen had taken him for his entire life savings. He looked up at the doctor. "I'm lucky you say."

"Oh my yes, you are one lucky fellow to be sure."

"What happened to me?"

"You narrowly escaped a massive attack of your heart. But we saved you!"

Singh's sing-song voice and enthusiasm suggested that Leon was the first one. "No kidding," he responded flatly.

"Certainly, for there you are and here I stand." Singh laughed loudly at his own joke and slapped his thigh with Leon's chart. "That woman from the carpet place gave you the CPR until the paramedics arrived and shocked your ticker." He pointed proudly at Leon's singed chest.

Leon recalled the confused woman from Mattress World. Singh must be referring to her. He figured she, if anyone, had saved his bacon and made a mental note to go back and thank her if he made it out of this place alive. "Where am I?"

"You are a guest of the Melbourne Space Coast Medical Center, a division of the Havenwood Healthcare System, and the Challenger

Cardiac Care Center, or C-4 as many interns like to name us." Singh reached into the breast pocket of his white coat and produced his card embossed with a replica of the Challenger soaring toward its doomed fate.

"What happened here?"

"When you arrived, you were a very, very sick man. They sent you straight to my catheter lab and I swiftly ran a very long one from here," he pointed to Leon's groin, "to way up here into your heart."

Leon felt his nausea returning.

"I was very much pleased to find your heart still beating despite a big blockage in your LAD, which is not a good thing I'm not ashamed to tell you."

"LAD?"

"A most important artery to the heart but I was able to open it with great skill, lucky for you." He laughed again like a school boy whose friend had just farted in music class. Eventually he regained control of himself and proceeded. "I then placed a stent much like this ballpoint pen spring to keep it open." He attempted to demonstrate by squeezing the spring between his thumb and forefinger, but the tiny spring shot from his hand and rolled under the bed.

"That's going to keep me from having another heart attack?"

"Oh, my yes. I am mostly certain." Dr. Singh's voice echoed from somewhere under the bed as he searched on hands and knees for his spring.

"Will I have to take anything?"

"Ha, ha. You will have to take many drugs and in your country they are mostly expensive. But I cannot seem to find my spring."

"I don't have any insurance and someone stole my money."

"That most certainly sucks for you as my Americanized son would say. Ha ha. Here is my little spring!"

"You don't understand. I only have what's in my wallet. I can't pay for anything."

Singh popped up on the other side of the bed and held the small spring triumphantly over his head. "Here it is. And not to worry. I'm sure if you came through the emergency room, which you did, there is no money in your wallet if you even still have a wallet."

"That can't be."

"Oh yes, you're not in Calcutta any more, Toto. Ha, ha, ha. I say that to my wife when she backs the Mercedes out of the garage."

"What will I do?" The beeping monitor attached to Leon registered one hundred twenty.

"First, you must stay calm. This fast beepity beep won't do. We don't want this stent spring to go flying like my pen spring. Ha, ha." With that Dr. Singh took out his pen and began to scribble furiously on a prescription pad. "Secondly, MSCMC will have you file for indigency and then you can call the free clinic at the health department. They might be able to see you in two or three months if you say it's an emergency."

"When can I go home?"

"Oh, most certainly today, yes." He tore off a fistful of prescriptions and handed them to Leon. "You need a beta blocker, an ace inhibitor, this most expensive cholesterol drug, and, of course, Plavix. And don't forget to take a baby aspirin every single day."

"Don't I have to go to rehab?"

"If you had any money, most certainly yes, but since you have no insurance the nurse will give you a pamphlet and demonstrate some exercises. In a month you can work out with the tele man Richard Simmons!" Singh demonstrated by running in place and thrusting his hands over his head. "Like this. Ha, ha."

"That's it then?"

"Yes, everything I have covered." Then Dr. Singh scowled as if he had forgotten something. "Oh, yes. This will help! I have smartly invested in several McDonald's franchises. Take this coupon; it's good for a Number 3 Combo!" He handed Leon a greasy recycled coupon.

Several hours, two nurses, a social worker, and an administrator later Leon, still in his gown, stood at the hospital entrance, taxi voucher in hand. It seems the emergency room staff had not only lost his wallet but every stitch of his clothing. With everything that had happened it didn't seem to matter who saw his bare ass. When the taxi pulled up, he threw his prescriptions and exercise pamphlet into the trash receptacle and climbed in.

"Where to, fella?" asked the nonplused driver as he reached for the voucher.

"Dahlia Dunes. Hopefully there's still a seafoam Taurus parked there."

"Can't imagine why anyone would take it."

TWENTY NINE

Nero's meeting took place in the Pink Pony Lounge just off South Beach. It was a bar that time and most of its clientele had forgotten. On the outside, dark wood beams criss-crossed dirty white stucco that suggested an English Tudor motif. Lit up at night with soft spotlights strategically placed in the shrubbery, it might look almost inviting, but in the daylight it had all the charm of an adult bookstore.

The only light inside emanated from the bubbling pink neon lights behind the bar and an empty fish aquarium in the corner next to the cigarette machine. The whole place smelled of stale tobacco and mildew. Bennett could barely make out the figure of the man who had called himself Nero on the phone. He sat in the corner booth nursing a Miller Lite just as he'd said. Bennett made no sign of recognition but instead approached the bar and asked the bartender for a Michelob draft.

The bartender added nothing to the ambiance of the place. He wore a black silk vest and a pink pleated shirt sans tie or sleeves. His tattooed biceps seemed more appropriate on the bouncer than a bartender and Bennett guessed he served as both. The jagged scar that traversed his right eyebrow suggested that either he rarely sought medical attention or the management of the Pink Pony had signed on with a very bad HMO. Bennett concluded this was not a man he should engage in small talk about the Miami Dolphins, and he turned to the lesser of the two evils sitting in the corner booth.

"Nero, I'm Bennett Durant." He extended his hand and shook Nero's firmly as he started to slide into the booth in an effort to evoke an air of confidence as well as nonchalance. His butt stuck to the damp vinyl and the inertia of his upper body carried him precariously into

Nero's personal space. He caught himself just before they collided but not before he splashed his Michelob onto the table. *Shit*, he thought. *Great first impression.*

"Are you all right? You aren't on drugs are you? I can't use you if you do drugs. Too risky."

"I'm fine. My ass got caught on this fine Corinthian leather here. Sorry."

"Okay, so try not to make such an impression on that refugee from the World Wrestling Federation behind the bar. He doesn't need to fucking remember us."

Bennett shook his head and started to get up. "It's a scam isn't it?"

"No, honest. It's legit." Nero reached for Bennett's arm and pulled him back. "I got a letter from a lawyer in Orlando. We're processing commendations from the French government and distributing them to WWII GI's for a small processing fee. It would be so much more efficient on the Internet, but I frankly don't know jack shit about how to go about it. That's why I need a guy like you for just a few days."

"What do you want me to do?"

"Set me up a web site with those links or whatever and I'll pay you five c-notes now and another five when the job is done. Cash. You walk and nothing's traceable to you."

"Why can't the French set you up?"

"You really want to ask a lot of questions or do you want the fucking job? I'm telling you it's legit and that's all you need to know."

"I can do it. I don't suppose you can quote me anything about the equipment you've got?"

"No, but it's being delivered today. You can come by tomorrow and look at it. We're just north of here at the Heron Quay Towers, 34 B. Come by at three o'clock." Nero started to leave.

Bennett's brow furrowed as he ran his thumb nail through the label on his beer bottle. "How do you know I'll come?"

"You'll come. You didn't meet me in a dive like this because you got a good day job." Nero smiled broadly. "And don't over tip our wrestler." He turned and walked out.

Nero was right; Bennett needed the money. On the other hand, one screwup and he was a two-time loser back at Glades. But this was neat and clean. All he had to do was walk in, program the computer, and walk out. It certainly wasn't illegal to set up a web site. What did he care what they did with it after he left? What the hell. He slapped a buck on the table and walked out into the sunshine and the clean smell of the ocean.

While it took Bennett a little longer than he expected, the job was pretty routine. He arrived at Nero and Helen's place and found the computer still in its box. The condo had two bedrooms with a balcony overlooking the ocean and the pool. Its walls, furniture, and carpet were stark white. The only color in the room exuded from a peach accent pillow on the couch and a pair of color-matched porcelain fish on the coffee table. Helen fretted about where the computer, an inappropriate gray contrast to the rest of the décor, should be set up.

"Christ, Helen, what's the difference?" Nero exclaimed. "Just put the damn thing in the corner of the bedroom."

Helen bit her lower lip and feigned a pout for Bennett's benefit. Then she knelt down and picked up her small white dog. "Come on, Pookie, you and I will get ready for the beach. Stick it anywhere you little ol' damn please, Nero. I'm sure you men can manage without me."

"Have you got some sort of desk or table, Nero?"

"Damn, I forgot. You'll just have to go back and get one. Take Helen's Lincoln. Here are two bills and the keys." He pulled out a money clip with a thick wad of bills and peeled off two one hundred dollar bills.

"Look, you didn't say anything about all this set up," Bennett protested.

"What else you got to do, Bennett? So I'll owe you another bill. All right?"

Bennett shrugged and took the money. An hour later he returned with a large flat box containing the unassembled desk and spent the rest of the day building it and setting up the computer. By the time he finished, it was too late to call the Internet company to set up an account. He'd have to finish tomorrow.

By now Helen had returned from the beach and downed two whiskey sours which greatly improved her mood. She sat on the couch and tugged at her short peach terry-cloth cover up, then leaned forward revealing ample cleavage as she tapped a cigarette on the glass table in front of her. She leaned back and held it to her lips. "Bennett, do you have a light, dear?"

"Why, yes ma'am," he responded with mock chivalry. He couldn't discern Helen's exact age, but she effused an antiquated sexuality that reminded him of his mother's friends or a heroine from an old Bogart movie. Bennett suddenly sensed his own discomfort with the fact that he was aroused by someone probably old enough to be his mother. He lit her cigarette and turned away. "I've done all I can do today, Nero. I'll be back in the morning to finish up."

"Must you scurry off so soon, hon? Nero, make Bennett a drink."

"No, really. I've got a cross-town bus to catch. Thanks anyway." Helen bit her lip in a pout again as Bennett let himself out.

At the bus stop Bennett lit his own cigarette and gazed back at the high-rises on the beach. It was nearly five o'clock and a small parade of domestics began trailing out the side entrances of the building. Some walked in pairs or even groups of four but most of them marched toward his spot in solitary silence.

A few were black and he assumed that not many years ago they all were, but now most were dark Hispanics, who laughed and joked in Spanish. They spoke with a young and careless bravado usually reserved for their young men. As three of them approached, he could sense their eyes, penetrating and assessing. Then one spoke and the others laughed and looked away; Bennett wondered what insult she'd thrown at him.

By the time the bus arrived, his shirt clung to his back from the late afternoon heat. He found a seat, sat back, and closed his eyes, his thoughts returning to Helen and Nero. They were a couple of old cons who should have gotten out years ago, before they had pulled off one too many scams and had stooped so low they couldn't look each other in the eye anymore. He wanted to be rid of them because they reminded him of how he might end up. He wondered if his mother had made it out.

Tomorrow when he finished, he would head north and find honest work up around Melbourne. He heard a man with computer skills could find work in the space industry. Yes, that's what he would do. It made perfect sense.

His room was on the second floor of a converted sixties-style pink motel with outside corridors. When new it had attracted middle class families on their one-week escape from the New York and New Jersey winters. Then in the seventies, the place was trashed by the college crowds who had since moved on to Daytona and Pensacola, like termites destroying every building in their path. In the eighties while the national chains were buying up the beachfront, the Cuban immigrants bought these small mom-and-pop joints and converted them into cheap one-room efficiencies for the down-and-outers like Bennett Durant.

Men in dirty T-shirts leaned against the railings in the afternoon and smoked while they stared at the decaying urban landscape. It was as if they were still doing time – waiting for something they'd long ago forgotten existed. By night Bennett could hear them through the paper thin walls as they snored or smashed their beer bottles and beat their whores. He knew if he stayed much longer his dreams would fade like his worn red carpet and he would become one of them.

The night he left Nero and Helen he packed all of his belongings into an old gray Tourister he'd purchased at a thrift shop around the corner and walked down to the office to settle his account. BP wasn't at his desk. He had a one-bedroom apartment off the small twelve-by-fifteen foot lobby. Bennett banged the bell on the counter and waited.

Shortly BP stuck his head out the door. "What do you want, Bennett? I'm eatin' my TV dinner and watchin' the news. Your toilet plugged again?"

"No, I came to settle up. I'm moving out tomorrow."

"No shit." BP stepped out into the lobby wearing baggy Bermudas and a knit polo shirt that clung to his fat gut like the skin on a ripe grape, his belly button an outie.

"It's time I got a life." Bennett didn't want to get into a long conversation with BP who was always looking for somebody to listen to him rehash his life story. It supposedly included a successful career in the Navy SEALS cut short by disability. Bennett suspected BP probably assisted the cook in the galley, and serving a Navy SEAL in the chow line was the closest he ever got to the elite group.

"Where are you movin' to? I got to have a forwardin' address you know."

"I don't know yet. I'll drop you a line when I settle in someplace." As an ex-con, Bennett treasured his privacy. Keep to yourself and don't give anyone any information you don't have to – the unwritten rule.

"Suit yourself. You wanna stop in and have one for the road? I got a fifth of Jim Beam." BP began to shuffle through the file on the counter.

"Thanks anyway, BP, but I've got some packing to do," Bennett lied. He just wanted to get something to eat and go to bed. Mentally he had left this place weeks ago after he quit Roy, and now he wanted to close his eyes and wake up somewhere new. He paid BP in cash and prepared to leave.

"Well, good luck to you, boy. I kinda' hate to see you go. You kept to yourself and didn't make no trouble. I wish I had a whole place full of guys like you. It'd be like bein' in the Navy again. You know what I mean?"

"I'm not sure. I never served." *Although prison wasn't much different,* he thought. "You take care, BP. I'll send you a postcard from Alaska or whatever." He shook BP's meaty hand, turned away, and walked back to his room. Later he ate at the diner down the street, returned to his room, and fell asleep to Diane Sawyer talking about doctors who defrauded Medicare and the patients who turned them in for a reward.

THIRTY

Colonel Collins poured himself another straight bourbon as Michael entered the room. "You ever drink a Tom Collins, Michael?"

"No, Sir. I don't recall having the pleasure."

"Pleasure, shit. Ruins a damn bourbon. I don't trust anybody that doesn't drink their bourbon straight or on the rocks. You want one?"

"How could I refuse? Make mine with a little ice please."

"Did you know I was christened John Collins?" Without waiting for an answer the Colonel dropped three cubes into a glass and poured a generous splash of Maker's Mark over the top. He handed the drink to Michael and continued. "People would always ask if John Collins wasn't the name of a sissy drink for women. They always greeted me the same, 'Hey, John Collins. How's Tom Collins?'"

"That must have been very hard for you, Sir."

"You're damn right. I came to despise my own name. No man should have to live like that. I changed my name to Jack as soon as I got to West Point."

"It's often the curse of great men, Sir."

"What do you mean by that?"

"Look at Dick Nixon, for example."

"By God you're right, Michael. No respectable man should be burdened with a name like Dick but Nixon bore the burden well."

"I'm sure he did."

"In all our conversations he never brought the matter up."

"You must have been close, Sir."

"We were *simpatico*, Michael. Like brothers."

"I'll bet you have some stories to tell."

"It's all classified, Michael. I'll carry them to the grave. There'll be no books written by Colonel Jack Collins. I'm too much of a patriot to exploit my friends."

"That's a wonderful attribute, Sir."

"Thank you, Michael, but enough about the past. Any news on my money yet?"

"No, sir, but it's just a matter of time." Michael settled into the overstuffed leather chair in the Colonel's study. He sipped his drink and stared directly at the Colonel.

"You seem pretty damn confident about my money. What the hell happened?"

"The Feds got a tip on our deal with Estefan. Helen must have suspected something and ran with the money."

"What the hell is the Fed's problem? We're on their side."

"I can only guess they got suspicious when O'Brien's name came up. They're pretty touchy about any shipments to Ireland."

"Well, I hear Estefan goddamn dispelled those rumors."

"Spilled his guts, Sir."

"Why the hell haven't we heard from Helen?"

"She probably thinks you're in custody or at least under surveillance. You said she could be trusted."

"Yeah, but it's that prick Nero what's-his-name I'm worried about. You think he went to the ATF?"

"Could be. If he did, he doesn't plan to let Helen return your money. It's an interesting thought. I'll admit I didn't give him that much credit."

"Have our people come up with anything? That son of a bitch makes me nervous, Michael."

"We've covered the airports. They aren't trying to fly yet. Their other options are taking US 10 west then dropping into Mexico. But my guess is they'll head south and try to hire a plane out of South Florida for one of the islands. I'm concentrating our efforts in that area. They'll use your credit card soon and then we'll have their asses."

"They've got over two hundred fucking fifty thousand dollars, Michael. They don't need a credit card."

"It's a habit, Sir. They're not used to spending cash. Sooner or later they'll lay down a credit card just out of habit."

"I want to be there when you find them. You hear?" The Colonel's voice turned to ice.

"Yes, Sir."

"The goddamn army wouldn't let me shoot men for disobeying my orders. Well, we're not in the fucking army any more, Michael. Nixon would understand that. He knew how to get things done."

"Yes, Sir." Michael rose to leave before he had to hear more about what was wrong with this country and its modern army.

"Your father was army, right Michael?"

"No, Marines. He died in Vietnam right after I was born. I never knew him."

"That's right. You told me. Well, if they'd have let us fight that war without our hands tied, good men like your father would have returned home to raise their families."

"Maybe, Sir. I never knew too much about that war, being just a baby and all."

"Well, I was there. I know what I'm talking about." He paused and turned his back to Michael and stared out the window. When he spoke again his voice had softened. "Finish your drink, Michael, and find out what's going on with that credit card."

"Yes, Sir. I'll keep you informed."

THIRTY ONE

Pookie stepped out of the elevator ahead of Helen. He tipped his head back and sniffed the morning air disappointed that it lacked the scent of a female. Then he looked down and noted shiny slime trails across the sidewalk which renewed his interest in the outdoors. Stepping forward he began to sniff the trail and was about to take a test lick when his leash jerked him violently backward.

"No, no, Pookie! Bad dog."

Pookie hung his head in shame as Helen swept him from the walk. "That could be poison, baby."

"No, miss. It's jes the slime trail of the Cuba gold. Dis here is de poison." An elderly black man held up a box of snail bait.

"A Cuba gold?" Helen responded trying to conceal her surprise at finding the groundskeeper in front of her entrance. Everything spooked her since she and Nero fled to South Florida.

"Yes, miss." The elderly black man stepped forward and opened his hand revealing a large gold-colored snail shell. "It's okay. Dis one's dead but dere be many more. I bait dem every week but dey jes come back. Ate dat whole hibiscus dey did. Jes twigs now." He motioned slowly toward a bush of sheared twigs on the lawn. "I hear dey workin' dere way north up de coast eatin' everything dey find. Just like dem refugees demselves. I hear dat." He smiled a toothless grin at his own joke and turned to his work. "Keep dat puppy away now. Don't want him gittin' in da poison, miss."

Helen shuddered and held Pookie tight. "I'll be careful. Thank you." She hurried past the old man, tucked Pookie into the Lincoln, and started the engine. A bell chimed warning her that she was almost out of gas. "Dammit, Nero could have remembered that." But he always ignored the chime and insisted that they could drive for miles before they hit empty. Helen hated the thought of running out of gas, even though she was anxious to shop and get her mind off the Colonel and his money. She pulled out of the parking lot and into the Speedway directly across the street.

She gingerly exposed the gas cap so as not to break a nail and twisted it off. Inserting the nozzle she cursed Nero again as she began to fill the tank. Luckily she always carried Handi Wipes in the glove compartment. Who knows how many people had handled this pump just this morning. Maybe even that old man covered with snail poison. Helen shuddered again.

Eventually the fuel line bucked and shut off the flow. Not bothering to top off the tank, Helen returned the nozzle with some difficulty to its place on the pump. She quickly reached into her car for several wipes and rubbed her hands repeatedly. Then, just to be thorough, she wiped each of Pookie's four paws.

As she approached the attendant, a knot suddenly tightened in her stomach. She had forgotten to get any cash from Nero. Distraught she searched her purse and then looked up at the boy in embarrassment. "I thought I had some cash but I don't."

"Fine, we take credit cards," he responded without looking up from his magazine.

"I'll just run back home and get some."

"Excuse me. Does this look like a bank? We don't give credit and we don't give loans."

"But I'm just staying across the street ..."

"No. It's cash or credit; take your pick, lady."

Helen tried to catch his eye so he could see she was about to cry but he just kept reading. She thought about all the money in the trunk but couldn't bring herself to go get it. Besides, it would certainly draw attention.

Just then a family in a minivan pulled in and the driver began to fill up as his wife and three small children bounded eagerly for the door. Helen reluctantly reached into her purse and took out the credit card Colonel Collins had given her. What the hell. They'd be out of the country before he got his next statement. "Visa," she snapped.

"That's more like it." The acne-faced teenager finally looked up with a sarcastic grin and took the card.

Helen and Pookie's spirits improved immensely as they entered the expansive mall. Her heels and his paws echoed in unison as they clipped across the glazed white tile into the three-story glass atrium that constituted the mall center. Royal palms reached skyward from huge hand painted urns that bordered shining silver escalators, in turn separated by a two-story waterfall cascading into a pool at its base. Purple orchids floated in the pool and also adorned the flowing hair of deeply tanned models in glittering green mermaid attire. The developers had spared no expense to prove that this mall with its Dillard's, Macys, Foot Locker, Waldenbooks, and Orange Julius was different than any mall its customers had ever shopped. They had almost succeeded.

Helen didn't need anything in particular. She savored the presence of the other shoppers. Two dark Hispanic women in their early thirties wearing designer jeans, skin-tight pastel T's, stiletto heels, and dripping with gold jewelry stopped and with some difficulty stooped to pat Pookie who shamelessly rolled onto his back for a tummy rub. Helen smiled, and despite their heavy accents, was able to deduce where they sold fine jewelry in the mall.

Long-striding young mothers in peppy shorts outfits and Nike *Just do it* shoes whizzed past Helen with their strollers. They had turned shopping into a high caloric workout but their tired eyes betrayed their boredom. Helen speculated how long they would last, and how long before they discovered that sexual exercise in the form of an affair would be preferable to laps with junior in the mall.

As Helen and Pookie continued toward the jewelry store they passed intense businessmen speaking into cell phones and an elderly snowbird in an Orioles baseball cap and baggy madras shorts, which exposed varicose calves and pallid, bony knees. He stood dumbfounded in the middle of the corridor, his jaw slack, as he searched right and left for his mate.

She could think more clearly in this haven. The money in the trunk still bothered her and if she were stopped by the police it might as well be a corpse. If she and Nero didn't split for the islands soon, one or both of them would be a corpse in the Colonel's trunk. That much cash wouldn't be as easy to smuggle out of the country as Nero thought. That was his problem; he oversimplified.

Maxim's Jewelry Salon emanated all the opulence and conspicuous consumption the two women had promised. Men and women in tailored suits stood at attention behind a circle of locked glass cases. Absent were the countertop racks full of cheaply priced earrings and watch bands. Rolex bands didn't wear out and that's the only watch they sold.

Helen scooped up Pookie and approached the counter manned by a distinguished-looking gentleman. His hair was neatly trimmed and graying at the temples. Helen guessed his story would be that he had sold the family business in New York and retired in Florida only to discover boredom, or the family fortune wasn't sufficient to support him in the manner he had hoped. In any case, he appeared genuinely pleased that someone had actually entered the store to break the monotony.

He reached forward and patted Pookie on the head. "How are you today, Monsieur Poodle? May I show you something in a fine collar or are you looking for something for your fine lady friend?"

Helen smiled at the compliment. This man had evidently been a very successful jeweler. "Pookie and I are just browsing, monsieur. You certainly have beautiful things." Her gaze fixed on the collection of emerald adornments in the case below her. "Do people really buy these for their dogs?"

"And cats. We have many clients with significant disposable income. The chokers and a few of the bracelets make excellent companion collars."

"Like that emerald necklace? In the corner."

"Yes, an excellent choice. You have very discriminating taste, Mademoiselle." He continued to tease Helen and Pookie with his faux French accent. His broad smile revealed perfect white teeth, though most likely not his own. He placed a white velvet mat that matched the color of Pookie's coat on the counter as carefully as a waiter preparing to serve lunch then splayed the scintillating green choker over the top. "It is beautiful, no? And for your puppy, only two hundred and fifty thousand."

Helen let out a brief gasp more at the price than its beauty. "It's breathtaking." Suddenly the tension flowed from Helen's body, and she was at once in harmony with both her shopping discovery and the bullet that she sensed whizzing toward her head. "Do you take cash?"

THIRTY TWO

When Helen and Pookie returned from the mall, they were so pleased with themselves and their new purchase that they failed to notice the two men in dark glasses parked across the street near the Speedway. Helen did remember the poisoned Cuban snails and quickly swept Pookie into her arms as they neared the elevator.

Michael had gotten the call fifteen minutes after Helen had purchased her gas at the Speedway and dispatched two good men to the site within half an hour of the call. Frank, a former Miami police sergeant, and Vinnie, a former Special Forces corporal in Nicaragua and Colonel Collins' demolition expert, topped off their gas tank and Frank approached acne boy behind the counter. Vinnie picked up a biker magazine from the rack near the door where he could survey the pumps.

Frank slapped a five dollar bill down on the counter. "Slow day, huh kid?"

"No shit. We got a price war going with a station up the street and they just lowered theirs. The Pakistani that owns this place says no more. He doesn't get it."

"Yeah?"

"People around here will drive ten miles out of their way to save a penny on gas."

"You sound like you know the business."

"I had two semesters of marketing at Nova over in Davie."

"No shit?"

"Yeah, but I needed a break so I took some time off to work."

"They really bust your balls, huh?"

"No kidding."

"Listen, I was sent out here to look for somebody. Maybe a smart guy like you could help me."

The kid looked over at Vinnie then back at Frank who had just flashed some sort of badge. "Sure, but this is a pretty quiet neighborhood."

"You can't be too careful. I'm from the white collar crime division. You got a woman out here using phony credit cards." Frank slowly pulled a creased facsimile of Helen and spread it out on the counter. "Have you seen her?"

"Holy shit! My boss is gong to be so pissed," the kid exclaimed. "She was in here this morning. Hell, not more than an hour ago. Rich bitch type with a poodle; said she didn't have any cash."

"That could be her."

"Real pissed that she had to pump her own gas. Probably hadn't done it twice in her life. Kept wiping her hands with a tissue."

"She's a kept society broad but it's all a front," Frank responded. "Doesn't have two nickels to rub together."

"Well, she's being kept at those condos on the beach." When the kid pointed at the white stucco building across the street Frank and Vinnie couldn't help but smile at their good fortune.

Two hours, four cups of coffee, and two trips to the Speedway bathroom later, Vinnie saw Helen's blue Lincoln approaching from the south. He nudged Frank awake and pointed toward Helen. "There she is, Frank."

"Yeah, that's her. She's turning in."

"So now what?"

"We phone in and wait for the Colonel." Frank reached in his pocket for his cell phone and flipped it open. "He wants to be here when we bust them."

"What for? We can handle this."

"He's always bitching about how soft the army has gotten and how in the old days you could be shot for not following orders. I think he has a hard on to shoot somebody."

"No kidding? You think he's ever shot anyone before?"

"Are you kidding? He's an officer and officers just give the orders. They never shoot anybody. You ever see an officer shoot anybody?"

Vinnie hesitated, as if Frank really cared what he'd seen. "No, I guess I haven't."

"Of course not, unless you consider the men that they send out on suicide missions. Wait …" Frank held up one finger. "Hello, who is this? Michael? Hello, Michael, we found them down here on the beach. That's right." Pause. "Nope, no sign of the cash." Frank proceeded to give Michael the address and assured him they would continue their surveillance until the Colonel arrived. "Okay, Michael. Good-bye."

"They're coming. We're to wait. You want any coffee, Vinnie?"

"No, it's hard on my stomach. Get me a Dr. Pepper and a couple of hot sticks."

Michael entered the Colonel's study and found him pacing in front of the large windows that framed the twelfth fairway. He wore burgundy designer coveralls. They were short-sleeved and zippered with a stitched-on belt that clasped at his waist. On his feet he wore white cross trainers. Since leaving the army, this outfit had replaced his battle fatigues. All that he needed were the gold eagles on his shoulder flaps and his last name stitched over his left breast pocket.

"Sir, they've been found." Michael handed the Colonel a folded slip of paper with the address on it.

"Dammit. I knew it! Was it Frank?"

"And Vinnie."

"I can always count on Frank but that Vinnie needs more discipline. Thinks with his dick. He better not foul this up like he did the Estrada assassination. They're on surveillance, right?"

"Yes, Sir. They won't move in until we arrive and then only to provide backup."

"Good. Have they brought armaments?"

"They have a piece for you, untraceable of course."

"Excellent, Michael." The Colonel clapped his hands together. "It was the credit card wasn't it?"

"Yes, a tough habit to break."

"I knew the boys at Langley wouldn't let the mission down. I told you we had nothing to worry about."

"I'll get the car."

"No, have someone else bring it. I want you to stay here, Michael. You're my aide de camp and aides don't go into battle."

"But, Sir."

"You'll stay here and hold the fort; be my alibi if I need one."

"Yes, Sir." Michael concealed his disappointment well. The Colonel didn't care about the money. Michael could see that he had been bored and restless the past few months, hoping for an exercise like this to come along. "Be careful and don't take any unnecessary chances."

"Excellent thinking! Instruct the driver to take the back roads to avoid being seen on the interstate. This is a covert operation, Michael; we can't be too careful."

"Prudence, Sir."

"We'll call it just that. Operation Prudence. Record that in the day book." The Colonel paced the room with an agitated energy. "In 'Nam they called me *Suicide* Collins behind my back but I was strong and they were weak, Michael."

"Sir?"

"No mission was too tough for my men. I demanded prudence just like all the rest but it took sacrifice to get the job done. Good boys laying down their lives to halt the spread of communism and blow the hell out of the domino theory. Your father should have fought with me, Michael. Then you would have known the glory of his sacrifice."

"I'll get the driver, Sir," Michael responded bitterly.

THIRTY THREE

Frank noticed the Colonel in the rear view mirror as he crossed the street and disappeared around the north end of the condo complex. He decided not to get out of the car or tell Vinnie but rather let the Colonel do his own thing. That was ten minutes ago. Now the Colonel had retraced his steps and surreptitiously approached Frank's car from the rear, as if in his bright coveralls he didn't stand out like a Minnesota tourist on the beach.

Eventually he stormed the car, opened the rear door, and slid quickly into the back seat, scaring the piss out of Vinnie. Vinnie had attempted one too many covert operations for Uncle Sam and tended to get skittish on big jobs like this.

"And you guys call yourselves soldiers!" the Colonel gasped as he attempted to catch his breath. "I've been in the zone for twenty minutes and have already reconned the condos in question."

"Good work, Sir," Frank replied nonplussed.

"Jesus, you gave me a scare," muttered Vinnie as he fumbled for a cigarette. "Now I gotta take a piss."

"Stand down, soldier. We've got a mission here." He turned his attention to Frank. "We need to reconnoiter which unit they are in."

"I've already taken the liberty, Sir."

"Excellent, did you tail the woman or that asshole Eyetalian?"

"No need, Sir. The woman took the elevator to an upper floor, so I inquired at the office. I told the manager I wanted to rent an upper unit on the water that allowed pets and smoking. She said she had two but one of them was occupied this week and the other is being repainted."

"Superb recon, Frank! We've got them. Let's deploy. Did you bring my weapon?"

"We're not sure they're alone or even if her friend is with her. No one else has come or gone since we got here. But if we are going to bust in there, I would do it now before traffic picks up. That or wait until after dark."

"We do it now. They won't be expecting us in broad daylight. Give me my piece, Frank."

Frank rolled to his right and opened the glove compartment, taking out a small caliber pistol with a silencer, and passed it back to the Colonel.

"Be careful, it's loaded," blurted Vinnie. "Jesus, keep it out of sight! It's not a goddamn flag."

"Listen, soldier, I was handling weapons before you were whelped." The Colonel pointed his finger at Vinnie; it was so close to his nose that Vinnie was beginning to look cross-eyed. "You don't worry about your C.O. Just do your damn job and protect my flank."

Frank watched as the Colonel tried to slip the gun into his waistband before he realized that he didn't have one. Then the Colonel tried to jam it into his pockets but they weren't deep enough to hide both the gun and the silencer. Finally he shoved the gun back at Frank. "Here you take it and be sure Vinnie boy covers me."

Frank fought the urge to shake his head in disbelief and took the gun. "Fine. Let's do it." Frank and Vinnie slipped on their dark glasses and they all climbed out of the car and crossed the street.

Helen heard the knock at the door. "Are you expecting Bennett, Nero? I'll get it." Pookie looked up briefly from his food bowl and cocked his head as she passed the galley kitchen. "It's okay, baby. It's just Mr. Durant." She opened the door and stood face to face with the Colonel and two men she had never seen before.

"Hello, Helen. I believe we have some unfinished business."

"Sir," was all she could utter. Her heart pounded against her chest wall like a bass drum and it felt as if someone had a vice grip on her throat.

Nero rounded the corner. "What did you forget?" He paused

when he realized who stood at the door. Helen, still struggling for air, searched his face for some clue to his thoughts.

"Oh, it's you," Nero snapped, as if the janitor had just arrived. "You set Helen up, you bastard." Now he was in the Colonel's face like a fierce miniature Doberman oblivious to its own inadequate size. "It's lucking fucky I went along. If it weren't for my quick thinking, we'd all be in jail right now."

The Colonel pushed his way past Nero into the condo while the other two stone-faced men stepped over the threshold still blocking the door. Helen reluctantly followed Nero into the living room as he nipped at the Colonel's heels. Someone quietly shut the door and twisted the dead bolt.

From the kitchen Pookie had sensed the fear in Helen's voice and knew something was amiss, but decided he'd better finish his food first in case the intruders had brought their own food-stealing dog. Once convinced he had devoured every morsel, Pookie trotted around the corner with his fangs bared to greet Vinnie and Frank with as fierce a growl as he could muster.

"What the hell is that?" Vinnie croaked.

"What's it look like, Vinnie? It's a miniature attack dog in a necklace," Frank replied.

"Looks like a fag dog to me. Wearing a green necklace."

Pookie growled again. He couldn't understand the words but knew when he was being insulted. He decided to bite the antsy one called Vinnie first. Just as he prepared to lunge, he felt Helen's hands yank him off the floor as his feet clawed the air wildly.

"It's okay, Pookie. The bad men won't hurt you." Her voice sounded almost normal but he sensed a tremble suggesting something wasn't right.

"Put him away, Helen, or one of my men will have to wring his pretty little neck."

"No." Her voice strained again and Pookie began to squirm. "I'll shut him in the bathroom. He'll be all right. Just don't hurt him." Helen hurried Pookie into the bathroom and set him on the rug, then switched on the overhead fan. "You'll be all right, baby." She reached down and gave him a pat on the head and closed the door. Pookie cocked his head and wondered about the small tear he had detected in the corner of her eye.

When she returned to the living room the Colonel was looming over Nero, who now sat meekly on the couch, his bravado evaporated. "Sit down, Helen. Here next to Nero." He pointed at the couch with a small gun adorned with a silencer. Helen swiftly complied. She wished her heart would stop pounding, certain it was visible through her white blouse.

"You know I didn't set you up, Helen. You took my money and didn't try to contact me. You disobeyed my orders."

"There wasn't time," Nero interrupted.

The Colonel's eyes widened with rage as he sucked back the saliva from the corners of his mouth. "You shut the fuck up, dago. I'll deal with you later."

He turned again to Helen, gulping air in an attempt to compose himself. "My organization, unlike the rest of the ineffectual businesses in the country, is successful because everyone knows his job and follows orders. We aren't losing market share to our former enemies the Japs and the Krauts because my people are disciplined, efficient, and effective." The Colonel paused and inhaled deeply before he continued.

"Not many women are cut out to work for me, Helen, but those that do are shown no favoritism. No personal days to have their periods or to visit their counselors. No slack cut because they are the weaker sex. Everybody in my outfit carries their own weight. You're no different than Frank or Vinnie over there." He waved the gun toward the two men at the door. "To fail in the line of duty is sometimes admirable, but to fail because you deliberately disobeyed and went AWOL is unforgivable."

"We just took evasive action," interrupted Nero. "Anyone in their right mind …"

"I thought I told you to shut up." The Colonel shoved the barrel of the silencer against Nero's right nostril. Nero winced and withdrew, his toupee sliding forward as his head struck the wall.

The Colonel laughed the laugh of a small gleeful child as he swiped the hairpiece off Nero's head and held it high over his own. "You ever play capture the flag in Dagoland? You just lost dago boy." The Colonel began to dance what faintly resembled an Irish jig as he continued to wave his prize.

"Sir, we do have some time constraints," Frank said.

"At ease, soldier," the Colonel snapped. "I'm not through with Helen yet." Frank stepped back. "That's better."

"There's a soldier that can follow orders, Helen." The Colonel cast Nero's rug to an unsuspecting Vinnie and leaned over Helen, his breath hot. As he spoke Helen felt a drop of spit strike her cheek. She grimaced but made no move to wipe it away.

The Colonel swallowed hard as he fought to regain his composure, then continued. His voice took on an eerie detached monotone like a valium-loaded mother lecturing a small child. "Your insubordination has sabotaged everyone in this organization. My competitors will now think they have the edge. If you go unpunished my entire organization will within weeks be headed down the same path of moral decay as the rest of this once-great nation."

His short lecture ended and his voice began to rise again. His eyes widened as his head twitched hard to the right. "So I ask you, Helen, where's my damn money?"

Helen suspected what the Colonel was capable of but she had never seen him like this. Nero might not realize it yet but they were both about to be murdered by this madman if she couldn't calm him down. But giving him his money wouldn't be enough. *God, don't let my life end this way!* she prayed.

In the distance she heard Pookie calling for her. It was just a soft whine. For some insane reason she remembered a saying she had seen in a mall. *May I always be the kind of person my dog thinks I am.* Sadly she knew she had failed. Then strangely her thoughts shifted to Rick Brindle who'd said he could help. Men never returned, except the Colonel. Her thoughts drifted further. This room was too white. It needed more color and …

"Quit stalling, Helen. Where the hell is it? Do I need to do Nero here first to show you I mean business?" He placed the gun at Nero's temple, his hand shaking. Helen heard a soft sound and noticed an expanding yellow stain forming around Nero on the white couch cushion. Her first reaction was to say *No, no bad dog!* But then in horror she realized Nero was peeing on the couch not Pookie.

"No." Helen was desperate now. "I'll make you a deal."

"No!" the Colonel screamed. He turned the gun on her now. "No more fucking deals. No compromising plea bargains. No goddamn excuses, soldier!"

Helen saw him point the gun at her chest and watched helplessly as he squeezed the trigger. No noise, just sudden pain as she felt herself gasp. Then a warm rush. Blood oozing over the back of the couch sticking to her blouse. She tried to look at Nero, to reach for him – then nothing.

"Oh God!" Nero cried. "What the fuck have you done? Helen?"

"I said stay out of this," spit the Colonel. He turned the gun on Nero and in a fit of rage emptied it into his twitching body before Frank and Vinnie could reach him.

Frank took the gun from the Colonel and began to wipe it clean with his handkerchief. "We don't have much time, Sir. I'm going to sweep the condo while Vinnie checks the car."

"Yes, Frank. That's right. Go ahead." The Colonel's voice, now spent of its rage, was softer and more distant.

"Have a seat here in the bedroom, Sir." Frank spoke softly as he escorted the Colonel to the bedroom. It wasn't the first time he'd helped a man after his first kill. The Colonel wasn't so different.

"Why did she disobey me, Frank?"

"We'll never know that now, Sir." Frank moved quickly about the room as he spoke searching for something large enough to hold two hundred fifty thousand dollars.

"They're bleeding all over the white couch, Frank. Is there any blood on me?" His voice was trance-like now as he rubbed his hands across his overalls looking for fresh blood.

Vinnie walked over to Nero's body and carefully placed the stray toupee over his face. "I hate it when grown men piss their pants. It ain't right. We saw it hundreds of times in Nicaragua." His brief tribute to Nero over, he left the condo to search the car.

Eventually Frank noticed the Colonel staring at the bodies on the couch and broke the silence. "It's best not to look at them, Sir."

"Are you sure they're dead?"

"No doubt about it."

"I loved her once you know."

"No I didn't, Sir." *Damn*, thought Frank. *I've got to get this bastard out of here before he does a complete mind fuck.*

Just then Vinnie returned from searching the car. "The car is clean except for an empty suitcase."

"Shit," said Frank. "Check the other bedroom but I'll bet she stashed the cash somewhere this morning. I'm moving the Colonel out of here now. Meet us at the car, Vinnie." He turned to the Colonel. "Sir?"

"Yes, soldier."

"I'm moving you to higher ground."

"All right, Frank. You take point and move the men out."

THIRTY FOUR

Bennett Durant rose at 7:00 a.m. the next morning. Showered and shaved, he was eager to start his new life. His computer job on the beach was taking longer than expected but he should be able to finish today and move on. He stepped out onto the balcony and scanned the parking lot. The potholes formed small reservoirs of rainwater from a storm that had passed through during the night. The sun melted the haze in the East but the air remained damp and cool. Beer cans and broken whiskey bottles marred the scene in the lot below and a chronic smoker around the corner coughed up what remained of his lungs.

Undaunted, Bennett walked down to the corner to buy a paper. He folded it under his arm and walked briskly back to his perking coffee as he imagined himself the proud husband and father about to kiss his cheerful wife and beaming children good-bye. Just like Ward Cleaver. Life was good – or at least it would be.

At first he couldn't believe it when he heard the knock at the door. No one ever visited and he had settled his bill with the office. Rising from his dinette with his coffee cup in hand he opened the door. He stood face to face with a familiar-looking woman who might have been in her mid thirties and weighed over two hundred pounds. Pretty hair and a nice face. Too bad, he thought.

She brushed back a strand of loose blond hair which she wore pulled back and spoke in a breathy voice from climbing the stairs. "Oh, Mr. Durant. I'm so glad I found you before you left." Crossing the threshold she enveloped him in her arms, her large bosom and perfume conjuring memories of Bennett's grandmother.

Bennett backed away and brushed at the coffee that had spilled down his shirt front. "Excuse me. Have we met?"

"Mr. Durant, you saved my life!"

Bennett felt a flicker of recognition. "Are you the lady from the beach? The one with the broken vacuum cleaner?"

"Yes, the one who would have died of carbon monoxide poisoning if it hadn't been for you."

"You were lucky. I didn't do anything. In fact I was supposed to return it the night before."

"Oh, I knew it. It was fate, Mr. Durant. Fate!" Verbena threw her hands up over her head and Bennett backed further away to avoid another embrace. "It's just like a Thomas Hardy novel; he was my favorite in high school. I read *The Return of the Native* three times. My theme paper explored the divine forces in nature that controlled events in the characters' lives, and I compared it to Buddhism and the web of life."

"I'm afraid I've never read Mr. Handy. But you don't have to thank me, Mrs. Dewitt. I just happened to be in the right place at the right time."

"That's just what I'm talking about."

"Fine, but you'll have to excuse me. I have to go to work." Bennett walked over to the sink and began to dab his stained shirt with a wet cloth.

"But you don't work for that vacuum place any more. I checked." Verbena glanced over at the faded green suitcase by the door. "You aren't leaving are you?"

"As a matter of fact I am. I have to finish some computer work for a couple over on the north beach, and then I'm heading up to Melbourne to find some permanent work."

Verbena's face fell. "But I haven't had time to thank you properly. I must do something."

"No. Thanks anyway but it's not necessary. Really."

Verbena paused and Bennett sensed she was desperately trying to think of a way to continue the conversation. "You don't have a car do you?" Verbena asked.

"No," Bennett replied, immediately wishing he had answered in the affirmative.

"Good. Then I'll drive you." Verbena clapped her hands and smiled.

"It's no problem. The bus goes right by the place."

"No good, Mr. Durant. You're going with me." With that Verbena walked over and picked up Bennett's suitcase. Bennett dutifully followed but wished he had time to change his coffee-stained shirt.

Verbena struggled with the suitcase until they reached the parking lot where she set it down. She puffed and pointed to a dark blue Buick Electra sporting several significant dents in the side panels.

"It was my father's car. He took such pride in it when he was alive. Eldridge took good care of it, too, but I never was much of a driver. Everyone seemed to think they should chauffeur me and I guess I just let them. I'm afraid I put those dents in it since Eldridge passed on."

Bennett shuddered at the thought of riding with this woman. "Would you like me to drive?"

"No, I have to learn to do for myself. But thank you."

"At least let me put my bag in the trunk."

Verbena hesitated. "Well, I guess that would be okay." She walked to the trunk and fumbled with the keys. As Bennett threw in the suitcase and slammed the lid, Verbena dangled the ignition key over her head in triumph and shouted, "*Andale!*"

It didn't take Bennett long to learn that no good deed goes unpunished. Verbena shifted the car into reverse and stepped hard on the gas. He quickly grabbed for his seat belt and narrowly averted striking his head on the dash just as she slammed on the brakes to avoid a utility pole.

Verbena lurched forward into traffic oblivious to the other morning commuters, who honked and swerved before slowing long enough to flip Bennett and Verbena a single-digit salute. Bennett slid lower in his seat and fixed his gaze straight ahead.

Once in traffic, Verbena seemed to have decided it was safer to drive fifteen miles an hour under the speed limit. Cars began to stack up behind her, their drivers desperately checking their rear view mirrors for an opening in the left lane. "I love the oldies channel," Verbena said as she switched on the radio. "How about you?"

"Sure. I particularly like the Stones."

"Oh," Verbena commented with a tone of disappointment in her voice. "I meant Glenn Miller or Tommy Dorsey. Or …" She couldn't conceal her amusement. "Spike Jones. He's so funny. Like *You Always Hurt the One You Love*. I love that one with the guns going off." Then her face suddenly reddened. "I'm sorry. My God. That's essentially what I did to Eldridge – leaving the car engine running in the garage. Oh dear, I guess one does hurt the one they love."

"Maybe. I've never really been in love," Bennett replied. "I suppose I hurt my mother though. Lord knows my father hurt her plenty before he left us."

"You hurt your mother because you went to prison?"

"How did you know that I'm an ex-con? Is there anything you haven't discovered about me?"

"Roy told me when I went to look for you at his shop. He was pretty upset that you left him after he gave you a job."

"That's a laugh. He helped me? Did he tell you his brother was a parole officer who'll ship him another down-and-out sucker to slave for minimum wage? They've got a racket going."

"Oh, I'm sorry I mentioned it." Verbena sounded sad and a little hurt. "I didn't know. He seemed nice enough."

"Well, you can't trust anybody. Remember that, Verbena."

Verbena smiled. "You remembered my name."

"Yeah, well, I'm good at names. Verbena isn't one I'd forget."

"Just the same, you remembered."

"Forget it. But you'd better speed it up a bit or I'll be late."

"I can't talk and drive fast at the same time, so you'll have to be quiet if you want me to go any faster."

"Fine by me." Bennett closed his eyes and pretended to sleep while Verbena edged the speedometer up another five miles per hour. He had an uneasy feeling this ride to work wouldn't even the score.

When they finally pulled into Heron Quay's parking lot, Bennett sat upright and pointed to Helen's Lincoln. "That's their car; they must be home. You can let me out here and be on your way."

Verbena found three open stalls near the Lincoln and then angle parked the car. "Daddy always parked like this to avoid door dings." As she turned off the ignition she turned to Bennett and continued, "I'm going with you to help."

"Oh Christ, are you crazy? These people expect me alone. They won't like it. Besides, what can you do?"

Verbena's lower lip began to quiver. "If you go in there alone I'll never see you again. You saved my life and I owe you more than a ride to work. Besides, I could even drive you to Melbourne so you wouldn't have to ride that smelly bus."

"Verbena, I appreciate all you're trying to do but it's not necessary. You should just go home."

At the mention of home Verbena began to sob uncontrollably. "I don't have a home. They say I owe back taxes and they condemned it to make room for a new Ramada Inn. I don't have anywhere to go."

Verbena's wailing made Bennett nervous. He glanced around to see if anyone was watching. All he saw was the elderly black caretaker who seemed to have busied himself pruning a nearby hibiscus. "You must have somewhere to go. Don't you have any friends?"

"No, all my friends except Tom were friends of my parents and they're all dead or in the Home. I'm a homeless person like they talk about on TV, except I don't even know where the shelter is." Verbena sobbed even louder.

"Verbena, get a hold of yourself. Why can't you stay with Tom?"

"Because he's a homosexual! Eldridge says he's a pervert and probably an Obama Democrat, and that I shouldn't trust him."

The gardener's head turned toward the car at the word homosexual. "No disrespect to the dead but I don't think Eldridge knew what he was talking about. Most of the gays in South Florida are very friendly and polite. In fact, they make excellent waiters."

"Tom's not a waiter. He's a writer with one of those blocks." With that Verbena blew her nose with a resounding honk. Now the caretaker looked up and it appeared as if he was about to approach the car.

"Jesus, I don't need to attract any more attention. Okay, Verbena, if you'll quit crying right now, you can come along and I'll think of something for you to do. Just do what I tell you, okay?"

Verbena looked up and smiled broadly. "Okay."

"When we finish, we'll drive over to Tom's to talk to him. Then you can drive me to the bus stop and we'll be even."

"We could never be even, Bennett."

"Please, let's not go there right now."

Bennett got out of the car and walked toward the elevator; Verbena followed a short distance behind. Neither spoke in the elevator as it ascended to the third floor. When they reached the condo Bennett noticed that the door wasn't completely shut so he knocked and opened the door as he spoke, "Hello. It's just me. Is anyone here?" Silence. Bennett stepped over the threshold into the foyer opposite the galley kitchen and Pookie's empty dog dish. He thought he could see Helen and Nero sitting on the couch. "Hey, I hope I didn't interrupt something but the door was open."

From somewhere in the condo he heard Pookie's whine.

Getting no response Bennett walked directly into the living room. The sight of Helen and Nero's bodies draped over the bloodstained couch, heads thrown back with their cold lifeless eyes staring at the ceiling, hit Bennett like a sucker punch in the stomach. "Oh, dear Jesus in heaven," he whispered.

Then he remembered Verbena and turned to tell her to go back but it was too late. She stood there, her hands at her face and her mouth open as if to scream, but nothing came out. Bennett saw in her face the stark horror she must have felt inside and rushed to her side. "Come in here. Don't look any more." He shut the door and slowly guided Verbena to the bedroom and sat her down on the edge of the bed, where she held her catatonic pose with hands raised in front of her open, silent mouth.

Bennett got down on one knee. "Listen, something has happened here and you must believe I had nothing to do with it. Do you understand?"

Verbena slowly nodded her head. "Call … police … 911." Her tiny voice sounded flat and dispassionate.

"I can't do that just now, Verbena. I could be in serious trouble here. I'm an ex-con, remember? I worked for these people and was likely noticed by the neighbors. My fingerprints are all over this place and the car. I need to make them go away. Do you understand?"

Verbena nodded and Bennett slowly lowered her hands to her side, her gaze fixed on the door to the living room. "Murder … Get away."

"That's right. I must get away." Bennett could feel beads of sweat forming on his forehead and the palms of his hands. He shouldn't have allowed Verbena to follow him here and dreaded having to return to the bodies in the living room. He stood up slowly so as not to startle Verbena.

"Dog …"

"What?" Bennett asked.

"Dog." Verbena pointed deliberately toward the bathroom door.

"That must be Pookie. The killers probably shut him in there. We'll get to him after I've looked around. He's a good dog, Verbena. He won't hurt you."

Bennett rose, patted Verbena on the knee, and returned to the living room. He tried to avert his eyes as if it was just a bad movie, but the odor of early decomposition lingered in the room like a dirty rumor. It became readily apparent that if he didn't face the reality of the macabre scene before him, he would surely vomit and spew chunks of telltale DNA all over the white carpet.

He slowly forced himself to view the remains of Nero and Helen, and then inched closer to the couch in search of the gun. Maybe it was one of those murder suicide things. Florida's elderly did it all the time. No gun – must have been murdered.

Bennett turned toward the entry. He felt better now that his mind was working. The intact door jam suggested no forced entry, so Helen and Nero probably knew their assassins. The place had been tossed but in a subtle, professional manner rather than a desperate rage. Nero and Helen had something someone else wanted very badly. Something so important it was worth dying for.

Despite his fascination with this puzzle, Bennett felt a greater need to extricate himself from the playing field. What had he touched besides the computer and the desk? The tools to assemble it. A drink. The cigarette lighter? Of course the bathroom. He went to the kitchen where he found a dish towel and began to proceed methodically.

As he approached Helen and Nero again, he imagined they were still alive. Just another retired couple having cocktails their heads thrown back in laughter with no more enemies than the winner of last night's bingo pot at the Polish American Club. He moved quickly around them as he swiped the glass top of the coffee table and the cigarette lighter.

Next he found the tool box by the desk where he'd left it and rubbed off each tool. He proceeded to do the same to the computer and keyboard. Dumbfounded Verbena still sat silently on the bed as if she had just awakened in someone else's nightmare.

Finally Bennett returned to Verbena and resumed his position on one knee. "Verbena, I need your help. I know you think that you owe me but you don't. At least I don't feel that way. But I need to get that car out of here and take it somewhere so I can remove my fingerprints. Then I'll have to dump it where no one will find it. Can we go back to your place and put the Lincoln in your garage while I figure this out? I'll understand if you say no. Just give me a head start before you call 911."

Verbena spoke slowly and deliberately. "But we have to save that little dog."

"It would be best if we left him."

"I won't leave him here. He could starve. My parents never let me have a dog; they thought I wouldn't take care of it." Her voice was distant and childlike.

"All right, we'll do it your way."

Verbena rose from the bed and approached the bathroom door. "Are you okay, little puppy? I'm coming for you." She opened the door slowly and disappeared behind it. "Oh, what a pretty little dog. Let's go home."

Bennett shook his head in disbelief as he picked up the car keys from the dresser. "Let's get out of here you two." Verbena inched out of the bathroom with Pookie in her arms; her right hand shielded his eyes from the carnage in the living room.

Once outside, Bennett found Pookie's pet carrier in the back of Helen's car and transferred it to Verbena's. Then, acting as nonchalant as possible, he opened the door of Verbena's Buick and assisted Pookie and her inside. The two were suddenly inseparable. Pookie looked up passively at Bennett with tear-laden brown eyes, and Bennett suspected that he knew he had seen Helen for the last time. Yet despite his grief, he seemed to sense security in Verbena's soft, fleshy arms.

Verbena mechanically set the dog aside and started her car. As the engine roared to life she suddenly shivered as if she had been jolted. Turning to face Bennett she spoke. "I've done this before. Let's go."

Perplexed, Bennett found himself looking back at a different Verbena. In her eyes he detected a murderous indifference that he had witnessed before in women just prior to their time of the month. A look that said, *Don't mess with me, mister!*

Bennett turned and without another word scrambled into Helen's car. He let Verbena take the lead as he followed her south along the beach. If he could just clean up this car and ditch it, he could resume his plan to head north. He had counted on the rest of the money from Nero to stake him in Melbourne until he found a job, and now he was down to nothing. Unfortunately, Verbena wouldn't be any assistance in that department.

THIRTY FIVE

When Bennett and Verbena arrived at her beach place in tandem, Bennett had the car radio tuned to a local station to hear breaking news in the murder case, but to his relief he heard nothing. He planned to ditch Helen's car after dark, so he hoped that the bodies wouldn't be discovered until tomorrow. It was the most he could hope for.

After he parked Helen's car in Verbena's garage, he ran back to Verbena and helped her out of the car. Supporting her by the arm, he walked her toward the cottage. She clung to Pookie as she staggered in silence with all the grace of a beached sea turtle.

The cottage hadn't changed noticeably since Bennett's last visit except for the absence of the furniture. Verbena had apparently cashed it in piece by piece at the local resale shop. The scent of mildew permeated the hot and heavy air, and Bennett wondered how long Verbena had been without the power to run her air conditioner. Clearly the real estate vultures were circling. Bennett sat Verbena down at the kitchen table, then walked over and pulled back the faded curtains and opened the window.

At midday even the beach was oppressive and the open window provided no relief. A few foolhardy souls were scattered along the beach stretched out on their brightly colored towels, glistening like Oscar Mayer wieners on the grill. Bennett jerked his head north, then south, expecting to glimpse flanking SWAT teams but none materialized.

Apparently unfazed by the heat, Pookie darted from room to room and sniffed out every corner of his new digs before he trotted back into the kitchen with a pair of men's boxer shorts in his teeth. He stopped and looked at both Bennett and Verbena, as if expecting reproach.

Ignored, he began to growl and shake his quarry violently from side to side.

Unsure of what to do next, Bennett returned to the kitchen table and sat beside Verbena in the only remaining chair. He started to reach out and touch her arm but she withdrew and stared at him like the stranger he was. Tears formed in the corners of her eyes and began to roll down her cheeks.

"Did we – Eldridge and I – look like those murdered people?" Her voice was almost a whisper.

Her question stunned Bennett, who realized that except for the blood that's exactly what Verbena had looked like stretched out on her recliner. "No, it wasn't like that at all," he lied.

"I – I murdered him!" she blubbered as her corpulent frame convulsed like an apostate at a revival meeting.

"You what?" retorted Bennett.

"I murdered Eldridge," Verbena wailed.

"Jesus, not so loud." Bennett sprang to his feet and slammed the window. One of the Oscar Mayers rolled over. Pookie dropped the shorts and fled.

"He's gone and I should be dead, too, just like those people."

"But the paper said it was an accident. It wasn't your fault." He paused. "Was it?" All he needed now was to be named as an accessory in a triple homicide. He imagined a judge issuing one of those life-plus-forty-years sentences. God, he hoped his mother was dead and wouldn't read this in the papers.

"Eldridge was going to sell this place. I was so depressed. It was just like *Jude the Obscure,* only I didn't die."

"Who the hell is this Jude guy? My God, is the mob involved in this, too?"

"*Jude the Obscure* is a Thomas Hardy novel. They all die! I hated that book." Verbena sobbed uncontrollably. Her encounter with those corpses had apparently uncorked an avalanche of guilt.

"Are you saying that you purposely left the car running to murder Eldridge and take your own life at the same time? That's just plain stupid."

"I don't remember. I try and try but I just can't remember. And don't call me stupid. Eldridge thought I was stupid."

"I'm sorry, but I don't think you're capable of murder. It was an accident. You're just upset from all you've been through." Bennett wasn't sure if he was struggling to convince her or himself.

Verbena's sobs shifted to snorts and sniffs. "Are you sure? You're an ex-con; you'd know these things. Right?" She smiled weakly then swiped a flabby forearm across her nose and sniffed hard. A large tear rolled to the end of her nose, paused, then splattered on the table below. "Right?"

"Absolutely. Us cons have a sense about this kinda' shit." He hitched up his pants in false bravado and returned to the window searching expectantly for cops in SWAT gear like in the movies. "You don't have what it takes to be a killer. Trust me, woman."

"Oh, Bennett, I knew you were a good man." Verbena picked up a dish towel and with a loud honk blew her nose. "It's fate just like in a Thomas Hardy novel – out of our control but meant to be."

"Tell me something, Verbena; did any of Thomas Hardy's characters end up happy?"

"Diggory Venn got what he wanted but most of them ended up dead."

"Great. Doesn't sound like the odds are in our favor."

"Oh, I'm sorry, Bennett. I didn't mean that would happen to us. They're just books."

THIRTY SIX

Tom Poole, Verbena's artistic neighbor on the beach, had been born Thomas Jamison Poole in the Hilton Village subdivision of Newport News, Virginia, to James and Odessa Poole. He was an effeminate child coddled by his mother and largely ignored by his workaholic father, a bean counter in the shipyards. Tom showed no propensity for athletics, preferring instead to read books or to write plays for the neighborhood children to perform, selling tickets for a nickel. It never bothered him to dress up and play the part of a girl. In fact, he found he preferred it.

In high school he joined the Thespians and only shuddered briefly when his father said, "My God, I thought you said you joined the Lesbians!" With a skinny body lacking any muscle definition, he was relegated to the character parts and played old men, professors, and ministers.

Like Verbena he found himself quite smitten with the quarterback of the football team, despite his Baptist upbringing. At night his unconscious desires surfaced in his dreams to torture him. He never shared his fears with anyone, but instead convinced himself that since people had no control over their dreams, everyone must have dreams like his.

After high school his father wanted him to save money by attending Christopher Newport College while he lived at home. But Tom appealed to his mother who in turn convinced his father to let him cross Hampton Roads to Norfolk and attend Old Dominion University. In exchange Tom gave up his bedroom so his father could turn it into a home office and deduct it on his income tax.

At Old Dominion Tom majored in English and befriended a shy female nursing student who appreciated his feminine side and who seemed relieved not to have to fend off any sexual advances. He assumed that with marriage he would develop normal sexual desires and have a family.

The marriage ended in disaster. Tom should have realized it when he took more interest in the bridesmaids' dresses than the tuxedos. His wife, a nurse, eventually made the diagnosis and promptly ran off with a naval ensign whose red Miata boasted a bumper sticker: *Submariners do it deeper*.

By the time his wife left and Tom came out, only to lose his job at the Baptist day school, his father James had already died of a coronary. Odessa, who loved her son deeply and had once loved her husband, felt relieved that he had died before learning Tom's secret. James had left her a great deal of money which made it easy to scoot Tom out of town and finance his novel of discovery. She just prayed it would never be published.

"Knock knock. Did someone mention books?" Tom stood at the screen door. "Hi, Verbena. I noticed your car in the driveway but didn't see any new dents, so I assume you got back safely." He paused. "I'm sorry. I didn't know you had company."

"That's all right, Tom. Come in and meet the man who saved my life."

"No kidding?" Tom fumbled with the door and burst into the room. He wore red swimming trunks and a floral print shirt with a matching red hibiscus pattern. Except for the fact that a teenager wouldn't be caught dead in that outfit, he looked about sixteen years old. He grinned and extended his hand. "If it hadn't been for you I would have lost my good friend. I'm Tom."

"Just luck, or fate as Verbena would have it." Bennett took Tom's hand and sensed he was being studied. He couldn't tell if it was because Tom probably knew he was an ex-con or if he wondered how Bennett would be in bed. He shook off the thought and took back his hand.

"Hey, what's that?" Tom asked. Pookie stood in the doorway to the living room with the shredded boxer shorts dangling from his mouth.

"Looks like a little poodle." Pookie squealed with delight for the first time that day and trotted over to Tom. "The little fella likes me."

It figures, thought Bennett. "He's mine. We're pretty much inseparable." As Bennett reached down Pookie let out a low threatening growl and bared his tiny fangs. "He does that when he's hungry." Bennett forced a smile.

"Allow me." Tom reached past Bennett and lifted Pookie who had dropped the shorts at his feet. Pookie squirmed with delight and licked Tom's face. "I'll be back. I'm taking this pup to my place for some food." Before he reached the door he turned to Bennett. "Whoever lost this dog and that nice car you parked in the garage will be looking for them. I hope you haven't placed Verbena in jeopardy. She's had a hard enough time." With that he turned and left.

"I guess we didn't cover ourselves very well," Bennett said to Verbena.

"Maybe we should just tell him the truth."

"We can't just go around telling everyone we see, like it was some sort of end-of -season sale at Dillard's."

"You said I should forget what Eldridge said about his being gay and trust him."

"I meant baking cookies together or maybe a walk on the beach. That's a little different than asking him to keep secret a double homicide."

"But if he hears it on the news, what's he going to think? He might turn you in."

Verbena paused and looked as if she was about to cry again. "I'm so frightened. I wish I had a Moon Pie."

Bennett walked over and put his arm around her shoulder, resting his hand on her silky hair. She had beautiful hair, and when she wasn't sobbing, a pretty face. Her eyes were as crystal blue as the waters of the Caribbean and, despite her weight, he detected the high cheek bones of a model. "I'm sorry I got you into this and you're right about his reaction to hearing this on the news. We'll have to tell him."

Verbena looked up and smiled. "You two are the only friends I have. I don't want any secrets between us." She dabbed her eyes with the dish towel.

"Then that's how we'll do it." He paused. "You really like Moon Pies, huh?"

Verbena nodded.

"I haven't had one since I was a kid. I didn't know they were still around."

"The man at the Winn-Dixie orders them for me by the box but without any money I've been too embarrassed to go back."

"Well, the first money we get I'll buy you one. How's that?"

Verbena smiled a slow smile and rolled her eyes up at Bennett. "You mean we're going to stay together?"

"Just until we both get enough money to be on our own."

"That's going to take awhile."

A few minutes later they looked out the window and saw Tom and Pookie. Tom had fashioned a leash out of a necktie and was trying to lead Pookie across the hot sand. Pookie danced gingerly as he pulled Tom toward the shade of the porch. Once there he hunched his back and defecated with results quite impressive for such a small dog. Satisfied he was finished, Pookie kicked the sand with his back feet to cover his deed and capered over to Verbena's porch.

"This dog must have been cooped up awhile. He was starving," Tom said as he reentered Verbena's kitchen.

"Sit down, Tom. We need to explain our situation," said Bennett. Tom obediently sat at the kitchen table across from Bennett who proceeded to relate the story from the minute he met Nero, Helen, and Pookie to the discovery he and Verbena had made that morning.

Tom sat motionless while Bennett explained. His eyes widened, first like Orphan Annie's and then like Moon Pies, when Bennett got to the part about finding dead bodies on the couch. "We didn't want to involve you, Tom, but Verbena was afraid you'd think the worst if you heard it on Channel Eleven."

Tom got up from the table and began to walk around the kitchen oblivious to Bennett and Verbena. Suddenly he began to bang his fist on his forehead. "Once I took a class on writing crime fiction at the junior college. They could charge us with being accessories after the fact." He frowned and began to pace the floor again.

Verbena looked over at Tom and shrugged. "He does this when he gets writers' block."

Tom stopped again this time with a big smile on his face. "This is going to make a great book!"

"What?" Bennett and Verbena responded in unison.

"Think about it. Ex-con, suddenly impoverished oversized rich girl, and gay guy team up to solve murder mystery on Florida's Treasure Coast."

"Who said anything about solving a murder?" Bennett interrupted. "We don't have a clue."

"It doesn't matter. It's fiction. I can solve it in the book if not in real life. This could even become one of those mystery series."

"Yeah, we'll call it *G is for Gay Guy*."

"Go ahead and make fun. Do you realize how few gay protagonists there are in fiction?"

"There's probably a reason for that, Tom. Like, it won't sell."

Tom looked hurt. "You two are so smart. Between the two of you, you don't have enough money to pay attention. How do you plan to fill up your getaway gas guzzlers? If you don't need me, you at least need my money. So what's your plan?"

"It's not that intriguing," Bennett replied. "I need to clean the fingerprints off their car and lose it. Then I'm off to Melbourne to get on with my life."

"What about Verbena?"

"I'd hoped she would follow me in her car to the drop site then drive me to Melbourne."

"Excellent. Keep it simple. Only we'll make it a threesome. Since you may have noticed that Verbena's driving skills are a bit weak, I'll drive her car. When we get to Melbourne, I'll loan you some of Mother's money until you can get settled."

"Thanks, Tom, but you don't have to do that."

"Forget it. You saved my friend's life; it's the least I can do. And for this, I get the book rights. Don't forget."

"No problem. Have you got any cleaning supplies?"

"Yes, yes. Come with me. I have some simply fabulous lemon-yellow Playtex gloves you can borrow," Tom mawked. "Yellow will look stunning against your skin tones. We gay men are known for our neatness; it's the cleanliness that seems to give people problems. TTFN, Verbena. I'll bring your friend back shortly."

"Ta Ta for now, Tom." Verbena smiled for the first time in hours. "I'll take care of Pookie." She scooped up the white fur ball. "What a beautiful green collar, Pookie. It looks real. Where on earth did you get it?"

Pookie looked up at Verbena with soft brown eyes that said, *I'll never tell.*

"Take good care of that dog," Tom whispered. "He's an eyewitness."

THIRTY SEVEN

Tom, cleaning supplies in hand, joined Bennett in the garage. In his swim suit, Tigger T-shirt, and pink Crocs he reminded Bennett of a high school debater at the team car wash. Bennett looked in the bucket. "What's that smell?"

"Murphy Oil Soap. I don't have a product just for cars."

Bennett looked down at the bright pink Crocs again and raised an eyebrow. "I guess we can make do."

"What do you plan to do with this car when we're done neutralizing the evidence?" Tom asked in a clinical voice as if he were probing Bennett's criminal mind.

"It's not that big of a deal. I figured we'd drop it off at a mall during business hours. It'll probably be days before anyone notices and another week before the connection is made. But you're the writer; maybe you have a more creative idea."

"Actually, I did envision a more cinematic, if you will, scene."

Bennett looked up toward the garage's exposed trusses and sighed. "Let's hear it, Spielberg."

Tom's voice became breathy with excitement. "I picture you and me along some dark deserted drainage canal, our hard sweating bodies straining against this slowly moving machine. Mosquitoes buzzing around our head on a dark and moonless night. Rolling thunder and lightning in the distance foreshadowing the danger that lies ahead."

Bennett shook his head. "Jesus, I liked you better with writers' block."

Verbena came up with the compromise. "Let's drive north toward

Melbourne but get off at West Palm and park it in one of those areas that's always on the television show *Cops*. Someone will surely steal it, there'll be a great chase scene, and when they're caught the police will find only their fingerprints."

"You're a genius, Verbena." Tom gave her a big hug. "It will work, Bennett, and it makes great copy."

"It sounds fine to me. Good thinking, Verbena." Bennett looked at Verbena and smiled. She was smarter than he had given her credit for and probably smarter than a lot of people thought. Tom, on the other hand, remained an enigma for the moment. His gayness continually played on Bennett's mind. He had the impression that Tom was sizing him up. But was it because he considered him sexually as Bennett would another woman, or was he concerned with Bennett's qualifications as Verbena's friend? In any case Bennett felt as self-conscious as a woman wondering if her lipstick was on straight.

"We'll leave late tonight," Tom continued. "After we dump the car, we'll swing over to A1A and follow the coast north. We'll hold up in some old motel on the way after we wake up some grouchy old guy in a sleeveless T-shirt and suspenders. His wife will peer over his shoulder, her hair in rollers and her face all smeared with cold cream. She'll be wearing one of those old robes that looks like it was made from a chenille bedspread.

"The scene will be a weathered pink stucco motel with just eight units in a single row and a neon sign flashing the name Vista del Mar, The Flamingo, or The Palms. I'll add some night-blooming jasmine whose scent will provide a stark contrast to the tension in the air.

"Remember, we can't park directly in front of our unit. That way if they come for us they'll hit the wrong place and we can escape before they catch us."

"Hello, Tom, are you there?" interrupted Verbena. "Who is going to come for us?"

"Well, maybe the killers. Maybe we have something they want."

"You're dreaming, buddy. I don't know why they killed those two but why would they look for us? They don't even know we exist," snapped Bennett.

"Be careful what you say, Bennett. Remember life can mirror fiction."

"Whatever. I never took any of those writing classes down at Glades; I don't know what the hell you're talking about."

"Bennett, I think Tom is right. This is an adventure and you shouldn't be so negative."

"It's easy for you two to say. I'm the one whose fingerprints might still be decorating that condo. If we get caught it's probation for you two and back to Glades for me. Pardon me if I'm not reveling in the adventure but I've got a little more at stake here."

Tom and Verbena looked stricken at Bennett's outburst. "Look, I'm sorry. I know you two are trying to help. I'm just a little edgy; that's all."

"That's okay, Bennett. I get a little carried away sometimes when my creative juices get flowing," Tom replied. "Why don't you two get some rest. You both look like hell. I'll go out and get some burgers, coleslaw, and beer and we'll have a cookout at my place tonight before we leave."

"That would be great, Tom. Thanks." Bennett suddenly felt very weary.

"Get some Moon Pies and Orange Crush, too," Verbena chimed in. "And dog food!"

THIRTY EIGHT

"So Mamma says, 'I won't send my boy to California or anywhere above the Mason-Dixon line for that matter. You take your daddy's money and head south to Florida. You'll be safe there. All that sun and sand has softened those Baptists a bit. But watch out for those Yankee transplants. They'll lose more than a night's sleep scheming how to get your money.'" Tom laughed and tossed back the last of his third can of beer.

"At least your mother cares. Mine kicked me out when I turned eighteen. I haven't heard from her since." Bennett took another bite of his hamburger and stared into the fire they had built on the beach.

"Did you ever try to find her?" asked Verbena. She peeled the cellophane off another package of Ho-Ho's since Tom hadn't found any Moon Pies.

"Why should I? She never cared."

"I don't know. I guess I'd try to find mine no matter what." Verbena stared into the fire. She'd never sat around a bonfire on the beach with friends her own age. She savored this moment even if the stories were sad. She smiled at Tom, who struggled to crush his beer can. He'd bought the beer rather than Dr. Pepper to impress Bennett.

"Anyone want another burger?" Tom asked.

Verbena and Bennett shook their heads. Then Verbena said, "We can take the Ho-Ho's with us."

"I suppose it's about time to make that road trip," Bennett said. He stood up and stretched a long stretch toward the starry sky. "This was a good idea, Tom. You're a good cook."

"They say *we* make great chefs and have the best restaurants."

Bennett smiled and Verbena, after looking blank for a few seconds, got the joke and scoffed at Tom. Tom helped Verbena up out of the sand as Bennett began to gather the trash.

At ten o'clock they began their trek north along I 95. Bennett drove the Lincoln and Tom followed in the Electra as he chatted with Verbena, who marveled at how many cars and trucks still populated the roads at this time of night. Having rarely ventured out after nine p.m., she was clueless about a world that worked in shifts.

Forty-five minutes later Bennett flashed his turn signal and took an exit ramp near West Palm Beach. At the light he turned east onto a well-lit boulevard, which promoted a new Holiday Inn Express and a Hampton Inn. They passed a Kmart anchoring a small strip mall with a brightly lit frozen custard shop adjacent to a darkened framing franchise, a beauty shop, an Allstate insurance office, and a store promising *Everything's a Dollar*.

At the next traffic light the scenery began to change. The hotels were the seedy stucco type with small neon vacancy signs flashing in the windows. There were liquor stores and pawn shops with bars on the windows and litter on the sidewalks. The streetlights were fewer and smaller now, their absence adding to the gloom.

Bennett passed a 7-Eleven that also doubled as a Greyhound bus stop and a gathering place for local youth. A few hundred yards beyond it he turned into the parking lot of a thrift shop and waited for Tom to park a short distance away on the street as he had been instructed. He turned off the car, leaving the keys in the ignition, and slipped off the latex gloves he had worn to drive. He exited the car unaware of the group of men who emerged from the darkness and walked toward him.

The deep voice startled Bennett. "What's your business here, Mister?" Bennett spun around fully expecting to face Darth Vader, light saber in hand. Instead he saw a muscular black man step into the dim light. The only hair on his face or head was a well-trimmed mustache that turned down at the corners of his mouth. He wore a sleeveless black T-shirt exposing mammoth biceps and a rippled abdomen. The shirt tucked neatly into clean white jeans.

If all this weren't menacing enough, he casually slapped a black

Louisville Slugger against his thigh as if it were a policeman's night stick. The men with him remained in the shadows. "This store is closed," his voice boomed again. "You hadn't oughta park here."

"I'm having some car trouble. I thought I'd better pull off the road and call AAA." Bennett hoped invoking AAA might somehow legitimize his presence. He didn't dare let his gaze drift over to where Tom and Verbena were parked lest they become involved.

"You should have gone to the 7-Eleven. They have a phone and the light's better."

"Oh, yeah. I missed that. Thanks." Bennett smiled sheepishly. He could feel the sweat trickling from his armpits as it ran down over his rib cage.

"People like you, the pimps, and the drug dealers, come down here and tempt our youth. We aim to stop you mother-fuckers and take back the night." As if on cue the rest of the gang stepped into the light.

"You've got it wrong. I'm not a dealer or a pimp." Bennett felt momentarily relieved to see the rest of the group was apparently unarmed. In fact one of the men was white and in his mid forties. He had a gray-peppered beard and wore a windbreaker with khaki chinos and boat shoes. He looked as out of place here as Bennett but a welcome sight in any case.

The leader sensed Bennett's relief and looked briefly over his shoulder. "Don't mind the white man. He's a Uni-friggin-tarian, a regular Boy Scout, but he won't save your ass." The Unitarian Universalist remained grim faced and Bennett began to think he was going to die.

"You think all the years I've lived here, I don't know what you're doin'? Let me tell you what you be doin.' You got the good job and fine wife but you have to own the car to show everybody you made it big. Then you spend too much, or maybe you dabble in cocaine or a little harmless day trading. Pretty soon you can't make the payments no more, but you're afraid to tell your woman or let the neighbors find out. So you sneak down here in the middle of the night in your well-insured mortgaged car and park where one of the brothers will surely see it - near a 7-Eleven. I'll bet you even left the keys in it for them."

Bennett swallowed hard wishing he could produce the keys.

"You end up with the insurance money, a warm hump from the

wife, and probably a promotion all on the back of one of our bloods who does the time for grand theft auto."

"It's not like that," Bennett tried to protest.

"I can tell by you sweating that it's close enough, boy. It's time you became a man and faced your problems." Bennett saw his grip tighten on the baseball bat and fought desperately to maintain sphincter control. The black man smiled. "Now you're in luck because we here are all men of the cloth or youth workers or parents, and God says we've got to let you live. So I'm going to give you three minutes to get back on I-95."

"Yes, sir."

"The little white Saturn behind you will be the Unitarian. Don't underestimate him."

"No, sir." Bennett scrambled for his car without looking back. His arms were still trembling as he clutched the wheel and propelled his car up the ramp onto I-95. He didn't even bother to put on his latex gloves, but he had noticed Tom discreetly circle the block and fall in behind the Unitarian.

The Unitarian broke off at the ramp and continued west while Tom and Verbena closed the gap. Suddenly Bennett slammed his fist against the dash. "Of all the goddamn exit ramps on I-95 I had to pick this one. Jesus H. Christ, is my luck ever going to change?"

Several exits north he exited at PGA Boulevard and turned into a combination Mobil Station and Dunkin' Donuts. Tom parked alongside and everyone got out. Verbena managed to speak first. "My God. What happened back there? We thought you were going to be killed."

"Are you all right?" Tom asked. "You don't look so good."

Bennett paused a minute to catch his breath, and debated briefly if he should tell them how he'd faced down a gang of dope-crazed killers. It would surely sound better in Tom's book. Then Tom killed the idea when he asked, "Who was the little bearded white guy driving the Saturn?"

Bennett sighed. "It turns out I picked the one neighborhood with its own vigilante posse. They were on to the plan the minute I stopped the car and not so politely asked me to take it somewhere else."

"Now what, Plan B?" asked Tom. "I think there's a mall near here."

"It's too late for that now. The mall is closed and the lot's empty. This car will stick out like Al Gore at a nude beach. We'll have to drive up to Ft. Pierce or Vero Beach and lose it in a drainage canal like we first talked about. But right now I need some coffee."

"And a doughnut," chirped Verbena.

Bennett ordered black coffee and Verbena got a hot chocolate and a crème-filled long john while Tom cleared off a table and swabbed it down with a napkin.

When they were all gathered at the table Verbena spoke. "You were so brave, Bennett."

"How could you tell?"

"By the way you didn't look at us that whole time. You didn't know if those people were going to kill you or not, but you never looked our way so as not to implicate Tom and me, or get us killed."

"Like I've always said, as much as I appreciate your help, it's not your problem. It wouldn't have been right to get you two involved." He looked into Verbena's deep blue eyes which effused devotion and hero worship mixed with infatuation. She'd get over it, but he couldn't remember how long it had been since a woman had looked at him like that, if one ever had at all. Maybe she saw something in him others didn't. It wasn't the worst thing. He grabbed her long john and took a bite; the sweet cream filling tasted good. He wiped the powdered sugar off his mouth and winked at Verbena.

Verbena blushed. Tom smiled at Bennett and gave Verbena a nudge before he spoke. "Do you know where to go when we get to Indian River County?"

"I had an uncle who used to raise citrus up there," Bennett said. "My mother would ship me off to him every summer as soon as school let out. I'd work in the groves until school started again." Bennett remembered riding with his uncle out on the dusty county roads through the groves at dusk. The roads were flanked by soft shoulders and wide murky drainage ditches.

His uncle would comment on those ditches. "A car slides in there it drops right out of sight. If no one saw it going in, they'd never find it. Hell, so many miles of canal in this county they wouldn't know where to start. I've lost more migrant workers that way. As soon as I pay 'em they go off and get drunk and the first thing you know they're gone leaving a wife and five kids. Some think they're just irresponsible and deserted their families but I know 'em better than that. They're resting at the bottom of one of these sons a bitches." Then he'd spit a wad of tobacco out the window into one of those canals as egrets picked their way along the bank.

"Don't worry, Tom. We'll find a place." Bennett took a swallow of coffee and said, "Let's hit the road."

North of PGA Boulevard the traffic thinned. Bennett placed the Lincoln on cruise control just below the speed limit so as not to attract the attention of any troopers. He tuned the radio until he found a country oldies station nestled between the Christian right and an all-night talk jockey. WOLD was paying tribute to Patsy Cline's greatest hits and the soulful sound of *Crazy* filled the car, now illuminated only by the soft glow of the dash lights.

It reminded him of when he was a kid and his mother, who couldn't afford a baby-sitter, would put his pillow and blanket in the back of their '61 Pontiac and drive to the bars leaving him there in the back seat for hours at a time. On the way home he would pretend to sleep as the radio played Patsy Cline, Whispering Bill Anderson, and Tex Ritter. Her long hair flowed over the back seat and he could still smell her perfume mixed with the cigarette smoke from the bar.

Sometimes he snuck along a book and read it with a flashlight he kept hidden under the seat. If he got really bored, he would sneak out of the car and watch the men stumble out of the bar to fight, or he'd follow a couple to another car and watch undetected as they groped each other and wrestled. Sometimes they became so violent they tore each other's clothes off. It would be years before he learned what they were really doing.

The woman, his counselor at Glades, continually directed him to talk about this part of his life. Bennett knew she thought it was gross negligence on the part of his mother and that it had clearly scarred him for life. Consequently, he never mentioned the *Leave it to Beaver* reenactments.

But he had never been afraid or felt he was in any danger. It was a time of mystery and adventure followed by a ride home in the dark when he and his mother were alone together, safe in their fortress of a car as Patsy Cline sang just for them.

If he listened to Patsy Cline for long, he invariably became aroused but not for Patsy Cline, because he couldn't recall ever seeing her. Rather her music conjured images of the night he followed his mother's friend, his Godmother Betty Lou, and watched her wrestle in the back seat with the man from the Texaco filling station. She was apparently winning because she was sitting on top of him as he moaned in pain.

Suddenly she peeled off her orange tube top, exposing her large, soft breasts in the moonlight. This made the man moan louder as if he was in more pain, and he began to squeeze her breasts hard causing Betty Lou to throw her head back and buck violently as if she couldn't stand any more. Then suddenly she cried out to God and fell forward on top of him out of Bennett's view.

Silence. Somewhere in the distance Bennett could hear Patsy Cline on the jukebox and could feel his own heart pounding as he feared one or both of them had been killed in the fight. Eventually, he heard soft laughter coming from the car and sensed that Betty Lou was not only safe but sublimely happy.

Thereafter, when he rode his bike to the Texaco station after school to buy a Coke, he found it nearly impossible to look the man in the eye. He had certainly lost faith in the Texaco slogan; *You can trust your car to the man who wears the star!* Eventually he started riding over to the Standard station.

Aroused once again Bennett was surprised to find his thoughts turning to Verbena. He had never been attracted to a fat woman. Maybe fat was too harsh. She didn't really have a double chin or really flabby arms. Her face was quite beautiful actually, especially when she spoke about his courage. Then he could envision her intensity and passion and it moved him.

After all, he had been courageous back in that West Palm parking lot. Ward Cleaver couldn't have done better. He couldn't think of another woman who had ever noticed his courage. That meant something, even if she did weigh too much.

Bennett decided that all this arousal and country music created too much confusion, so he turned off the radio and concentrated on the highway. His thoughts turned to sinking a car in an Indian River County drainage ditch.

They reached the Vero Beach exit just before 2:00 a.m. Bennett pulled off at the junction with Highway 60 and turned west past the Cracker Barrel, Steak 'n Shake, and the entrance to a factory outlet mall whose coral stucco buildings emitted an eerie glow under the fluorescent security lights of the parking lot. In less than a quarter of a mile, they were plunged into the desolate darkness of Route Sixty, a four-lane blacktop whose next connection with humanity was thirty miles away at the Florida Turnpike in Yeehaw Junction.

Retirees didn't venture out on this road at night, their visibility hampered by cataracts. Also, rumors abounded about drug deals that went down along this route, even though the shoulder was almost nonexistent, and swarming mosquitoes would suck a drug dealer dry before he could open and sample a nickel bag. But every retiree knew, probably from their 55 Alive driving classes at their condominium clubhouses, that where there were drug deals, there were carjackings which led to the inevitable – RAPE!

Fortunately, Bennett didn't have to drive far down this road of no return. He turned south on a dusty side road flanked by a large canal and orange groves. It appeared absolutely deserted, but Bennett switched to his parking lights and was relieved to see Tom do the same. No need to attract attention.

After a mile and a half Bennett slowed to a stop and waited for Tom to roll up behind him. Bennett got out and walked back to Tom. "I don't think we'll run into the Neighborhood Watch out here." The dome light was on and Bennett smiled over at Verbena. She was sleeping peacefully against the far window, her lips slightly pursed, her upper lip lightly dusted with powdered sugar. "But we'd better get a move on before the mosquitoes have us for breakfast."

Tom exited the car quietly and followed Bennett to the Lincoln. "Well, Tom, you got the scene you wanted." Bennett pointed to the lightning in the East. A few seconds later they could hear a faint rumble. "No jasmine out here but you can smell the oranges." Bennett inhaled deeply. "And cow shit. And rotted fruit."

"It was a dark and stormy night …" whispered Tom.

"Is that James Lee Burke or Robert Parker?" Bennett had had plenty of time to read in Glades.

"No, it's Snoopy." Tom smiled broadly.

"I didn't know he was a gay icon," Bennett shot back.

Tom's smile turned to a frown. "You can't forget I'm gay, can you Bennett?"

"No, I'm sorry but I can't. I mean I don't hold it against you. You're an all right guy and your sex life is your own business."

"But when you look at me, you don't see anything else do you?"

"No, but I feel badly about that, Tom. Maybe if we just give it some time, okay? Let's move this car before the mosquitoes notify the fire ants that we're here."

"What do you want me to do," Tom responded with resignation.

"I'll open the car door and steer. You push from behind."

It was a simple feat with the Lincoln in neutral and two men pushing. They eased it over the edge of the embankment and the car took over on its own, picking up speed silently as it rolled down toward the dark still water below.

It hit the water with a splash startling three sleeping egrets, which erupted skyward like flapping ghosts. Tom and Bennett watched in nervous anticipation as the car floated briefly then began to tip nose down and sink slowly into the water.

"Wow!" exclaimed Tom softly. "Did you ever see *Titanic*? It went down just like that. Slow and majestic."

"Yeah, but I bet they didn't forget to turn off the parking lights did they?"

"Oh, shit!" Ten feet below the murky surface they could just make out the faint glow.

THIRTY NINE

They returned to Verbena's car and Tom insisted on driving. Bennett, whose nerves were shot anyway, didn't argue. He climbed into the back seat, closed his eyes, and hoped the sunken car's battery would short out soon. He convinced himself that the lights wouldn't stay on long and by daylight wouldn't be noticed. Still, he could kick himself for not turning them off.

"Bennett, I think we should head east and take Highway 1 north. It will take longer but I don't think we'll get a hotel now anyway."

"Go ahead if you want." It didn't make much sense but Bennett was too tired to argue. "Are you okay if I sleep back here with Pookie?"

"No problem."

Pookie looked out the side window of his travel kennel and let out a low growl. Bennett growled back, then curled up in the far corner and fell into a fitful sleep.

Bennett awakened to the sound of metal tapping on glass and managed to open one eye before Pookie began to bark furiously. In the front seat Tom and Verbena jerked awake.

"Where are we?" mumbled Bennett.

"A 7-Eleven near the beach in Melbourne."

"Who the hell is tapping on our window?" In the light of the gray dawn, Bennett could just make out the face of an old man peering through Tom's window.

As Tom lowered the window the man who'd rapped against the glass with his wedding ring announced, "We ain't open yet. You having trouble?" He had a thin, deeply-lined face with ears that stuck out like a chimpanzee's. When he spoke his thick horn-rimmed glasses bobbed up and down his nose under a 7-Eleven baseball cap.

"No problem," replied Tom. "I'm a little low on gas and thought I'd better pull off the road."

"Not enough traffic here to stay open all night but I open early for the fishing crowd. I don't expect we'll see many today with this wind."

"Could I use your bathroom?" Verbena asked.

The old man stuck his head into the car to get a better look. "Certainly, young lady, let me just unlock the door and turn on the lights." He retracted his head like a frightened turtle and scrambled for the front door, keys in hand. "You all can come in. I'll have some coffee made in a few minutes if you don't mind the wait."

Bennett climbed out of the back seat and stretched while Tom put a desperate Pookie on his twine leash and trotted him around the side of the building. Bennett hollered to the old man, "Do you want me to bring in this bundle of newspapers?"

"I'd appreciate that, fella."

Bennett reached over and paused to read the headlines. *Elderly Couple Found Murdered in Beachside Condo.* In smaller print it said, *Police on lookout for missing vehicle.* Bennett threw the bundle up onto the counter and the old man cut the binding tape.

"Oh, now look at that," the old man said sadly as he shook his head. "Another murder; each time it's a little further north. I spec' crack heads looking for dope money." He moved away to make coffee.

"I suppose," answered Bennett absently as he picked up a paper and scanned the story. Helen and Nero had been identified by name from their drivers' licenses but their names were being withheld. All that police knew so far was that the condo was owned by an ophthalmologist in Orlando, and that they had rented the place for a week under an assumed name. According to the groundskeeper, they drove a late-model dark blue luxury car, but he knew nothing about the make or the plates. Since they found no evidence of a break-in, the police had no clues as to the motive.

"I'll turn on the pumps soon as I get this coffee perking, so you can fill 'er up."

"No rush," Bennett answered as he tucked the paper under his arm and placed three quarters on the counter.

Tom entered holding Pookie under one arm like a football. Dark circles had formed under Tom's eyes and patchy stubble adorned his chin. His skin had a sallow hungover look, and Bennett wondered if he himself looked that bad. "Did you get any sleep, Tom?"

"Maybe an hour out there in the parking lot. That means you got maybe two and a half."

"I'll feel better when we find a place where I can shower and shave."

Just then Verbena appeared from the bathroom looking radiant. She carried a small tube of toothpaste and a toothbrush and had obviously combed her hair and applied makeup. The sight of her made Bennett feel worse. He excused himself to the restroom and combed some water through his hair where a rooster tail stuck up in back. Then he splashed his face with cold water, but decided he didn't look any better than when he walked in.

At the counter, Verbena clutched Pookie and talked to the old man as he poured three coffees. Her fingers caressed the green stones on the dog's collar. Outside Tom stood by the pump and refueled the car. "Bennett, this gentleman says we should head west of here to find a place."

"It's pretty pricey near the ocean but a lot of new apartments are going up out west near the interstate. That's where the good jobs are, too," the old man said.

"Did you work in Melbourne?" Bennett asked.

"No, not me. I worked for forty years for Hershey Chocolate up in Pennsylvania. We made the Kisses, probably a billion of 'em during my time. My wife and I moved down here after I retired but the togetherness next to drove us crazy. Now I work here days and she works the evening shift at Wendy's. She gets to watch her soap operas and at night I can watch *Wheel of Fortune* and *Millionaire*."

"Doesn't sound much like retirement," Bennett said.

"I tried the usual stuff. I even learned to crochet Mt. Rushmore into a rug. I still got it nailed to the wall in the den but I think I missed people. So once a month the wife and I drive over to Disney World for the day and just walk around the hotels and gardens. They're like ant hills with everyone scurrying to pack as much as they can into a week's vacation. Then at night before we come home, we go down to the boardwalk and watch the fireworks. That does it for us."

Verbena sighed and scratched Pookie's ears. "I've never been to Disney World. My parents hated crowds, so we always passed Orlando and drove straight to the beach."

"Well, now that you folks are moving here you'll have to go. It's only an hour or so away and those fireworks are really something."

Verbena blushed and averted her eyes from Bennett and the old man who continued. "You've got a really pretty face. I'll bet you could get a job with those Disney people. You're real friendly, too, and they like that."

Verbena smiled. "That would be a dream job, a job that really mattered, working for Walt Disney World."

Just then Tom burst back into the store, credit card in hand. "That coffee smells good." He reached for one of the Styrofoam cups and raised it in a mock toast before taking a sip. "To a new start," he said.

"To a retirement with real fireworks," Bennett replied.

"To a real Mickey Mouse job," Verbena chimed in.

FORTY

ATF agent Rick Brindle rolled out of bed and headed straight for the front door and the morning paper. The eleven o'clock news had alluded to a late-breaking double murder near Ft. Lauderdale. It was Tuesday, only a week since he and Nixon had bungled their stakeout in Melbourne. Helen and her predicament hung over his head like an afternoon storm cloud.

He opened the door just as the neighbor's cat was about to pee on his paper. The yellow tabby bared its fangs in anger, then leapt from the porch into the yard where it proceeded to take a dump on Brindle's mangy lawn.

Never able to keep track of all the foliage-eating pests of South Florida, Brindle had neglected treating the lawn for cinch bugs, while the snails made a smorgasbord of the flower beds around his house. As Rick looked around he realized his place was one junked auto short of a crack house. No wonder none of his neighbors spoke to him.

He took his paper and crawled back into bed. He found two paragraphs on page three of the *Miami Herald* – just another routine murder. Whoever covered the crime beat must have been in a hurry to get to the Monday night Dolphins game against Buffalo. The double homicide occurred north of Deerfield Beach at a beachside condo. Except for a missing car, there was no sign of forced entry or robbery. Names were being withheld pending notification of next of kin.

Brindle had a sick feeling in the pit of his stomach. Helen had tried to run with the Colonel's money and this is just the sort of repayment he would exact.

Good old Colonel *Suicide* Collins, the war hero who passionately argued that no mission was impossible for his men. No one had ordered more men to their deaths since General Pickett at Gettysburg. But at least Pickett watched with horror and remorse instead of sitting behind a desk waiting for the next politician to pass through so he could kiss his ass.

Now a wealthy civilian with political connections and a penchant for right-wing causes, he was untouchable. Brindle and Nixon hadn't been reprimanded for their fiasco because, after all, illegal arms trade did come under the jurisdiction of the Bureau. But his superior mentioned in an offhand manner that selling guns to unseat Castro wasn't really a serious crime. We were really at war with the drug dealers down here. Brindle and Nixon would do better to focus their activities on areas more consistent with the mission statement of the regional office.

Rick decided he'd better shower and get down to the office. Once there he'd call Nixon and see if he could learn anything from his friends at the police station. Easily reached on his pager and cell phone, he could normally linger over breakfast and his paper and then drive in after the rush hour. This morning he decided to shower and go right in to find Nixon. As he left the house, he tucked the sports section under his arm and left the rest.

At the office he picked up the phone and dialed Nixon. "Merritt, this is Rick. Did you read this morning's *Herald*?"

"Sorry, the kids and the dog beat me to it. All I saw was the business section. Why, you got another ad in the personals?"

"Listen, this is serious. A couple got murdered in Deerfield Beach and I can't help but wonder if it wasn't the two I followed from Denny's last week."

"Hell, Rick, that's over. Besides, if they neglected to return the money, they'd certainly be smart enough to skip the country."

"I've got a bad feeling about this one, Merritt. I wondered if you could call your friend and get an ID."

"I can try. We aren't as popular down there as we used to be. Any one of their people goes down from an AK-47, and they hold us responsible for letting it get into the hands of the bad guys."

"Well, see what you can do."

"Fine. I'll get back to you."

Brindle hung up the phone and picked up the sports section.

Buffalo had walked all over the Dolphins. The Marlins were worried about their unaffordable payroll despite the fact that the Dodgers' new pitcher made more than the entire Marlins team put together. Florida and Florida State's football teams were ranked number one and two in the country for about the tenth year in a row. In other words, there was nothing new in Florida sports. Rick put down the paper and read his memos with half interest.

Suddenly the phone rang. "Rick, I got those names for you. He was Nero Venditto, a small-time con artist, and her name was Helen Wilson." Rick closed his eyes tightly and slowly shook his head. "It seems they were both wanted for questioning in Melbourne regarding a scam that cleaned out some rube from Iowa."

"That's them."

"Well, just to be sure check the fax machine. I got them to fax over copies of their drivers' licenses. I never got a close look at him."

The copies were poor but it didn't matter. Rick recognized Helen and was pretty sure Nero had driven the getaway car. This time Rick walked down to Merritt's office. He wondered how his and Helen's lives could have taken such different directions. His mind flooded with *what ifs*: *What if she had come to him? What if he had protected her? What if he couldn't?*

"There's no doubt who they are and who pulled the trigger." Rick threw the photocopies down on the desk.

"It all makes sense except for the car. The Colonel's people wouldn't touch the car."

"Maybe they couldn't find the money in the condo, so they drove it somewhere to strip it down."

"I suppose, but if that's the truth the locals might as well quit looking for it. It'll be scrap by now. I suppose we'd better call homicide and fill them in. It's their baby now."

"They won't be able to pin anything on the Colonel. We can't prove he was in on the gun deal, and they can't even talk to the man unless they have a solid case. He'd have them all working sanitation in less than twenty-four hours."

"Well, as you recall, Hoss, we've been respectfully invited to leave the man alone." Nixon called people *Hoss* when he was taking his just-plain-folks routine to its highest plateau. His father was a third-generation Memphis lawyer in a firm founded by Merritt's great-grandfather.

Rick was all too familiar with Merritt's dysfunctional history. Merritt had been rebelling against his bloodline since the sixth grade. He'd hung out with the wrong crowd and in football shunned the offensive backfield for a blue collar job on the defensive line. After high school he rejected a scholarship to Vanderbilt choosing to walk on at Mississippi State. Eventually, as if he hadn't pissed off his father enough already, he quit law school despite a straight-A average and joined the ATF.

His problem now was that, having burned his bridges behind him, he couldn't afford to cross the people at the top. His last trip to Melbourne with Rick had filled his screw-up quota.

"I'm not letting the Colonel get away with murder. I'm heading back to Melbourne for a few days."

"Why don't you just save yourself some time and walk up to his front door and shoot him, you dumb ass. Then pack your bags for Fargo, North Dakota, because that's where you'll be stationed next. I hear they make the agents do body cavity searches on all the cattle and hogs crossing the U.S.-Canadian border."

"I might just do that." Rick's voice had the chill of a police morgue slab.

FORTY ONE

"Michael, did you see this damn article?" asked Colonel Collins.

"Yes, Sir. I read it this morning."

The Colonel stood up from his half-eaten breakfast and tightened the sash on his robe. "Did you notice anything unusual?"

"No, Sir. Not unless you count the fact that two supposed tourists were murdered in their rental condo and no one noticed for two days. It's not the sort of *get away from it all* the Chamber of Commerce would promote." Michael still harbored bitter feelings about being left out of the mission.

"Michael, that's not what I mean. Their car is reported missing and we didn't take it."

"Maybe someone hot wired it and stole it from the lot."

"Instead of a BMW? I doubt it. I think someone else knew about the money and where it was hidden. When they found the bodies they took the car and the money and ran."

"It sounds plausible, Sir."

"You're damn right it's plausible and I'll tell you something else." The Colonel stepped so close to him that Michael could smell the pool's chlorine on his skin and see the stubble on his unshaven face.

Michael internally struggled to hold his ground. "What would that be, Sir?"

"There's no mention of Helen's damn dog: not dead, not barking, not missing, nothing. Whoever took the car entered the condo and took the dog, too!"

Michael turned away. "You're absolutely right, Sir. Good thinking on your part." The Colonel had become his old self again. When he returned from Deerfield Beach he had looked old and fatigued. He kept going over and over his mission.

At first he insisted that it had been a military mission. "Search and destroy!" he cried out in his sleep. He promised to recommend Frank and Vinnie for the Silver Star.

Later he began to weep and call out for Helen. "Helen, why did you disobey me? Helen, I'm sorry; we can still make a deal."

Michael did his best to cover for him. He secluded the Colonel in his room and stayed at his bedside throughout the night. He took the calls and gave the orders, telling everyone the Colonel had a fever and probably the flu.

"Michael, call Frank and Vinnie and have them start looking for the dog and the car. They know both of them by sight."

"Fine, but we have no idea where they went or who they are. They could be out of the country by now."

"I don't think they planned to go far since they took the dog and the car. I want my money, Michael," the Colonel hissed.

"Yes, Sir."

"While you're at it call my niece. Helen took that damn mutt to the clinic where she's a receptionist. See if she has any more information to share."

"Any word on the guns, Sir?"

"Damn Feds impounded them, of course."

"But we'll get them back."

"As soon as we can set up another dummy storage outfit, we'll make a successful bid to warehouse them as evidence."

"Then the storage outfit files for Chapter Eleven and everything disappears."

"You know the drill, son. The NRA has Congress by the short hairs, so no one really cares if my guns are out of circulation or not."

Frank and Vinnie were less than thrilled to get the call from Michael. "Fuck this!" Vinnie exclaimed as he got into Frank's car and slammed the door. "We go with him on the hit like a couple of goddamn babysitters and watch while he fucks up the whole thing. In another ten seconds that woman would have given up the money, and we wouldn't have to be drivin' around stickin' our necks out trying to find a hot car."

"Don't forget the dog, Vinnie." Frank smiled; he'd hooked Vinnie deeper.

"Fuck that dog." Vinnie slammed the dash with both fists. "He was about to make lunch outta my leg. He's the one we shoulda' iced, not the woman. Shit!" Vinnie slid down in his seat and leaned against the door sulking. "Son of a bitch," he muttered.

"I don't hold to killing a woman." Frank was serious now. "I haven't slept for shit since this happened, and having to look for that car and dog isn't going to help."

"Neither will the Jim Beam you had for breakfast," carped Vinnie. "You better stay on the wagon, pal, or we don't work this together."

"Mind your own damn business."

"Yes, sir, Mr. Kicked Off The Force For Intoxication On Duty." Vinnie pulled his Marlins cap down over his eyes and stared straight ahead.

Frank didn't respond. His head hurt and deep inside his inner child, or whatever the hell it was called, screamed for more poison. He hadn't a clue where to look for the right toy poodle in South Florida. White poodles were more prevalent than hookers and dope dealers.

FORTY TWO

Melissa *Missy* Melnick, the niece of Colonel Collins and former beauty queen, had worked for the Melbourne Veterinary Clinic for the past year. Three years earlier she had been crowned National Peanut Princess in Dothan, Alabama. The scholarship money allowed her to attend Auburn as a pre-vet student.

At Auburn she pledged Tri Delt which, until Missy joined, had considered itself one princess short of a full court. Missy convinced her new sorority sisters to campaign for a local chapter of Jimmy Buffett's Save the Manatee Club as their chapter service project.

Good grades impress vet school admissions committees; sincere and perky peanut princesses are fine as long as they have the grades. Missy didn't. After brief consideration, the committee encouraged Missy to consider a career as a veterinary assistant. Later three of them called her. Two offered her a job as their assistant at the vet school and one asked her out to dinner.

Disillusioned with the rigors of academia, Missy dropped out of school and prepared to move to Orlando where she hoped to get a job with Sea World rescuing manatees. She soon discovered two things: graduate students in biology are a dime a dozen and get all the good animal jobs, and her parents would cut her off without a cent if she moved to that wicked city.

In her hometown of War Eagle, their family preacher had reminded her parents of the church's boycott of Disney for promoting the gay lifestyle. He had it on good authority that God's plan for Orlando included plague, pestilence, and total annihilation.

Missy and her parents finally compromised on Melbourne. Her

parents were comforted because she would be under the watchful eye of Uncle Jack. Missy consoled herself that she would be near the ocean and only an hour from Sea World. It didn't take any time at all to find a veterinarian in need of a perky peanut princess who loved animals.

Missy hadn't heard from her uncle or any of his emissaries for a long time and Michael's call surprised her. "Hello, Michael. What can we do for you? Did you finally buy a pet?"

"No, Missy, I'm afraid not. The bylaws at Premier Island don't allow dogs the size of Labrador retrievers. How have you been?"

"Oh, fine. We're pretty busy now that all the snowbirds have roosted." Missy felt uncomfortable talking to Michael on a personal level. At the Colonel's insistence she dated Michael when she moved to Melbourne. To her discomfort, the specter of her uncle manipulating Michael behind the scenes confused Missy. She couldn't be certain if Michael was more interested in her or advancing his career.

"The Colonel wanted me to call and ask you for a favor," Michael continued before Missy had a chance to respond. "Do you recall a white toy poodle belonging to a woman named Helen Wilson?"

"Pookie."

"What?"

"Pookie is the dog's name. I keep a list and when I go home at night I memorize the names of all our clients' pets."

"That's a lot of names."

"Right now 1,285. It's hard because a lot of the names are the same: Whitie, Spot, Cookie, Princess, Duke, even Missy. You'd be surprised."

"It does sound demanding, Missy."

"What does Uncle Jack want to know? I have to be very careful what I tell you. We have very strict rules about animal confidentiality at this clinic. Animals have the right to privacy, too, you know."

"I'm sure, with all that interbreed socializing and the resultant unwanted pregnancies. But don't you think these fathers need to be exposed and forced to take some responsibility for their pups?"

"Michael, you never take me seriously."

"I apologize but this is serious, too. Helen was murdered in Deerfield Beach and the Colonel is devastated."

"What? Oh my God. That's terrible. What happened to Pookie? Is he all right?"

"He's …"

"Just a minute, Michael. I have another call coming in." Michael was instantly cut off only to get the recorded Missy telling him to please hold because, *Your call is important to us.* She went on to advise him to keep current on his pet's heartworm medicine and reminded him that this was National Pet Week and their clinic carried a full line of gifts and accessories.

"Michael, I'm back. Where's Pookie?"

"Missing I'm afraid. He wasn't mentioned in the paper and the Colonel wants to find him. He's not a dog lover but he feels it's the least he could do for Helen. They were old friends."

"I'm so sorry, Michael."

"He has all his people on the alert even though it's probably hopeless. He wondered if Pookie's record contained any identifying or useful information."

Missy thought long and hard. She had taken a night class at community college on animal ethics but this situation had never come up. She didn't know what to do.

"Missy?"

"I'm thinking, Michael."

"Pookie's life may be in the balance."

"You're right." Missy hesitated. "I'll do it but I'll have to pull the record on my lunch break and call you later."

"Good girl, Missy. You have the number."

"Yes. Later, Michael. I've got to go now."

FORTY THREE

Amazingly, Tom found a place for the three of them on the south side of Melbourne near Palm Bay. It was an apartment complex with a wing catering to industries that occasionally brought in their sales people for two weeks of training, or hired systems analysts who stayed for months on end running up large consultant fees and demanding something homier than a Motel Six.

It was a slow time for Dartmouth Square, so the manager agreed to show them a unit. Attired in a blue blazer, a white blouse, and a red skirt accented with a red, white, and blue scarf at her neck, her patriotic attire and trim figure reminded Verbena of a stewardess.

"I've got a golf cart right outside and I can drive you over. It's just a short distance. It's a tight squeeze but we'll all fit." She appeared to size up Verbena as she spoke. "You can ride up front with me and we'll put the boys in back."

Just outside the office sat a white canopied golf cart bearing the Dartmouth Square crest. A small cushioned bench seat had been bolted in back and faced the rear. Tom and Bennett would fit snugly shoulder to shoulder. Winking at Bennett, Tom hopped aboard and patted the seat next to him. "Come on; this will be fun."

Bennett frowned but didn't create a scene. They'd been looking all day and this was their best prospect. He sat down and growled as Tom snuggled against him.

Verbena caught their perplexed chauffeur glancing into the rear view mirror and quickly commented, "You boys behave yourselves back there." Then she smiled blandly at the manager-stewardess and changed the subject. "Have you worked here long?"

Palm trees lined the narrow blacktop that wound through the complex around small irrigation ponds identified as lakes. The year-round rentals backed up to the lake and were two-story gray wooden structures, each with its own small porch or patio.

Verbena tried to assess the ages of the tenants by the items they displayed: red and yellow plastic tricycles, full-size bicycles, neatly arranged pots of geraniums, boogie boards, or empty patios with curtains drawn.

The executive building consisted of eight units at the far side of the property, fronting a drainage ditch and an empty field canopied with high-voltage power lines. Miraculously a few red pines had been saved during construction and provided some shade. Here each porch and patio featured the same white five-dollar plastic table with three matching molded chairs.

"Here we are!" their guide announced cheerfully as the cart rolled to a stop in front of a kiosk containing mailboxes. Bennett quickly jumped free of Tom and busied himself creasing the front of his slacks. "Follow me and watch out for snakes. Just kidding." She laughed nervously but seemed to be inspecting the landscape very closely as they approached the model.

As promised, the executive units were furnished. The style suggested early Holiday Inn surplus with lime green and orange the dominant color scheme. Each had two bedrooms with twin beds, a galley kitchen that included a microwave and dinette, and a living room set with a television. The carpet color hovered somewhere between mud brown and asphalt gray. Other than the twin beds, Verbena saw nothing that hinted at anything but an oversized motel room.

The manager began to chatter away as she opened the drapes to the expansive view of the drainage ditch and the power lines beyond. They were welcome to use the pool and lighted tennis courts at the clubhouse as well as attend the Saturday morning free coffee and doughnuts social hour. Small pets were allowed if kept on a leash. The utilities were included in stays under one month.

This vacant unit could be rented for the next two weeks for seven hundred and fifty dollars payable by cash or major credit card. The parking spaces were assigned, each unit being entitled to two. As a special offer she would waive the one hundred dollar security deposit if they signed today. Twenty minutes later Tom signed on the dotted line assuring Bennett he could write it off as a business expense while researching his book.

"I'll pay it all back when I get on my feet. Don't worry."

"I won't."

"You're so sweet, Tom. I don't know how I'll ever pay you. But I'm going to get a job." Verbena spontaneously leaned over and kissed Tom on the cheek and then quickly pulled away blushing. She had never kissed a gay man before and feared she had offended him.

As if he sensed her embarrassment Tom reached over and kissed her back. "It's allowed, Verbena. Thank you."

FORTY FOUR

Bennett lay on the orange couch watching *Jeopardy*. It had been a week and he still hadn't found a job. The big corporations hired through temporary services and the positions were usually data entry, which paid just over minimum wage. Since everyone wanted to do business with the space industry, background checks for national security purposes were often mandatory. Bennett had a feeling convicted felons' applications stood out like a fart on the space shuttle.

Tom sat at the dinette, as he did every day, typing incessantly on his laptop. Of the three, his mood was the best. He declared he had overcome his writers' block and discovered a new inner voice. It didn't hurt that he had also discovered a new boyfriend at Office Depot while picking up a BC-20 ink cartridge and a case of twenty-pound copy paper.

Tom and Bennett shared a room but Tom's cheerful humming and whistling grated on Bennett. He constantly nagged Bennett for an in-depth interview so he could crawl into the psyche of an ex-con trying to acclimate himself back into society. Bennett couldn't decide which he hated more, the nagging or the wistful sighs Tom made every night just before dropping off into the deep sleep of an innocent child.

Verbena stretched as she exited her room having finished her second nap of the day. Alex Trebek had just announced the Final *Jeopardy* answer.

"Do you want me to make the macaroni and cheese now?" she asked, directing the question to neither Tom nor Bennett. "I've got those little cocktail wieners to put in it and I can boil some frozen corn."

"I'd love to stay just to appreciate the color spectacle of the macaroni juxtaposed with the corn, Verbena, but I have a date," Tom replied without looking up from his keyboard.

Bennett got up and turned off the TV. The bald accountant from New Jersey had this *Jeopardy* all wrapped up. Bennett had been pulling for the horny-looking housewife from Marshfield, Wisconsin, who wore a skin-tight party dress she probably made ten years ago in 4H. She preceded each selection with, "I'm going to get lucky tonight, Alex," but she never got a question right.

"Sounds good to me, Verbena, but I'm going to take a shower first," Bennett said.

"Bennett, you're so easy to cook for."

"I was in prison, remember? They wouldn't give our chefs time off to watch Emeril." He winked at Tom and left the room.

Tom smiled at Verbena and then looked at the clock. "I'm going to be late. I'd better shut down and get going." Tom hit *save* and then *exit works*. "Do you mind if I take your car, Verbena?"

"No, that's fine, Tom. I don't need it."

"I might not get home tonight."

"Oh, I'm sure there's enough gas in the car, Tom." Tom looked up at Verbena and she suddenly realized her mistake and blushed.

"I'll see you in the morning, Verbena. Try to get Bennett to loosen up. I think he's getting depressed."

"I don't think I know how to loosen up a man, Tom. You'd be a lot better at that than I."

"I don't think Bennett would appreciate my efforts in that department."

"Could you teach me?"

"I'll take that as a compliment, Verbena, but my approach just isn't going to work in this case. You've got a good start with your cooking, though. When he's full get him to talk and listen to him. That always works and I've got to go."

"Thanks, Tom. You smell nice; I think he'll like it. And watch out for the snake."

"I saw him yesterday through the window. He must be six feet long. Scary as hell but not poisonous."

"I hate any kind of snake," Verbena shivered.

Verbena needed to know where she stood. She could go back to Deerfield Beach with Tom for awhile but she had lost her own place. If Bennett wanted her to stay in Melbourne with him, she needed to look for a job so she could pay her own way, but she needed a sign from him before she began to look. It wasn't fair to Bennett to assume she could stay.

"You ever trust anyone, Bennett?" Verbena asked. They had eaten the macaroni and cheese with the cocktail weenies and the frozen corn and were just finishing their Sara Lee turtle cheesecake. Verbena had taken Tom's advice and was trying to get Bennett to talk.

"I used to trust my mother but she booted me out when I turned eighteen."

"That must have been hard." Verbena reached over and cut herself another sliver of cheesecake.

"I should have seen it coming. When my father ran off with the A&W car hop, she promised everything would be all right. Just like when she left me in the dark while she toured the bars."

"My parents never went to bars," Verbena replied as she licked her fingers and picked up a fork.

"By the time I was in high school, she mostly drank alone at home. She'd get too loud in the bars and embarrass her friends or begin to hit on their husbands. Pretty soon she didn't have any friends. I worked at the Winn-Dixie to help with the rent and would occasionally steal beer and Salem cigarettes. She and I would sit out on the front porch trying to catch a cool evening breeze just smokin' and drinkin.'"

"Sounds like you got along fine. I'm surprised she kicked you out."

"I think the booze did it. The more I worked the less she did, and the more she drank."

"Did you try to stop her?"

"Not really. My counselor at Glades said I enabled her by bringing home the money and stealing the stuff for her. *Enable* is a big AA word you know. I was only sixteen. What the hell did I know about enabling?"

"You just wanted some attention."

"Anyway, one day I told her I wanted to go to college. She acted like I'd just asked to be an apprentice axe murder. I suppose by then she knew I was her meal ticket and the thought of me leaving scared her to death.

So she said, 'We'll see.' She began to sulk, and then the night of my eighteenth birthday she got really plastered and started to scream and yell. She told me to pack my things and get out of the house. She said she wasn't responsible for me any more. Like she ever was. So I packed my stuff and hit the road. I never even finished high school."

Verbena swiped her finger across a now empty dessert plate and began to suck on it thoughtfully. "Gosh, do you know what happened to her?"

"Later at Glades when I was working on my GED, I met a kid from my hometown. He said she'd moved in with another old drunk who used to manage the Texaco station, and they were successfully drinking themselves into oblivion."

"I'm sorry." Verbena reached over and touched Bennett's arm.

"Don't feel sorry for me." Bennett sniffed hard. "She knew I was in Glades but she never wrote or tried to call me, not once."

Bennett looked down at Verbena's sticky fingers resting on his arm and began to slowly trace them with his own. "All my subsequent acquaintances with women have been just brief sexual encounters."

"Eldridge's and mine were very brief, too." She felt her throat tighten and her words became breathy. Bennett slowly traced up the inside of her index finger pausing as he reached the apex of the 'v' where the finger joined the next digit. Verbena gave an involuntary shudder and reflexively tried to cross her fingers.

Bennett withdrew. "My counselor said I'm afraid of intimacy and commitment because of my mother. She tried to get me to understand that the alcohol betrayed us. After losing my father, my mother had her own insecurity when it came to intimacy."

"It sounds logical." Verbena hadn't heard another word but was intensely aware of a throbbing sensation emanating from the depths of her pelvis. She uncrossed her fingers.

"It may seem logical but my gut screams *How could she choose the booze over me?* Can you answer that?" Bennett stared deep into Verbena's blue eyes as if they held the answer.

"Maybe you need to work on that intimacy thing."

"We're a strange pair, Verbena. I find it hard to believe we are destined by fate like your author said."

"But I know we are." Verbena smiled coyly at Bennett and took his hand and tugged him to his feet. "I want to kiss you, Bennett Durant."

Bennett resisted. "I'm not a good risk, Verbena. I'm attracted to you, too, but I can't trust it."

"Just trust the moment. We'll worry about the rest later." It was a quote from a soap opera Verbena had seen the day before. It felt a bit melodramatic but she went with it anyway.

They embraced gently at first both fearing the other would pull away, and then as their tendered kisses were accepted it seemed as if all the years of stifled frustration and rejection surfaced in both of them at once. Bennett's hands kneaded Verbena's large soft breasts as she fumbled at his shirt buttons, both still kissing as they stumbled toward Verbena's room and her twin beds.

They arrived and Bennett, already breathless, said, "Wait," and pushed her away. Then he began to yank his still-buttoned shirt over his head as he tried to kick off his shoes. Verbena picked up on his cue and turned back the bedspread and thin cotton blanket. When she looked back, Bennett had shoved his pants down around his ankles and was kicking frantically to get them off. He wasn't wearing any underwear and it looked as if a flagpole had sprung from his midsection. Verbena's last thoughts before Bennett pulled her back onto the bed were, *Damn you, Eldridge Dewitt, all men are not created equal.*

Bennett had not had a big woman before and everywhere he put his hands there was more than he could imagine. It was the sort of feeling a starved man gets when he stands before an all-you-can-eat smorgasbord. He implores his stomach to outlast his desire to consume it all.

Verbena participated willingly, her hands first on his back then squeezing his butt. She finally took him in hand and sighed deeply before sliding all of him inside her. They moved awkwardly at first on the small bed but eventually found each other's rhythm. Having not had a woman in over two years, Bennett spasmed and exploded quickly and cursed his inability to go the distance. In fact, it wasn't until the third time they had sex that night that he lasted long enough for Verbena to reach her own reward.

Later, out of necessity, they clung to each other to remain on the twin bed. Entangled in the sheets, their bodies glistened under the soft glow from the security lights in the adjacent parking lot. Finally Verbena spoke. "It's never been like this for me. I don't mean to speak ill of Eldridge but I don't think he ever loved me."

"Don't say that Verbena. You're putting yourself down." Bennett reached for a cigarette.

"If he did love me, Bennett, he had no passion for me. Nothing like this." She squeezed Bennett so hard he hoped she would release in time for his next breath.

"What happens now?" Bennett finally got the courage to ask.

"About us you mean?"

"Of course about us. What else?" Bennett trembled. He tried to prepare himself for *This was nice; we'll have to do it again sometime.*

"If it's all right with you, I'll stay here with you and find a job." Verbena spoke haltingly as if she was struggling with her own demons.

"Are you sure?" Bennett asked, his future suddenly looking brighter.

"Mother, I've never felt like this in my whole life, with or without a condom. I'm not leaving now."

"Did you just say *Mother?*"

"No, I said, 'Do you think we could do that again or would it be too much *bother?*'"

Pookie lay on the living room rug near an empty Cheetos bag. Pookie shouldn't have eaten so many but he couldn't stop himself. Just thinking of it made his stomach cramps worsen.

If he threw up he might have to go to the vet. Last time he bit the vet and the vet called him a little cocksucker when Helen wasn't in the room. Pookie didn't believe there was such a thing as an AKC registered cocksucker and he didn't want to see that vet again.

FORTY FIVE

The next morning Bennett and Verbena arose to find Pookie lying beside an empty Cheetos bag with a telltale orange stain on his forepaws and face. He had vomited several times on the rug.

"Oh my God, Bennett. I think he's overdosed or something." Pookie opened one eye and thumped his tail weakly against the carpet.

"Damn. In all the excitement I forgot to put them away last night."

Just then Tom returned from his all nighter. "What's that smell and what happened to Pookie?"

"I left the Cheetos out last night and he got into them. I think they made him sick."

Verbena had already rushed to the phone book to look for a veterinarian in the Yellow Pages. "There's one near here on Palm Bay Road. I'm going to call them."

As she dialed Tom looked beyond Bennett and into Verbena's bedroom where Bennett's clothes were still strewn across the floor along with the bedspread and blanket. "Looks like someone had a tough time getting to sleep."

Bennett flushed but couldn't help smiling. "Yeah, it just sort of happened."

Tom shook his head as he reached for the paper towels and began to clean up Pookie's mess. "Dogs and heterosexuals are such slobs."

"Yes, Miss. We can come over right away. Do you think he will be all right?" Verbena sounded desperate and when she hung up the phone Bennett noticed tears had formed in her eyes.

"The receptionist said to bring him right over. It's called the

Melbourne Veterinary Clinic. Hurry, Bennett. Put on some clothes and comb your hair. Tom, you finish cleaning up Pookie's mess while we change. And take off that green collar so he can get some air." Verbena hurried into the bedroom and slammed the door.

Pookie didn't move because he didn't think he could without throwing up again. Those Cheetos had tasted so good going down. How could they make him so sick? They were taking him to that vet, the one who called him a cocksucker. He wished he could run and hide but it was no use.

Bennett drove and Tom sat up front next to him while Verbena clung to Pookie in the back seat. The clinic was only a few minutes east of Dartmouth Square. Palm Bay Road posed as a major east-west artery separating Melbourne on the north from Palm Bay to the south and provided access for both to I 95. The land on either side, all lowland and scrub pine, had been scraped clear and made to look like Anywhere, USA. It boasted a Wal-Mart SuperCenter, Walgreens, Albertsons, Outback Steak House, Home Depot, BP convenience station, and various sprawling apartment complexes with names like The Pines, Garden Lakes, and Orchid Trail. Their names were enticing but, to Bennett, the complexes looked mediocre at best.

As they crossed Babcock Street Verbena said, "Slow down, Bennett. It's very close now. There it is! Just past the Wendy's on the left. Wait! You're passing it."

"I can't turn here, Verbena. There's a median strip for Christ's sake."

"You can make a U-turn up there." Tom pointed to a turn lane ahead.

"Fine. Hang on everybody." Bennett braked hard into the turn lane, then yanked the wheel to the left and hit the gas pedal. The tires squealed as the big boat of a car fishtailed around the turn and drifted toward the soft shoulder. Bennett fought to bring the Buick back under control while irate morning commuters swerved around him. They blared horns and flipped him the bird.

"Up yours!" shouted Bennett.

"Clever retort. That should pacify them," Tom carped as he clung to the door handle.

Once they came to a stop in the parking lot, Tom jumped out and opened the back door for Verbena and Pookie. Pookie took one look at the building and let out a low growl. "It's okay, baby," Verbena cooed. Bennett remained in the car for a moment and combed back his hair in the rear view mirror. Verbena noticed his shirttail hanging out, but still perturbed over his snapping at her about the median strip, said nothing.

They were greeted by a perky young girl who looked like she could be a beauty queen. Her thick blond hair cascaded over her shoulders while her soft green eyes reminded Verbena of key lime pie. Her name tag said *Missy* and was pinned to a forest-green smock embroidered with a menagerie of tiny animals. As was often the case, Verbena wondered if that's what she would look like if she were thin.

Her concern for the bundle in Verbena's arms seemed genuine. "We'll take him right back as soon as I can get some information. Are you all together?"

"Yes," they responded in unison.

"Who's the responsible party?"

"I guess that would be me," Tom answered. He proceeded to give her their Melbourne address and phone number, then produced a credit card.

"What's the dog's name?" Missy smiled at the squirming white bundle in Verbena's arms.

"Whitey," said Bennett just as Verbena said *Pookie* and Tom said *Puffy.*

Missy looked at them perplexed. "Which is it?"

Bennett scowled at Tom and Verbena, then turned back to Missy. "I'm sorry. We each have a pet name for the little fella, but Whitey is his registered name. He was sired at the Cumberland Kennels in Indiana," he added with authority.

Missy was stricken at the sight before her. Although languishing and not groomed to his usual standards, the poodle lying prostrate on the counter was indeed Pookie. In college she had struggled to memorize the table of chemical elements and the anatomy of the fetal pig, but she never forgot a face whether animal or human.

The man talking, the one they called Bennett, lied easily, as if he had been doing it all his life. The overweight woman seemed genuinely upset about Pookie while the other man stood there taking it all in as if he was just along for the ride.

They didn't look like murderers but how else would they be in possession of Pookie? Missy's first instinct was to call the police but Michael had specifically requested she call him first. The Colonel had more experience in these matters and would know what to do.

"One of you can bring Whitey and follow me. The other two will have to wait here." Missy struggled to keep her composure.

"I'll take him back," Verbena responded, her voice reflecting a measure of desperation.

Tom and Bennett quickly agreed and sat down leaving an empty chair between them. Bennett picked up the morning paper and Tom sifted through an assortment of dog and cat lover magazines. Bennett looked up and smiled at Missy.

Finally she spoke. "Are you from Indiana, Mr. Durant?"

"Indiana?"

"You said Whitey hailed from Indiana, so I thought maybe you did, too."

"Actually Cumberland is my hometown; that's very astute on your part."

"You've picked up a nice Southern accent. You must have been down here quite awhile."

"Cumberland is in southern Indiana. Folks come down from Ft. Wayne and say we all speak with a Southern drawl, just like y'all. I have been detained in South Florida for the past two years due to my business activities." Bennett turned and smiled at the one named Tom.

"And what about you, sir?" Missy sensed herself easing into the role of interrogator. Michael would be pleased by what she was learning.

"My home is Virginia," Tom replied. "The Tidewater area."

"I have an aunt in Richmond."

"Imagine that, just sixty miles up the road."

"Are you down here on business, too?"

"I'm a Southern writer; I go where my mood and imagination take me."

"That sounds so exciting. Do you write about the manatees?"

"I'm considering a piece on that at just this moment. I can't believe you mentioned it."

Now the one called Bennett glared at Tom.

Missy continued, convinced more than ever that these men, especially the sensitive writer, couldn't be killers. "You must cross over to the other side."

"What?"

"I'm afraid crossing over isn't his strong suit," interjected Bennett smiling.

"But you must go over to the Gulf side where the red tide is killing all the manatees. At least they think it's the red tide. I read it in the last issue of the *Save the Manatee Club* newsletter. I think I have it here somewhere in my desk." Missy began rummaging through her desk drawers as her head disappeared behind the counter. "The club was founded by Jimmy Buffett you know."

"The *Let's Get Drunk and Screw* guy?" Bennett reacted with mock surprise.

"Excuse me. He wrote other songs and that's not even the right title." Missy popped up from behind the counter, her face feeling hot and flushed. "Here it is." She handed the newsletter to Tom. "You can keep it; I've read it."

"Thank you. I'm sure this will be most helpful. Mr. Durant and I may just drive over to the Gulf tomorrow and see what we can dig up on the matter."

Just then the door opened and a large black woman entered carrying a pet kennel much like Pookie's. She wore a navy blue dress and matching shoes and a light blue scarf on her head. Missy immediately turned her attention to the woman. "Hello, Mattie. How's Bathsheba?"

At the mention of the name, Mattie dropped the cage to the floor and wailed, "I think she's deaaad! Lord, what am I goin' to do?" Missy jumped up from her chair and ran around the counter. She dropped to her knees and, peering into the plastic box through the portal in front, looking up briefly to notice Bennett shift in his chair to get a better look down the front of her smock.

"I called her and called her but she won't move. She's dead; I just know it." Mattie covered her face with her hands.

"Don't cry, Mattie." Missy stood up and wrung her hands. She wasn't having a good day. "We'll take Bathsheba right back to Doctor." Missy picked up the cage and escorted Mattie around the corner into an exam room.

Verbena and Pookie appeared before Missy returned. "Pookie will be fine. We have to give him Pepto-Bismol every two hours today and tomorrow. And no more junk food." Pookie lifted his head and stared sadly at Verbena, then sighed and returned his chin to the cradle formed by her arm.

Tom and Bennett stood up and joined Verbena at the counter to wait for the bill. Missy emerged momentarily from the exam room. "The doctor is coming, Mattie," she said with concern as she returned to her desk. "Whitey will be okay?" she asked Verbena.

"Yes, the doctor says he'll be fine. Here's the charge slip." They could hear the doctor enter the exam room and address Mattie.

"I'll add this up and charge it to your card." She smiled her sweetest smile at Tom, the one who wrote about manatees. Moments later she handed him a charge slip and a pen. "Sign here, please."

As Tom's pen touched the paper, they heard a harsh hiss and yeoooowl emanating from Bathsheba's exam room. A man's scream followed. "This cocksucker's alive! He damn near took my hand off!"

"Oh, dear. Excuse me. I have to help the doctor. Keep the yellow copy," she called over her shoulder as she disappeared down the hall.

Bennett looked down at Pookie and could have sworn the dog smiled.

A few minutes later they were all back in the car, driving back to their apartment. Bennett noticed that the seafoam Taurus that had been parked in the clinic's lot had also pulled out and headed in the same direction. Good Lord, thought Bennett, what kind of idiot would buy a seafoam-colored car?

FORTY SIX

"Michael, I'm sure that dog is Pookie. I never forget a face, animal or human. It's six o'clock and I've had a really bad day." Besides dealing with potential murderers, she had to drive her boss to the emergency room to have thirty stitches taken in his right hand. When they returned to the office, she spent the rest of the day rescheduling his surgeries and then broke the news to Mattie that her cat Bathsheba had been dropped from the practice. However, they would forward her records without prejudice. Now Michael doubted her.

"Did you get their address?"

"Yes, Michael. They live just down the road at Dartmouth Square."

"You didn't call the police or tell anyone did you?"

"No, Michael," Missy sighed. "I did just as you asked and called you the first chance I got."

"Good, Missy. I'm sure the Colonel will call the police as soon as he's sure Pookie is safe. He's afraid if he calls the police first, the dog might be sent to the pound pending the outcome of the case. It's the least he can do for Helen. Pookie is all right, isn't he?"

"Michael, I told you his medical records are confidential. He has a right to privacy, too."

"I'm not asking for a diagnosis. I just want to know if he is all right."

"I'll only say that he left with the people that brought him."

"Then he can't be too sick."

"He'll be fine if they quit feeding him Cheetos."

"What?"

"I can't say any more. I have to go, Michael. Good-bye."

"Thanks, Missy. Your uncle will be very grateful."

The Colonel couldn't believe Michael's news. "I've got half my men including a Special Forces assassin and a Miami detective looking for this dog, and you're telling me my bimbo niece tracked him down?"

"That's it, Sir, but the dog did sort of find her. A bit fortuitous I'd say."

"And she even got their address?"

"Right here." Michael held up a sheet of paper with the Dartmouth Square address on it.

"Good! Call those two incompetents down in Lauderdale and get them up here. In the meantime have someone keep an eye on those people so we don't lose them again. We're going to get my money, Michael."

"Yes, Sir."

Vinnie contemplated new employment. For the past week he had followed Frank from one broken-down bar to another in the quest for a little white poodle. Frank formulated the plan: buy a drink, offer a reward, and tip heavily with the Colonel's money.

By lunch time, Vinnie took over the driving while Frank slept off his morning's work in the back seat. Then Vinnie drove further south and spent the afternoon quizzing idle prostitutes with their own poodles. What they accomplished was that Frank fell further from the wagon as Vinnie indulged in sexual fantasy involving hookers.

When Michael summoned them north, they followed his directions to a barbecue joint on the west side of Palm Bay. It was a low wooden structure stained dark brown and surrounded by an unpaved parking lot. Untended oleander shrubs loomed blossomless near the entrance. At nearly two in the afternoon the lot, which at lunchtime filled with carpenters' pick-ups, plumbers' rusting vans, electricians' trucks, and assorted other maintenance vehicles, stood nearly empty. Vinnie read the sign that denoted the early bird special didn't start until four o'clock.

Michael slipped off his sunglasses and waited for his eyes to adjust to the dimly lit interior. The aroma proffered a mixture of barbecue, molasses, and stale tobacco; everything about the place suggested grease. He tried to slide into a red plastic booth in the corner, but his pants stuck to the cushion. A weary waitress approached Michael and handed him a laminated menu adorned with a milieu of fingerprints.

Michael rested his elbows on a clean paper placemat and began to rub down his silverware with his napkin. He chose to meet Vinnie and Frank here because it wouldn't be busy this time of day and they kept it dark, probably so as not to disturb the cockroaches.

The waitress returned, and he halfheartedly ordered sweetened iced tea and a pork sandwich basket that included coleslaw and fries. It was small consolation that his meal wasn't a numbered combo and the waitress didn't ask him if he wanted to super-size it.

By the time his overflowing green plastic basket arrived, Vinnie and Frank materialized in the doorway. They stood for a moment getting their bearings and then walked over and sat down opposite him.

"My God. You look like hell, Frank." Michael couldn't help but notice Frank's unshaven face, the dark circles under his eyes, and the rumpled cotton sport coat that looked as if it doubled as a pajama top.

"Good to see you too, kid." Frank fumbled through the side pocket of his jacket and fished out a single crooked cigarette, which he proceeded to light despite the visible tremor in his hands. "Vinnie says you got the mutt."

Michael looked over at Vinnie who rolled his eyes and picked up a sticky menu. "That's right. By an amazing coincidence they walked right into the vet clinic where the Colonel's niece works. She ID'd the dog."

"She's that beauty princess," Vinnie responded. "Maybe we should go over and talk to her. A nice change from the hookers."

"I've got all the information you and Frank need, Vinnie. You don't need to contact Missy."

Vinnie leered at Michael. "You been dippin' into that, Michael?"

"Right, Vinnie, and the Colonel would have my balls run up the flag pole at reveille."

Vinnie smiled and leaned back in the booth as he spread his arms resting one behind Frank, who looked as if he was about to doze off.

195

"Blonde top to bottom and one hundred percent pure virgin. Just the kind of girl Frankie and I won't be taking home to Mother."

"I wouldn't even consider impure thoughts about the Colonel's niece if I were you, Vinnie."

"Easy, Michael. We're all friends here." Vinnie lifted his hands in mock surrender.

"Fine, let's get down to business."

"But I tell you, Michael, I know her kind. One day you'll find yourself sitting on the john reading Playboy with your dick in your hand, and there she'll be lookin' back at you – lyin' naked on satin sheets, touching herself in her private recesses, and lookin' at you like she really wants it. That's the kinda' tease she is, boy."

"Shut the fuck up, you little prick." Michael stopped himself short of reaching over and grabbing Vinnie by the throat. "You and your lush partner don't have the luxury of another screwup, so you'd better listen."

"Don't be so touchy, Michael. You've been living with the Colonel too long. Don't take life so serious. Right, Frankie?" Vinnie nudged Frankie who awakened briefly only to nod off again.

Michael stared hard at Vinnie. "And you've been around the Colonel long enough to know what happens to screwups."

"So what are the orders for Frankie and me?"

"It's simple. The Colonel wants you to pick up these three quietly tonight and bring them to his place for questioning. Obviously we don't want to attract any attention. As usual, the security people at Premier Island won't ask any questions. The tough part will be abducting them quietly."

"No problem, Mikie," Vinnie said. "It's a standard MO for an old School of the Americas boy like me. We should be out of there by 1:00 a.m."

"Fine. It'll give Frank here some time to rest and sober up."

"Fuck you, Michael. Your hands are always clean. You're never around when the dirty work gets done."

Michael smiled coldly, then spoke as if he hadn't heard Vinnie. "We'll expect you in the morning. Then we'll see who has the last word." He rose and threw a twenty down on the table. "Lunch is on me, fellas."

"What about the dog?" Vinnie asked.

"The Colonel doesn't give a damn about the dog."

FORTY SEVEN

Rick Brindle took a week of personal leave, his own car, and his Smith and Wesson and drove north to the entrance of Premier Island between Vero Beach and Melbourne. A gated community wasn't easy to monitor, but Rick had the foresight to check the DMV tag numbers on all the cars registered to Colonel Jack Collins. It didn't take long to pinpoint a well-dressed young man who appeared to be the Colonel's errand boy and messenger. At six-forty each morning he left the compound in the Colonel's BMW and purchased him a paper and a cappuccino for himself at a nearby Snatch 'n Go.

Despite his initial success, his stake-out hadn't been easy. He sat alone for long hours. Once, the sheriff's deputy pulled over to investigate. A smart-looking kid in his early twenties, he was easily impressed by Brindle's badge and offered to help if he could, but Rick politely declined. One man's job in jeopardy was enough.

Initially he tried to live out of his car, but after two days he couldn't stand his own smell and craved a shave with foam and hot water. He rented a room near the Snatch 'n Go in an eight-unit complex run by a retired schoolteacher and his wife from Vermont. The room reminded Rick of Vermont itself. It was immaculate with sturdy straight-lined maple furniture and an extra charge for every service such as local calls and HBO.

The cuisine at the Snatch 'n Go consisted of breakfast burritos, corn dogs, and pepperoni and cheese stuffed hot dogs prepackaged in cellophane. He unwrapped and microwaved them on the premises.

By the second day he was on a first-name basis with Tigerton at the checkout counter. Tigerton was a chain smoking, leather-skinned Florida cracker who was probably ten years younger than his weathered features suggested.

"You ain't a government man are you?" Tigerton asked.

"No, I'm an insurance investigator. I do background checks on people applying for life insurance." Rick felt certain that Tigerton knew nothing about life insurance and wouldn't press further on the subject. To make it look official he flashed his Dade County library card, feeling equally certain that Tigerton was unfamiliar with libraries.

"I knew it." Tigerton smiled. The few tobacco-stained teeth he still retained gave the overall impression of a broken picket fence.

"How's that?"

"I was raised in the hills of Kentucky. I learned to spot a Revenue man before I could walk." Tigerton's trembling hand reached for another cigarette, which he lit off the butt he was about to put out.

"I didn't know you still had trouble with the Feds up there."

"Lord, yes. Once they cleared out our stills they started after our guns. If we don't stop them, they'll be after our coonhounds next."

"As citizens we've got to be constantly vigilant of our rights."

Tigerton cocked his head to one side and squinted at Rick. "You ain't part of one of those vigilante groups are you?"

"No, sir. I'm just a concerned American. I don't know word one about the militia."

"Militia? I weren't saying nothing about no militia. We got us a fine militia."

"Here on the barrier island? You're joshing me, Tigerton."

"No, not here. You gotta' go inland where there's more skeeters than people. That's where we assemble. We got a fine camp out there in the scrub pine and palmettos, and it'd take an army of coonhounds to find us."

"That sounds more like it." Rick was taking mental notes. The information he collected here might come in handy when his boss found out he'd been stalking the Colonel.

"But we got some supporters around here. You'd be surprised who slips money our way. There are some big fans of that Charleston Heston fella,' God rest his soul. You know the ones?"

"Sure. The NRA's about one clip short of a full magazine."

"What?" Tigerton cocked his head like a coonhound again.

"I'm just saying Heston was a formidable figure if you know what I mean." Rick winked at Tigerton.

Tigerton drew back a bit. "Sure, course I knew that."

"So you're the pick up man?"

"You seen anyone else around look like they can handle it?"

Rick looked around the empty store then back at Tigerton. "Now that you mention it, I haven't seen anyone with your abilities."

"I got a man comes in here from that there Premier Island place about once a month carrying a briefcase. Except for the briefcase he looks like a fruit picker in his cutoff shorts and them boat shoes worn right through the toe. You'd never know he had money until you look out at his sports car and the dame sitting there wearing enough gold jewelry to fill Ft. Knox. Course she wouldn't be caught dead inside this place."

"So what's in the briefcase?"

"I'm gettin' to that. You see he fills his tank then walks in here carryin' that thing and sets it down here at the end of the counter so's to pay for the gas. He hands me cash and walks out of here without the case. I take it in back and open it and it's full of cash, ten maybe twenty thousand at a crack."

"Whew, that's gotta help meet the old militia payroll."

"Damn straight it does. But here's what tickles my ass with a feather. I get all these welfare folks, pickers, and colored landscapers in here buying lottery tickets every day. They think their troubles are just a day and a ticket away from being over. And that makes perfect sense."

"But?"

"But this guy, with so much money he can't give it all away, buys a lottery ticket, too. He's already hit the damn jackpot and still wants more. Can you believe that?"

"No such thing as being too rich I guess."

"He's living damn proof of that."

"I notice one fellow in here every morning dressed pretty well."

"That would be Michael."

"Muscular young fellow with black hair. He drives a black BMW."

"That's him. He works for some retired general or something. Comes by every morning to buy one of them papers." Tigerton pointed to the *New York Times*. "Says the general expects it on his breakfast tray."

"The general sounds like a pain in the ass."

"I never seen him but Mike's all right I guess. He likes to chew the fat while he waits for his cappuccino to cool. Seems like a sissy drink to me."

"Sounds like a nice boy."

"It's a tragic thing though. His daddy got himself kilt in Vietnam when Mike was just a baby. Broke his poor mother's heart. Mike tells me she spent more time in one of them funny farms than out. His grandparents practically raised him."

"It sounds like someone raised him well." Knowing first name and background of the Colonel's errand boy wasn't critical, but Rick liked having a name attached to his quarry. In part he felt he had an edge now but it was more than that. Stake-outs were boring and this was like adding a stick of gum, something Rick could chew on while he sat and waited for Michael to move again. He worked it over and over in his mind wondering what it must be like to be raised without a father or to have a mother who couldn't cope. Did Michael see the Colonel as the father he never had? If so, how could he have made such a lousy choice?

Rick's first real break came near the end of the week. Michael left the complex just after noon and headed north on A1A toward Melbourne. He took the first causeway west and worked his way over to a barbecue joint near I-95. Michael looked like the fruit smoothie and bagel type; this place in the middle of the afternoon was out of character.

Deeming it too risky to follow Michael into the restaurant, Rick pulled into a busy McDonald's across the street and positioned his car to monitor the entrance. The place looked deserted this time of day and Rick hoped that if Michael were meeting someone, he had arrived before them.

Shortly thereafter another car rolled into the dusty lot and two men got out. The overweight one in a wrinkled suit appeared to be drunk. The second man looked younger. He was trim with a military haircut, dark skin, and a swagger to his walk that, if he were military, suggested Special Forces. He wore a dark polo shirt adorned with at least two gold necklaces, off-white linen pants, no socks, and black Italian loafers.

Rick reached over the front seat and grabbed a file containing an assortment of names and grainy photos of men assumed to be on the Colonel's payroll. He fumbled quickly through the collection almost certain he had seen a photo of the young stud before. Suddenly there he was staring back at him. Vinnie DiOrio: Special Forces, School of the Americas, weapons specialist, suspected arms dealer, and enforcer for the Colonel. "Bingo," Rick whispered.

Less than ten minutes later Michael exited the restaurant alone and climbed into his BMW. Rick made a quick decision to switch his surveillance and wait for Vinnie and his partner. He watched as Michael drove off in the direction of Premier Island.

He waited another half an hour, hungry but not daring to run into the McDonald's for a cheeseburger. Fifteen minutes later the two exited and headed west toward I 95. Rick backed out quickly and cut across the drive-thru lane and followed several cars back. Vinnie eased into the right lane ahead of Rick and onto the northbound ramp toward Melbourne.

As usual, traffic soared bumper to bumper at seventy-five miles an hour. Rick accelerated up the ramp, but heavy traffic forced him to brake and slide in behind a Yellow Freight semi. He lost sight of Vinnie and couldn't change lanes. Frustrated, he backed off the semi as best he could hoping to get a glimpse ahead. Just as he was about to change lanes, he spotted Vinnie up ahead. He was drifting onto the exit ramp at Palm Bay Road. The trucker also signaled an exit, allowing Rick to shield himself from view.

Vinnie had no reason to suspect he was being followed, so Rick had an easy time keeping up with him on Palm Bay Road. Eventually Vinnie turned into a development entitled Dartmouth Square. Rick followed as long as he dared, then pulled into a parking stall. Vinnie proceeded slowly past a building that bordered a canal. He seemed to be pointing something out to his partner. He parked near a mail kiosk and walked over as if to check his mail but he didn't have a key. Shortly he returned to his car and they drove off.

Rick contemplated following but realized that Vinnie had been casing this particular apartment complex for a reason and would most likely return tonight for whatever he was after. Rick decided to return after dark and wait. Whoever resided in that apartment building must be of great interest to the Colonel and Rick Brindle intended to find out why.

FORTY EIGHT

Rick had been parked in a dark recess of the Dartmouth Square parking lot for five hours. Along with keeping an eye out for the arrival of Vinnie and his friend, he remained watchful for the security guard who cruised by periodically in his golf cart. He had cracked open a window and ducked out of sight at the first sound of the cart's soft whirring engine. It was now almost midnight.

Vinnie's car rolled silently into the parking lot, but Rick caught a glimpse of it just before Vinnie doused his parking lights and coasted into a vacant spot in front of the building he had been casing earlier. Vinnie and his associate slipped quietly out of the car which apparently had its dome light removed. They walked nonchalantly to the door of a lower unit and entered, pausing no longer than if they had a key. The unit remained dark, but Rick thought he could detect the rays of the Maglite bobbing behind the blinds.

Rick waited another minute and then eased himself out of his car and approached the building. He found a place in the shrubbery that lined the building and positioned himself in the shadows still clueless as to Vinnie's intentions. With a black sky overhead, the only light emanated from a dim yellow lamp over the mail kiosk thirty yards away.

For the first time since leaving Ft. Lauderdale, Rick realized how isolated and helpless he was. The night air hung warm and damp against his already limp shirt. His Smith and Wesson weighed heavily in the small of his back as he felt the sweat roll down around the hammer and cylinder. He wished he had convinced Nixon to come along.

Negra, the six-foot female snake, quietly coiled herself four feet away from the man in the shadows and seethed. The two other men had interrupted her feeding earlier and now she would certainly have to wait longer. It wasn't fair.

The construction of the apartments had relegated her to this corner of the property near the drainage ditch. Here frogs, toads, and small lizards still bred, and Negra could find enough food to survive. She had adapted and languished near the low-lying shrubs during the day when the humans were about, foraging at night while they slept.

Negra accepted her restrictions and on the rarest of occasions slithered out on a warm sunny day only to retreat at the terrified shrieks of an unsuspecting tenant. But now they'd welched on the unwritten deal by walking about in the dark and scaring away Negra's dinner. She wasn't poisonous but she could still raise hell when she was hungry.

For Vinnie, breaking into these apartments was as easy as slipping into any hut in Central America. He had done it hundreds of times and could do it with his eyes closed. Frank, on the other hand, preferred kicking in a door while armed with a sawed-off twelve gauge shotgun. Subtlety was not his forte and Vinnie sensed his impatience. He had kept Frank off the booze for almost twenty-four hours but now Frank had the abstention shakes. Vinnie wished he'd allowed Frank a shot of Jim Beam before they left the motel.

The room was dark except for Vinnie's Maglite, which he flashed sparingly. He found the closed bedroom doors and listened for the sounds of sleeping. Vinnie saw no sign of the dog and that variable bothered him the most. They planned to sweep him up at first sight and muzzle him with duct tape. Vinnie wanted to take him to the Colonel just to demonstrate how good he was and then watch what the Colonel did with him.

Vinnie suspected someone would be sleeping with the girl, which meant one of the men would be alone. He wanted him out of commission first. Then they would go after the other two. An educated guess told him that the room at the end of a short hallway had only one occupant. He entered the room and Frank followed. With his light he quickly assessed the location of his target and the fact that the dog was absent.

He slipped out his gun and swiftly crossed the room, then placed the gun barrel at Tom's temple. Tom started to shift then awakened. Vinnie in turn flashed the halogen light directly into Tom's eyes and covered the startled victim's mouth. "Not a word and you won't get hurt."

Frank stepped forward as he struggled with the duct tape. Hands shaking, he tore a piece off and put it over Tom's mouth. "Now sit up," he rasped. When Tom complied, he wrapped the tape around his mouth and head, then taped his hands together in front of him.

"Tape his feet together for now while we get the other two," Vinnie ordered Frank. Then he leaned down to Tom's ear. "We are all going for a little ride. If you so much as fart in here while I'm collecting the others, I'll come back and put you away. Do you understand?" The captive nodded as a tear rolled down his cheek. "Come on," Vinnie whispered.

At the next door Vinnie quietly tore off a piece of tape for what he assumed would be the dog. Then he opened the door and flashed his light again. The dog had a twin bed to himself on the left and opened one lethargic eye at the sound and the light. Vinnie rushed Pookie and quickly enveloped and bound his snout. Frank moved to the bed, his gun already drawn, and waited as the two lovers awakened and began to untangle. "Is that you, Tom?" a male voice asked.

"No, lover boy, it's us." Vinnie flipped on the room light and stood with his gun pointed at Pookie's head. "No one make a sound or the dog gets it, then both of you and the guy we tied up down the hall. One, two, three, four."

Frank motioned them to sit up and began to tear off strips of duct tape. The big woman's eyes were wide with fear, but her partner seemed a little more experienced and was taking stock of his predicament. Vinnie needed to keep an eye on him and made a mental note to kill him first if the situation required it.

"What about the money, Vinnie?"

"Forget about it for now. If it's here, we'll come back for it when they tell us where it's hidden. We can't risk waking anyone."

Frank gathered the three captives in the living room while Vinnie held the now-agitated but muzzled Pookie. Vinnie spoke to the assemblage. "We are all going for the proverbial little ride. If you cooperate when we reach our destination, you might live to tell about it. Now let's take stock of everyone's belongings so no one accuses us later of stealing anything."

Vinnie looked at the motley group and smiled. He could relax now and loosen up. "We have one pair of yellow and purple striped bikini briefs," he said as he pointed to Tom. "An extra-large Tickle-me-Elmo night shirt for the lady and a pair of green fitted boxers on her friend. Sorry, folks, but neither time nor prudence allows you to dress more appropriately to meet the Colonel."

Bennett's mind raced as he sifted through the clues as to what had transpired. He suspected their captors had something to do with the deaths of Helen and Nero, although he had no hint as to how they'd been discovered. One of them mentioned some money, which Bennett didn't have and had never seen. It must be a lot or they wouldn't bother with a kidnapping attempt in the middle of the night.

The one in charge seemed very professional despite his crude language and he worked with military precision. Still, Bennett couldn't rule out drugs as the cause of this. The second captor didn't look well and had the shakes, which might prove useful if they tried to escape. Since none of them had been blindfolded, Bennett had no illusions about seeing the sunrise. All he could do was wait and watch for an opening.

Negra's frustration level had peaked. She was still three toads short of a full stomach and had grown weary of watching the man in the shadows. She eased out of her coil and glided away from the building toward the sidewalk just as the door of a nearby apartment opened, and five humans walked out. *Too late to stop now* thought Negra. They'll just have to wait until I cross the walk.

Frank didn't feel well at all and he needed a drink. His skin crawled and burned as if fire ants had built a nest just beneath the surface. His throat was parched, his eyes watered, and his hands shook. He had just enough sense to realize that if he didn't get a drink soon the hallucinations would return: Vietnam in Technicolor with snakes swarming in the rice paddies.

As he led the group along the walk in the dark, Frank couldn't help but step on Negra's back. The shock of the crepe sole resting on her spine ignited a fury in the queen of the black snakes. It was as if that shoe unleashed the anger and frustration of a lifetime of being pushed into the far corner of advancing civilization. In a flash Negra snapped back. Wrapping herself around Frank's fleshy ankle, she ascended his leg under his pants cuff.

Frank made a sound that started as a low moan and evolved through several octaves of a long ooooooohhhh!! and ended in the high-pitched scream of a wounded animal as Negra reached his groin. Discharging his gun overhead he ran straight for the drainage ditch. His oafish form disappeared into the darkness followed by a loud splash.

Vinnie and his captives stood paralyzed by what they had just witnessed, but Pookie wiggled free from Vinnie's grasp and made a break for the parking lot. A bullfrog croaked in the vicinity of Frank's disappearance, then was choked off mid chorus. Silence.

Rick Brindle witnessed the entire event, incredulous at the sight of what he thought had been a garden hose uncoil itself and stretch across the walk. He recovered before the others and stepped quickly behind Vinnie placing his Smith and Wesson in the small of his back. "Drop your gun, Vinnie."

"What the fuck? Who …?" Lights were coming on now and they could hear the sound of glass patio doors sliding backwards on their tracks.

"Do it," Rick snapped, "or you're a dead man. The rest of you don't move either. We're all going to see the Colonel and I'm going to find out who killed Helen. Now move. Everyone in Vinnie's car."

A voice came from somewhere above. "What the hell is going on down there?"

"It's all right," Rick responded. "Just another neighborhood drug bust. Go back to bed."

Rick heard the voice again as the glass door rolled back into place. "I told you that queer and his friends were trouble."

When they got to the car, Rick motioned for Vinnie to get behind the wheel and opened the back door for Vinnie's three captives. "Vinnie will chauffeur while you three ride together in back."

"Where the hell are we going?" Vinnie grumbled.

"I'm sure the Colonel is expecting you and we don't want to keep him waiting, Vinnie."

"I don't know what you're talking about."

"The hell you don't. Now drive us to Premier Island before I shoot you and take these folks myself." Vinnie shrugged as if Rick was nuts but started the car and headed for Palm Bay Road.

Leon had slept fitfully the past two nights in the back seat of his Taurus. In the first place, he had nowhere else to stay. Secondly, he was almost certain that the dog he'd followed from the vets to Dartmouth Square was Helen's Pookie, despite the fact he had never seen his companions before.

Pookie and the vet clinic were the only leads he had to Helen and his money. As soon as he had returned to his car and jump started it, he had gone straight there to set up surveillance. Hope had all but faded when three people rushed in with a white toy poodle. Unfortunately he hadn't been able to get a closer look at the little mutt and he still could be wrong.

Despite his quandary, Leon couldn't help but ruminate about that pen spring Dr. Singh had thrust into his coronary artery. The chest pains were gone but what insured that the hardware would remain in place? What would happen now that he'd tossed his prescriptions?

Maybe at best all he could do is rescue his pension only to have that spring bust loose. He couldn't stop the horrible fantasy of it lodged deep in his brain. He'd be left drooling and speechless in a nursing home with a rubber tube in his penis.

Suddenly shots rang out. Leon jerked and peered over the back seat in the direction of the apartment. Someone screamed and ran toward the drainage canal where Leon had periodically snuck to take a leak. It appeared that two other men with guns had bound and gagged the two men and the woman he'd followed from the clinic.

Then, to his amazement and delight, he saw Pookie dashing full bore across the parking lot toward him. He could have sworn his muzzle was duct taped, but Pookie passed him and crawled under a shrub near the car.

Lights came on in another apartment and he could hear voices. Leon strained to hear but all he caught was *drug bust.*

Now the two men pushed their three bound suspects toward a parked car in his row and he quickly slid out of sight. His heart began to pound like a jackhammer and Leon was convinced that little spring would bust loose any second. He struggled to check his pulse rate like the nurse taught him but found it impossible. Beads of sweat formed on his brow but strangely he felt no chest pain.

Car doors slammed shut and the engine started. Leon slowly pulled himself up to peek again and witnessed the car back out and head toward the Palm Bay Road exit. When he looked down, there stood silver-snouted Pookie who nonchalantly lifted his hind leg and pissed on his front tire as if nothing had happened.

The car disappeared around the corner and Leon threw open his door and jumped out. "Pookie! It's me." The muzzled poodle looked up and growled.

"Come on, Pookie. We've got to find Helen. Leon, who felt a bit like Timmy in a surreal Lassie episode, swept up Pookie and scrambled into the front seat. "Sorry, pal, but the duct tape stays. We've got to catch the bad guys." The Taurus engine roared to life and an invigorated Leon began the pursuit.

At Babcock he frantically searched right and left fearing he had already lost them. He couldn't make out the car, but he could see taillights in the distance headed in the direction of the beach. He concluded that it had to be them and turned left. Pookie lay next to him on the front seat and pawed at his restraint.

By the time they crossed the causeway and turned south along the beach it became obvious to Leon that if this was a drug bust they weren't heading for a police station or sheriff's office. Something more sinister was afoot. Pookie nudged him in the ribs and Leon wished he had a more substantial weapon than a toy poodle.

Eventually Leon slowed as the car ahead turned off into a gated community. The sign read Premier Island but he couldn't recall Helen ever talking about it. He slowed until the first car cleared the gatehouse then followed.

A guard stepped out with a flashlight and Leon rolled down the window and blurted, "How ya' doin'? I'm wit dem." His Nero impression was the best he could come up with. He took a deep breath and held it.

The guard flashed his light in Leon's face then at the muzzled dog. "All right, go ahead." He motioned toward the large iron gates as they rolled back.

Leon let out his breath but his quarry had disappeared. "I'm a new soldier for this outfit and got a little behind. They just said something about being near a friggin' clubhouse." In Iowa every small town had a grain elevator on the railroad tracks. Directions to any place could be given using it as a point of reference. Leon had learned that in Florida the grain elevator had been replaced by the clubhouse.

"The clubhouse is straight ahead; take a right and follow the road. Sorry to have held you up."

"Forget about it." Leon accelerated through the gates toward the clubhouse.

He turned right as instructed and doused his headlights. Certain he was out of sight of the guardhouse he stopped the car, and for reasons that would never be clear to him, he peeled the duct tape off Pookie and tucked him under his arm like a football. "Come on, Pookie. Let's find the bad guys." Like two blind pigs in search of an acorn they proceeded together down the dark street.

FORTY NINE

Rick glanced over his shoulder at the three hostages sitting in the back seat. They reminded him of the three monkeys: See no evil, hear no evil, and speak no evil. "I'm sorry but I'll have to leave you three tied up. Someone in this car knows who killed Helen and I plan to find out before the night is over.

Incidentally, my name is Rick Brindle and I'm with the bureau of Alcohol, Tobacco, and Firearms. In case you are unaware, our chauffeur is Vinnie DiOrio, scum of the mercenary soldier world. You three must have something either he or Colonel Collins wants or he would have slit your throats while you slept."

Vinnie grunted. "So where's the rest of the posse? ATF's aren't usually dumb enough to work solo."

"Don't worry, partner. I'm covered. Backup is just a whistle away."

"For your sake you'd better be right," Vinnie sneered.

"Just drive."

Vinnie saw through his bluff; Rick was sure of it. The problem was that he had no idea why the Colonel wanted the three bound passengers in the back seat. It occurred to him that they may have stumbled upon Helen and Nero and killed them for the money. Subsequently, the Colonel tracked them down to extract his money and his pound of flesh. His only option now was to take everyone to the Colonel and see how it all played out.

They arrived at the Premier Island gatehouse forty minutes later and were ushered through without so much as a glance from the security guard. "The Colonel has a lot of friends and support inside this place,"

Vinnie said as he pointed back toward the guard. "Your rescue team won't get in this easily."

"Turn right at this corner, Vinnie," Rick replied without acknowledging Vinnie's comment. "His place is just past the clubhouse on the left in case you've forgotten."

"No, I wouldn't dream of taking you folks anywhere else. I have my orders."

"This is it; turn into the drive and cut the engine."

Vinnie did as he was told but the car's motion triggered the security lights, which reflected off the white stucco. Rick moved quickly to get everyone out of the car before they were discovered but two men stepped from the shadows with raised guns.

"I see you brought company, Vinnie. What happened to Frank?" The Colonel stepped into the light followed by Michael.

Vinnie smiled at Rick as he walked over and took his gun. He turned to the Colonel. "We have a guest from the ATF. I figure he's been tailing Michael then jumped us tonight at the apartments."

"And Frank?"

"Frank fell into a drainage ditch and we had to leave him. I'll tell you about the snake later."

"Snake?"

"Yeah, later. Like I said."

"But this agent can't be alone. Are you sure you weren't followed?"

"It doesn't make any sense, Sir, but he's playing Lone Ranger. There's almost no traffic on the road. We couldn't have been followed."

The Colonel frowned but apparently accepted Vinnie's explanation for the moment. "But what kind of host am I? Won't you all come inside? Get the door for the lady, Michael." The Colonel motioned toward the front door of his mansion. Verbena led the way followed by the rest.

Tears welled in Leon's eyes as he approached the large home bathed in security lights. As soon as they had exited the car, Pookie had promptly sunk his little fangs into the base of Leon's thumb and refused to ease off. Despite the excruciating pain Leon remained stoic. He couldn't risk a sound at this point.

Ducking behind a shrub he watched two men confront the original group with guns and escort them inside. Once they were out of sight, he and his attached poodle slipped out of hiding and carefully made their way toward the back of the house in search of a window.

Once they were all standing in the marble foyer the Colonel spoke again. "Vinnie, remove the duct tape from our guests' mouths."

Vinnie walked down the line and reached forward to unceremoniously rip the tape off the faces of Tom, Verbena, and Bennett as each emitted a groan. "What the hell is this all about and who are you?" Bennett demanded.

"In due time, my good man, but first you have something of mine I believe. I want it back." The Colonel stared long and hard at Bennett then Tom.

"Whatever it is give it to him, Bennett," pleaded Verbena. "I want to go home."

Vinnie snickered at her last comment. "Sure, we'll call you a cab or maybe have Mikie bring around the limo." Vinnie had returned to the far wall and leaned against it while he casually inspected his gun. He looked across the room and winked at Michael.

"I want the money Helen and that dago stole from me."

"We don't know who you're talking about."

"Au contraire. You have the lady's dog." He glanced at Vinnie who merely shrugged. "He was alive and locked in the bathroom when we left Helen and her friend."

"Ohh!" Verbena gasped. "You are the murderers!" She inched closer to Bennett.

"You have an amazing grasp of the obvious, chubby." The Colonel laughed and looked over at Michael.

"Leave her alone." Tom spoke this time but Vinnie pushed himself off the wall and slapped him hard before he could continue.

Verbena began to cry. "They're going to kill us all, aren't they?" She directed her question to Rick, who unfortunately had been thinking that very thought.

"It will be all right." Rick tried to sound convincing. "They just want their money." He tried to size up his situation. The three hostages stood in line to his left. Michael stood just out of reach on his right and Vinnie covered the left flank. The Colonel placed himself in front of them with his back to a set of French doors, but Rick had no idea where they led. Rick couldn't envision a plan of escape that wouldn't result in one or all of them being gunned down.

"That's right *kemo sabe*. We just want the fucking money."

"Vinnie, there's no need to be vulgar," the Colonel corrected.

Bennett stepped forward and addressed the Colonel. "I worked for that couple but these two had nothing to do with it. I found these people dead and stole their car. Those two never said anything about your money and I never saw it. None of us knows where it is."

"It's brave of you to step forward and take responsibility. I admire that in a man but I don't believe you. I think you found the money or why would you have stolen the car and run?" The Colonel stepped forward and stuck his gun under Bennett's nose. Bennett stood his ground in silence. "You act the part of a hero but you're a fool just like Helen and Nero. We don't need any heroes tonight. My guess is if you're dead, one of these two will give up the money real fast."

"Colonel," interrupted Vinnie. "Let's not make the same mistake we did with those other two. Give them to me. By the time I'm through with them, they'll give up their own mothers."

The Colonel frowned and turned slowly to face Vinnie. "I'm in command here, soldier. I'll decide who lives or dies. And I don't make mistakes. What happened down there was a tactical error in judgment. That's all. Do you understand me?"

"It's your party, sir. I just think we should slow dance with the fat lady first. Give her to me and in twenty minutes she'll sing. Then it'll be all over."

"This is a military mission, soldier. At ease." Vinnie shrugged and the Colonel, his face now wearing a contorted smile, turned his attention back to Bennett.

"Vinnie is actually correct in his limited fashion. The fat lady will sing but leaving three men alive to attempt some futile rescue would be a tactical error. I'll not risk needless injury to my men."

Bennett turned quickly to look at Verbena as if to say he was sorry.

"Ah, I see you care for the woman. Also admirable. This is what I will do. I will give you until the count of three to tell me where the money is. You will still die but I give you my word as an officer that the woman will not suffer."

"We don't know anything. It's my fault. Please let them go."

"One …" The Colonel cocked his forty-five and shoved it under Bennett's left eye. "Two …" Bennett squeezed his eyes shut and began to tremble. "Thr…"

From deep within Verbena there arose a primal scream. Her scream was echoed by that of a man who for all the world looked to Rick Brindle like a man with a white dog attached head first to his crotch. The man flailed wildly and fell backwards into the Colonel's pool.

Hands still bound Verbena threw herself against Bennett and landed with her full weight on top of him. "You'll have to shoot me first," she managed as she drove the wind out of Bennett's chest. "And I'm the only one who knows where the money is."

Bennett's head bounced on the marble floor like a new NBA basketball. "Verbena!" he screamed. As he slipped into unconsciousness, gun shots echoed sharply off the marble walls and a woman screamed. Then nothing.

FIFTY

Michael had envisioned this night for a long time. Finally, the Colonel had given him a gun and included him in the dirty work. He stood for an hour in the shadows with the Colonel listening to the soft whish-swish of the automatic lawn sprinkling systems emanating from the dimly lit neighbors' yards.

He felt the pounding in his chest as Vinnie rolled into the circular drive. Now with the opportunity, all he needed was an opening. He hadn't anticipated the arrival of the federal agent but how could he? If the hostages just remained calm everything would be all right.

They reassembled in the foyer, everyone tense and talking but Michael wasn't listening. His eyes darted from the Colonel to Vinnie, then the agent, and finally back to the Colonel. Suddenly Michael realized the Colonel fully intended to murder the young man he'd been addressing. Before he could react, the woman threw herself on top of the man. She knocked him to the ground just as what appeared to be an ATF backup agent screamed and fell into the pool. The Colonel took aim at the woman and that's when Michael shot him.

The woman screamed and Vinnie, whose attention had been diverted toward the pool, looked back at Michael in disbelief. That's when the agent in the foyer dove at him. Instinctively, Vinnie turned on his attacker. As he raised his gun and fired, Michael shot him knocking him back against the wall. The agent grabbed his leg and fell to the floor.

Michael walked over and kicked Vinnie's gun away as he slid down the wall and slumped into a pool of blood on the floor. Then he calmly walked past the perplexed agent to the dying Colonel.

The Colonel gasped. "Michael, what have you done?"

Michael knelt down and stroked the Colonel's head. "My father wasn't in the Marines in Vietnam."

The Colonel placed his hand on his blood-soaked shirt front. "Jesus, Michael. I've been hit."

"He was in your outfit and died when you sent him on a fucking suicide mission."

"Radio the base, Michael. They'll send a chopper."

"He obeyed orders because he was a good soldier but he never had a chance." Michael was sobbing now.

"I'll be all right, soldier. I'm going to get a medal. You'll see."

"His patrol was ambushed while you tossed back Jack Daniels with the general."

"At least the Silver Star."

Michael's hand trembled as he lifted his gun. "I've waited for this day since my twelfth birthday, the same day they put my mother in an asylum." Then he aimed his gun at the Colonel's head and pulled the trigger.

As Bennett regained consciousness he found himself looking into Verbena's tear-streaked face. The overhead chandelier created a halo effect around her head and he was convinced they were both dead. Except he had a crushing headache and had always assumed dead people felt no pain. "Are we dead?"

"No, honey, we're all right." Verbena squeezed Bennett so hard he felt his head would explode from the pressure.

Bennett winced. "What happened?"

"I'll fill you in on the way to the hospital. That agent has been shot in the leg and you need your head examined."

"No lie. I'm sorry I got you and Tom into this. Is he okay?"

"Tom's fine. He found a pen and paper and he's over in the corner taking notes while everything is fresh in his mind."

"We're even now, Verbena."

"What do you mean."

"You saved my life tonight."

"Actually Michael and Pookie did."

"I don't care who actually did. I remember you throwing yourself on top of me to prevent me from taking the Colonel's bullet. I hope this doesn't mean you're leaving me."

Bennett smiled at Verbena and whispered, "Pookie?" before he passed out.

EPILOGUE

One month later, Rick Brindle limped into his supervisor's office, but it would be two more weeks before the swelling in Leon Eckerman's testicles would recede and he could forego his bowlegged gait.

"Good morning, sir."

"Brindle, good to see you back." His supervisor rose from his desk and reached over to shake hands. "You've picked up a nice tan while recuperating."

"I believe I was suspended with pay, pending the investigation."

"I'm sorry about that but you weren't acting under orders. Y'all could have been killed."

"And one of our war heroes was."

"Yes, unfortunate I'm afraid." The supervisor averted his eyes and turned to look out the window with his back to Rick.

"The inquiry has exonerated you and you are to be reinstated."

"But …"

"But not here."

"Do I get a choice?"

"Either Des Moines, Iowa, or Ogden, Utah. It's the best I could get for you."

"Not exactly hotbeds of Bureau activity, are they?"

The supervisor turned back to Brindle. "You're lucky to have a job at all. You broke all the rules, nearly getting yourself and innocent people killed. Now one of the survivors is writing a book about it. He'll probably make you the goddamn hero."

"I doubt that."

"Next thing you know it will be a TV movie and we'll have the

Sixty Minutes news team bearing down on our asses. The department doesn't need this right now. Can you conceptualize that, Brindle?"

"I'm sorry, sir."

The supervisor sighed and returned to his desk. "Off the record, Brindle. It took a lot of guts to risk what you risked and you did a damn fine job. Hell, you were a hero. But that's not how things work in a bureaucracy."

"Yes, sir. Can I go to Utah?"

"That's home isn't it?"

"Yes, it's time to go home. I want to spend my spare time studying with the church elders. By learning their ways, I can better help my people. Somewhere along the way I got lost, and I want to obtain their blessing and reestablish contact with my roots. I'll be a better agent for it, sir."

"Just stay the fuck out of trouble, Brindle. You sound like you're joining the tribal police."

Three months later Mr. and Mrs. Bennett Durant sat in their newly furnished lanai overlooking the neighborhood irrigation pond. A mullet broke the surface and slapped back down three feet away. Bennett and Verbena waited expectantly for its next two jumps while a great blue heron worked the far bank near a group of ibis.

Their new home sat in the middle of a sprawling development just south of the Osceola Parkway between Orlando and Kissimmee and just five minutes from a Wal-Mart SuperCenter and a Walgreens. They'd had four models to choose from and the developer promised to break ground for the central clubhouse and pool by Christmas.

"Are you sure you won't regret not living on the beach, Verbena?"

"This is all I want, Bennett. And it's all ours thanks to Andrea Streator."

"She sure moved quickly to buy your place in Ohio."

"Andrea promises to make it the showplace of Waterford," Verbena said. "Her husband has been very successful."

"It won't be long and they'll be looking for a winter condo in Florida."

"Will the circle be unbroken?" Verbena giggled and wiggled her toes. She picked up a Moon Pie and began to unwrap it.

"Tom called today."

"How's the book coming?"

"He's almost done and his agent called and thinks he can sell it as a television movie. You know the ones: *The following movie is based on a true story …*"

"How's Michael doing?"

"He's better. He and Tom take long walks on the beach together and Michael seems to be working through it."

"He's lucky to have Tom."

"It was fate, Bennett. Just like you and me."

Bennett smiled and shook his head. No use arguing anymore. He reached for Verbena's hand. "I worry a little bit about all this. Our jobs at Disney don't pay all that much, even though you had the cash for this place."

Verbena squeezed Bennett's hand and asked, "Do you love your job?"

"It's great. I couldn't be happier."

"Me neither. So just do it and don't worry about how much money we make. It will be all right."

"I wish it were that simple, Verbena."

"But it is, Bennett. Pookie, come here, baby." Bennett could hear the sound of toenails clicking across the tile floor. Pookie leapt onto Verbena's lap and licked her face. "That's a good puppy. Now, let's show Bennett how to differentiate costume jewelry from the real thing by the settings and their little clasps. My daddy was in retail you know."

Stephen T. Dinkle, CEO
Havenwood Healthcare Systems
Melbourne, Florida

Dear Mr. Eckerman:

We trust you are feeling better, that your stent has solved all your problems, and you have resumed a normal life. As you may know, we at Havenwood Healthcare are ranked among the top 5,000 hospitals in the nation for cardiac care according to the Cardio-Elluta-Stent survey. This prestigious award has prompted us to purchase an air rescue helicopter, employ a dedicated bilingual crew, and break ground on our own onsite family stay hotel with shuttle service to Disney World.

Of course this aggressive expansion into an already saturated market costs money, which brings me to the topic of your outstanding bill of $75,984.69 (not including cardiology, anesthesiology, or transport fees). I realize it is impossible to place a value on a human life, even one as atherosclerotic as yours, but if you could see your way to settling your account in the next thirty days, we will wave the $84.69 and engrave a brick with your name to be placed in our new helicopter pad. To avoid foreclosure on your home, car, and irreparable damage to your credit score, please consider our generous offer.

And don't forget about our cardio aftercare exercise and group therapy program.

Sincerely yours in good health,

Stephen T. Dinkle, CEO